Rain mixed with tears as I fled through the forest

Half-blinded, I failed to see the horse and rider that stepped out of the trees and directly into my path. When I finally registered man and beast, my shrill cry of fear unsettled the horse.

I had one glimpse of a superb rider controlling the magnificent animal before I had to throw myself off the trail and out of the horse's path. In that one brief glance I saw a man with his face completely hidden by a hat.

I noticed no more before I landed facedown in a leafy azalea. Before I could move from the clutches of the shrub, I felt the cold bite of steel against the back of my neck.

A masculine voice behind me gave me a blood-chilling warning.

"Make another move and you'll die."

ABOUT THE AUTHOR

On a recent trip to Vicksburg, Mississippi, with writer/history buff Pat Sellers, Caroline Burnes toured several ''haunted'' plantations and the historic battlefields. That trip, combined with the incredible letter written by a Union soldier to his wife and read during the PBS series on the Civil War, sparked the idea for *Flesh and Blood*. Caroline believes that the past is alive, and never far behind us.

Books by Caroline Burnes

HARLEQUIN INTRIGUE

Don't miss any of our special offers. Write to us at the following address for information on our newest releases.

Harlequin Reader Service
901 Fuhrmann Blvd., P.O. Box 1397, Buffalo, NY 14240
Canadian address: P.O. Box 603,
Fort Erie, Ont. L2A 5X3

Flesh and Blood

Caroline Burnes

TORONTO • NEW YORK • LONDON
AMSTERDAM • PARIS • SYDNEY • HAMBURG
STOCKHOLM • ATHENS • TOKYO • MILAN
MADRID • WARSAW • BUDAPEST • AUCKLAND

For my parents, Roy and Hilda Haines, and
Marjorie Manvel. They live in my heart.

Harlequin Intrigue edition published September 1993

ISBN 0-373-22241-6

FLESH AND BLOOD

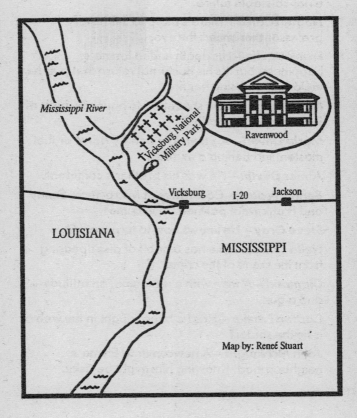

Mississippi River

✝✝✝✝✝
✝✝✝✝✝
✝ Vicksburg National
✝ Military Park

Ravenwood

Vicksburg   I-20   Jackson

LOUISIANA

MISSISSIPPI

Map by: Reneé Stuart

CAST OF CHARACTERS

Emma Devlin—A woman with a tragic past—and a not-so-stable future.

Nathan Cates—There's more to this history professor than meets the eye.

Frank Devlin—His death ended Emma's happiness, but it's his nocturnal return that puts her in danger of losing her life.

Mary Quinn—Does she return to haunt the halls of Ravenwood Plantation?

Marla Devlin—A pawn in a deadly game or the mastermind behind a murder?

James Devlin—He was his brother's confidant.

Benny Yeager—Co-owners of Micro-Tech, Benny and Frank were partners...in crime?

Steve Gray—He knows how to turn a profit.

Nella Colson—She has a habit of disappearing from the scene of the crime.

Diamond—A man with a nickname, an attitude—and a gun.

Carlton Frazier—Has he been caught in the web or is he the spider?

John McNaught—A newcomer to Emma's neighborhood. Knowing him might be risky.

Prologue

The brass bell jangled merrily as Frank Devlin pushed open the heavy glass door at Mason's Liquor Store and gave a good-natured grin to the store owner, short and plump Robert Mason, who stood behind the counter. Frank's long strides took him unerringly to the cooler at the rear of the store, where he searched through the cold bottles of champagne and wines, until he found the one bottle he sought and pulled it out.

"Thanks for chilling this for me, Robert. This is Emma's absolute favorite."

"Special occasion, eh?" Robert already knew. For the past five years on this date he'd gone through the same routine with Frank. The special champagne, the ritual of having it chilled and ready so that when Frank got home he could pop the cork without delay. The Devlins were two of his favorite customers. They were so much in love, even after five years of marriage.

"Emma claims that you call me up and remind me to do this," Frank said. He stopped near the selection of red wines. "She says you're a handsome rascal. She's also implied that I grew my mustache because she thinks yours is sexy."

"If Emma Devlin was my wife, I'd give her champagne for breakfast everyday," Robert answered. "She's a knockout, and you're a lucky man."

"You're not telling me anything I don't know."

The brass bell over the door jangled again. Frank selected a bottle of wine for the special dinner he knew his wife was cooking and turned back toward the cash register with a grin that quickly faded from his face. The wine bottle he held aloft was lowered to his side.

"Hit the floor, mister." The young man in a black leather jacket pointed a blue-black pistol directly at Frank Devlin's heart.

"Okay." Frank lowered his lanky frame to the liquor store floor. He had seen the look of terror on Robert's face. It was echoed on those of the two other customers caught innocently in what was surely an armed robbery. There were two robbers, both with guns and both wearing dark ski masks pulled over their faces. The second gunman was smaller, in a blue windbreaker.

"Take the money. Just don't hurt anyone," Robert Mason said from his prone position. "Take anything you want. Then get out. We don't want any trouble here."

"Shut up!" The leather-jacketed robber kicked Robert in the face as he lay on the floor. "When I need your permission, I'll ask for it."

The second robber, busy at the cash drawer, laughed. "That's right, you tell 'em, Diamond. We don't need nobody's permission!"

Frank could feel the grit of the floor against his cheek. He had no weapon. There was nothing he could do except wait for the robbers to take the money and leave. They were both young, and they both sounded unstable. Hopped up on some type of drugs more than likely. The best thing to do was to remain calm. If no one provoked them, they would probably take the money and some liquor and leave. Several stores in the downtown Jackson area had been hit by armed robbers lately. The Mississippi capital had never been a hotbed of crime, but the economic downturn and the high unemployment rate were taking a toll.

The young woman several feet away had begun to whimper in fear. Frank wanted to warn her to stay quiet. These robbers wouldn't need much to push them to another act of cruelty. They would certainly feed off the young woman's fear.

"Something wrong, bitch?" The robber called Diamond walked up to the woman's side. He nudged her in the ribs with the toe of his shoe. "You got a complaint?"

"No," she managed to gasp. "No problem."

"That's good. 'Cause if you had a problem, I'm afraid I'd have to solve it for you."

There was the sound of a gun cocking.

"You wouldn't like my solution!" The robber laughed, a high-pitched sound that mixed with his companion's deeper laugh and the soft sobbing of the woman.

Frank concentrated on their voices. If he ever heard them again, he'd know them. Diamond was obviously a nickname of some type. He carried an antique revolver. Frank looked at their shoes, searching for details that might prove useful when the police arrived. They were running shoes. Expensive. Brand new. He didn't have to ask where a couple of punks found the money to buy two-hundred-dollar running shoes. They did some running, but not for fitness reasons.

"Hey, this little mama's sort of pretty." The robber was still standing over the crying woman. He reached down and pulled her from the floor. She cried aloud with fear. "We got time for a little fun, cousin?"

The robber in the blue windbreaker had sacked up the money. He came out from behind the counter and stood on the other side of the crying woman. "Make it quick, before anyone else stumbles in here."

Diamond grabbed the woman by her hair. She hid her face in her hands and sobbed.

"Put her down." Frank rolled onto his side where he could look at the two men. He'd tolerated all he could. They'd gone beyond their original goal of robbery. If he didn't stop them now, they might kill everyone in the store. "Get the money and go. You don't want any trouble here."

"That's right, and we don't intend to have any." Diamond tugged the woman's hair until she cried out.

"You think you're gonna stop us?" The windbreakered robber ended his question on a sneer.

Frank held his position on the floor. He didn't want to challenge them, but someone had to stand up to them. With a bit of luck, they'd decide it wasn't worth the hassle. "Just take the money and go, before someone gets hurt."

"You giving orders to us?" Diamond asked. He raised his gun in a fast, practiced motion. His grip on the woman's hair loosened and she fell to the floor, too scared even to cry.

"You have what you came for. Be smart and go while you can." To Frank's relief, the gunmen started to back away, even though they both aimed their guns at him. The bottle of chilled champagne was still at his side, and Frank had a brief image of Emma. She'd be standing at the front window, looking out into the street and wondering why he was late. She wouldn't be worried about him—not yet—and he'd never tell her of this episode. He'd convince Robert not to mention it to her, either.

The robbers were at the door. The one in the leather jacket paused. "You know, you talk too much."

Before Frank Devlin could lift a hand in self-defense the bullet penetrated his brain. In a matter of seconds he was dead.

Chapter One

Grief is a peculiar emotion, as slippery as an eel. As deadly as a snake. It comes and goes in the dead of the night, or on the sunniest of days. It visits in the guise of memory, a dream or a too sudden thought of the future.

I know it well.

Before my decision to come to Ravenwood Plantation in Vicksburg, Mississippi, I thought I was beyond the anguish of first loss. There were times when the acuteness of missing Frank would take me unawares. I would suddenly miss him with an ache so deep that I had to stand and pace the floor.

Two years had passed since his murder, and I thought I had accepted his death. He was in a liquor store buying champagne for our fifth anniversary when he was killed in an armed robbery. A senseless act of violence. An act that changed my life forever.

I had adjusted to the grief, but I was completely unprepared for the guilt and desperation that came with Frank's first "visit" to me—after his death.

In all of our marriage we had respected and trusted each other. When Frank's ghost stood at the foot of my bed and accused me of betrayal, the terror was even greater than the pain. Not a fear of Frank, but a deep and gnawing concern that I had begun to lose my mind.

Self-doubt is almost as debilitating as guilt. Standing at the locked gate of the old plantation, I was filled with all sorts of loathsome anxieties. I was afraid, alone and confused. Once a proud and strong woman, I had been reduced to a superstitious creature willing to try anything to understand the nocturnal visits of a dead husband. Either I was going stark raving mad, or Frank's ghost had something important to tell me. Before I gave in to my fears of the former, I was going to make one last-ditch effort to explore the latter. Ravenwood was the place where I might find the key to unlocking Frank's words of accusation. I was a desperate woman.

I had come to find Mary Quinn, a young girl dead since 1863. But her love for a young man called Charles Weatherton was stronger than death, stronger than war. If my prayers were to be answered, her love would prove stronger even than a hundred years of time. It is said in Mississippi legends that Mary's ghost returns to earth to intervene in misunderstandings between lovers who've been separated by an act of violence.

I haven't taken on this mission lightly. I know that some people would call it macabre or morbid. Others would say that I am insane. I only know that I'm willing to try anything. Anything. To stop Frank's accusations of betrayal. I can live with my grief at his death, but I cannot live with his condemnation, especially when I have no idea why he thinks I've betrayed him.

Before I'm written off as a crackpot, let me assure you that when I first heard of Mary Quinn's ghost, I was a complete skeptic. Mary's legend is well known in Mississippi, part of the lore of the Old South. I'd never put much stock in such stories. They're rich in local color and emotion but often short on fact. But I was younger then, happily married, and immune to the type of tragedy that might make one consider looking to a spirit for help.

Life, and loss, have softened me. There are fewer blacks and whites and many more shades of gray. I suppose it could be said that now I want to believe. I need to believe in something, or someone.

My friends accuse me of still being in love with Frank. That, I suppose, is the brush with which I'll be tarred. I do still love him. Intensely. Ours was not a trivial love, not one easily dismissed by even the finality of death. Without being overly dramatic, I can say that I never expect to love anyone but Frank.

So why, then, has Frank begun to visit me in the dark hours of the night, pointing his finger and speaking of betrayal? Five years ago I would have laughed at the idea of a woman so desperate that she would consult a spirit. Today I find myself standing at the gates of Ravenwood Plantation.

Before I'm labeled a maladjusted hysteric, consider that I've done everything within reason to resolve my problem, including several trips to a highly acclaimed psychiatrist. He spoke to me of guilt and how it can manifest itself in dreams and visions. He has recommended "stringent rest," a contradictory term that escapes normal comprehension, but when translated from the shadowy jargon of psychiatry means institutionalization.

In our family, blood is thicker than mental disorders. After an attempt at psychiatry, I went to my mother. She loves me more than life and waits patiently for the grandchildren I will never give her. She said that Frank's "visits" are the subconscious twistings of my mind trying to tell me to let go, to accept his death, to remarry, to have those grandchildren she waits to spoil. To gain this end she has even enlisted the aid of Frank's family to convince me to get on with my life. She means well, but she doesn't understand. The Frank that stood at the foot of my bed and pointed his finger at me, dark eyes ablaze, was not shooing me into another man's arms. Not by a long shot. His exact words, delivered in a voice of wrath, were, "The past is never dead. I have suffered at the hands of those I loved. I am betrayed." I can't forget those words. And I can't twist them into some type of license to find a new life. I also don't believe that I'm losing my mind. So ruling out the extremes of psychiatry and motherhood, I'm left with few choices.

Now that reasonable steps have failed me, I'm taking the unreasonable. I have the key to Ravenwood—and two weeks to live in the old plantation without interruption. The house is generally open to the public for tours and is very popular, due to the legend of Mary's ghost. But each year, for two weeks in April, Ravenwood is closed in honor of the anniversary of Mary's death. These two weeks are mine. I must make contact with Mary, and she must help me to communicate with Frank.

I'm guilty of nothing, and I can't go on with Frank accusing me. Whatever he feels I've done wrong, I must explain to him so that he can rest in peace and I can continue with my life.

In a manner of speaking, Mary is my last hope. My last "sane" hope.

THE KEY TO Ravenwood's gates weighed heavy in my hand once I got out of my car and approached the wrought-iron fence. It was a work of art, iron twisted in curlicues that look as delicate as lace. With a grumble of protest, the gate opened. The driveway curved ahead of me, lost in a thicket of dark cedars and pristine dogwoods, a striking contrast of light and dark. Once my van was inside the fence, I got out and re-locked the gate behind me. There would be no need to leave the grounds. No one who could be stopped by a lock would be visiting me.

The scent of the paper-whites was as sweet as I remembered from childhood.

Ravenwood Plantation. I'd done my homework. The house was very old, dating back to the late 1700s when one wing of it was built by the original owner, Jeremiah Quinn. As the family prospered, the house grew. But the three-story structure has never been as awe inspiring as the grounds. From formal garden to acre upon acre of cotton and section upon section of woods, Ravenwood is one of the last remaining plantations.

The mini van I'd rented and stocked with two weeks worth of provisions cruised quietly down the winding drive. In the next few weeks as April's sun kissed Mississippi hello, the grounds would shift from the frills of spring to the vibrant colors of summer.

My family is "old Jackson," and I have several brothers who are in the legal profession. It was my older brother, Shane, who arranged for me to stay at Ravenwood. How he managed it, I didn't ask. It was one of those friends of a friend of a friend things, and I know Mama had a lot to do with it. She probably told Shane I was going off the deep end with nightmares and visitations. Anyway, Shane stepped in and took care of all the details down to the fact that I would not be disturbed by anyone for two entire weeks. I had to suffer his amused comments about my "new hobby of ghost hunting," but I got the key.

I drove around to the back of the main house. My quarters were to be in the newest portion, an apartment built above the old kitchen back in the 1930s. This was the only part of the house with electricity. Determined to settle in as quickly as possible, I hauled the ten sacks of groceries into the kitchen and my three pieces of luggage up the stairs to the bedroom.

From the moment I opened the door to the bedroom, I was enchanted. Three walls of the room were windows from waist level up. The fourth wall held the door to the bathroom and a fireplace. The bedroom was enormous. A cozy sitting area was structured around the fireplace and the bed, draped with coral mosquito netting and set up on a dais, occupied one sunny corner. If I remembered my history correctly, this room had been created according to the express wishes of Corrine Quinn, the last of the Quinn family to inhabit Ravenwood. A distant relation of Mary, Corrine had never married and had devoted her life to restoring and maintaining Ravenwood. It was her decision to open the house to public tours, and she laboriously documented the furnishings and repairs made to the original structure. Ravenwood had one of the most complete histories of any home in the state.

Although she was a spinster, there had been rumors that Corrine was not a saint. The house was her life, but she found spare time for pleasures and happy pursuits. She was reputed to have been a great beauty, and the only surviving photograph of her showed a slender woman with eyes that held the promise of mischief. She'd died at a young age in a riding accident. But her wishes had been followed in keeping Ravenwood open to the public—and closed on the anniversary of Mary's death. Corrine had been bold enough to give an interview to the local newspaper saying that Mary deserved a couple of weeks alone in her own home.

The chifforobe was empty, so I made myself at home, unpacking my bags and arranging my belongings in the room I would occupy for the next two weeks. I was anxious to race past the gardens and down the riverside trail that led to the old oak tree where Mary's ghost was said to visit frequently. Something held me back, though, some sense of propriety, as if I had to give Mary time to adjust to me, to sense that my intentions were sincere and that I honestly needed her help. I wanted to spend a few hours settling in to her home, learning a bit about her from the furnishings that had once made up her daily life.

So instead of rushing about the grounds, I made my way through the entire house, room by room.

The dimensions of the house dwarfed me. I'm average height, about five-six. During the days of the Civil War, I would have been a giantess of a woman. Miss Scarlett boasted of a seventeen-inch waist—and she was probably only four feet, eleven inches tall. The high ceilings of the plantation houses were designed for coolness, not the size of the inhabitants.

The staff at Ravenwood had done an impressive job. The bedrooms were filled with personal items from brushes to pantaloons in keeping with the period. I had to laugh aloud at the beds; they would have been barely long enough to contain my legs. In one bedroom a corset was laid out. No wonder Southern women swooned.

What price vanity! Or should I rephrase that to say, what price society does extract. Well, it would take more than a maid to wrestle one of those things on me. I'm afraid I would have failed miserably in the role of mistress of the plantation. Ha! Frank always said that my tongue would run an honest man away. I suppose that's another area of womanliness that I would have flunked. I do have an inclination to speak my mind.

I wandered the rooms of Ravenwood, wondering if Mary Quinn's ghost watched me. I've never been afraid of ghosts or haunted houses. I've never spent much time thinking about either. With my footsteps echoing on the beautiful oak floors, I hoped that such things did exist. How else, sanely, to explain Frank's reappearance?

Before I could imagine, the afternoon was gone. I had a feel for Ravenwood. For all of its magnitude, it had been someone's home. It had been loved and cherished. I was comfortable as I sat on the front porch in an old rocker and greeted the dusk. It occurred to me that for the first time in two years, I had not written a word. Not a day had gone by since Frank's death that I hadn't been able to pen some pithy remark or hone some sentiment that would fit perfectly inside a Hallelujah Hijinx card. The line specializes in sharp humor, and I had prided myself that I'd never lost a day's work over Frank. I had some peculiar idea that he would have approved of my refusal to buckle under to grief.

But today, I also knew that he would understand. Maybe it was time to take a breather. Maybe it was finally time to sit on the front porch and rock until dark had settled around me like a soft blanket.

When I picked up the flashlight I'd had the foresight to bring with me, I left the porch with reluctance. I had dinner to make and a fat, juicy novel to take to bed. There was also the little matter of the fireplace. Someone had laid it with seasoned oak. All it required was a match, and I'd brought a big box of kitchen matches for such a necessity.

After a light meal, I found myself curled before the warmth of the fire, my book opened but unread upon my lap. The sense of loss that struck was acute. I stood, the book dropping unattended to the floor. Why couldn't Frank be here with me to share this room, this fire, this soft spring night with just enough chill to make the fire welcome? Why, of all the people in the world, was it Frank who'd been killed?

As a million others who've lost loved ones, I went to bed that night with my questions unanswered.

The next day dawned brisk and beautiful. Pale pink light suffused the room, creeping in through the wall of eastern windows and ricocheting off the delicate webbing of the mosquito netting that I'd been unable to resist draping around my bed. It was like a fantasy to wake up swathed in that glorious coral bed. I was thankful that whoever had furnished the room had been of more modern size. The bed was more than adequate, with plenty of room to wallow and indulge. But this wasn't a morning for such activities. I intended to get up and scout the grounds for the old trysting oak of Mary Quinn and Charles Weatherton. I had the peculiar sense that during the night Mary had stood over me, weighing my cause. I would meet her this day. I knew it in my bones.

My hair is dark brown and straight, just below my shoulders, and I've taken to pulling it back in a barrette or ribbon at the nape of my neck. My mother says I'm not young enough or old enough to support this style and that it's simply a tactic to look austere and spinsterish. Most days I stay in the house and write, and since the grocery man or the postman haven't complained about my "do," I've been able to ignore Mother. I donned a pair of jeans and a cotton sweater, tied a ribbon in my hair and set out with a piece of toast in one hand and a cup of black coffee in the other. Perhaps I'd breakfast with Mary Quinn.

Walking through the gardens, I recalled the legend. There are a few variations on it, but only in specific detail. The content is the same no matter what version I'd heard or read.

In the spring of 1861 Mary Quinn was a seventeen-year-old girl, or woman in those days. Corrine, her descendant, favored her greatly in looks and attitude. Curly red hair, pale skin and green eyes. The ferrotypes of Mary reveal a lovely young girl with a square jaw and a humorous twinkle in her eyes. It was March, and Mary was attending a church social on the grounds of the Presbyterian Church in Vicksburg when she was introduced to young Charles Weatherton. Four years her senior, Charles had been to Europe and was reputed to be quite a charmer. He had completed his education and was heir to the Weatherton fortune, a firm that had grown up around the development of the railroad in the South.

While most of the eligible Vicksburg ladies had fallen victim to Charles's gray eyes and olive complexion, Mary was immune. She told him archly that as an only child, she had been well vaccinated with skepticism by her father when it came to male charm.

Charles was smitten. By the end of March, he had proposed to her at least fifteen times—and been declined. His sixteenth plea met with success, for as saucy as Mary's tongue could be, her heart was tender and she'd fallen in love with Charles.

Mississippi had already seceded from the Union, and Charles had joined the Confederate army. Mary had jokingly told her friends it was the combination of Charles's gray eyes and the gray of his cavalry officer's uniform that had finally worn down her resistance. Whatever the source of the attraction, their love was so deep and intense that no one who saw them together could help but feel the tender brush of their love. Even the most cynical of anti-romantics melted at the emotion that flowed between the two.

The proposal was approved by both families, and a wedding was hastily arranged. Charles was due to report to Richmond for his orders, and Mary wanted her wedding before he left. The entire town rallied to the cause and began the preparations for the April 14 wedding. But fate stepped in, and on April 3, Charles received orders to report to Richmond immediately. There was dire need for his services. Torn between his duty to his country and his fiancée, Charles hesitated. It was Mary who tied his golden sash of rank and walked him to his horse. He could not love her if he neglected his duty to his country, she'd said. She would wait for him. She would wait until eternity.

The quick war that everyone in the South had anticipated was an illusion. Though one Southerner might be able to lick ten Yankees, the Yankees were better trained and better provisioned. And there were so many more of them. The year passed, and then another. It was 1863 and the South was struggling for survival.

Mary received many letters from Charles. She would take them unopened to the oak tree where they had often sat holding each other in a tight embrace and planning their future after the war. When she read them, she could feel Charles beside her.

It was in February of 1863 that Mary received word of Charles's death. He had led a charge in a remote area of North Carolina and been shot down. He did not suffer. His death was instant. Mary's reaction to the news was completely unexpected. She said she'd known for three days that he was dead.

Instead of the terrible grief her family expected, Mary went on about her life as if she still believed that Charles would return after the war. She did not speak of the future, but she did not grieve, either. She continued to go to the oak tree where they'd had their trysts, and each time she returned, she seemed calmer, happier.

When Vicksburg came under attack, Mary's father, Canna, ordered her to remain in the gardens and not to venture along the riverbank to the oak tree. Union soldiers were straggling about the grounds of Ravenwood, and even desperate Confederates were dangerous. For the first time in her life, Mary disobeyed. No matter what her father said, she refused to give up her daily visits to the oak. Canna ordered a servant to restrain Mary. With all the agility of her quick mind and body, Mary was able to elude her keepers. At last, Canna ordered her locked in her room. Not even a lock on her door could prevent her from slipping away to the tree.

One clear spring day Canna followed his daughter. To his horror, he found her acting out the role of lover to empty air. She spoke as if Charles answered her, carrying on an animated conversation and even mimicking the act of hugging and kissing her nonexistent fiancé. The Yankees could not defeat Canna Quinn, but the sight of his daughter, his only child and heir, in such a condition, devastated him. He ordered Mary to be restrained in her bed.

Within three days' time she was dead. Once she could not go to the oak tree, she simply gave up the will to live. She had told everyone not to mourn her, that she was simply going to meet Charles and that he waited for her, as she'd promised to wait for him. She'd closed her eyes and died without a struggle. She was not quite nineteen years old. Her date of death was April 14, the second anniversary of the scheduled date of the wedding.

Out of compassion for other lovers separated by death, Mary's ghost is said to intervene in misunderstandings. She is said to be a messenger between the living and the dead. But only a pure love can attract her help.

There is certainly some misunderstanding between Frank and myself. I do not have the purity of Mary's love, I know that. It was impossible for me to simply will myself to stop living, though I did think about my own death in the first months after Frank's murder. Walking through the rose garden and past the fountain, I gave that idea some thought. Perhaps there is another kind of strength that allows one to survive a tremendous loss and continue to live. I've often thought that I'd rather be dead and allow Frank to live. But that in itself is cowardly.

Even through the worst of my grief, I never doubted that Frank knew how much I loved him. Not until lately. In the past month he has appeared to me three times. I wake up from a troubled sleep, and he is standing at the foot of my bed. He points his finger at me and makes his accusation of betrayal. I want to reach out and touch his hand, to feel his thick, black hair beneath my fingers. To pull him to me and tell him that I haven't betrayed him in thought or deed. But he makes his accusation and he fades. It is unbearable, and if I don't find the reason for his visits, I truly will become insane.

By the time I had mulled through the entire legend yet again, I found that I had arrived at the old oak. It was a live oak, an enormous presence that exuded a peace that invited me to sit beneath its branches on an old root. I settled in, wondering if Mary and Charles had shared this same natural seat. I felt as if they had. Setting my empty coffee cup beside me, I leaned back into the trunk of the tree and prepared to wait. I wasn't certain what to do to attract the notice of a ghost. Were there chants or songs or whistles that might help? I didn't know.

Lacking any specific behavior, I decided to wait quietly. The sun was warm and relaxing, and I leaned into the tree and closed my eyes. Fragments of dreams danced behind my eyelids. There were parties in Ravenwood, laughter, the crinkle of dresses, the clink of crystal. Charles and Mary danced before me, their love a palpable presence so that all other dancers stopped to watch them. I think I must have laughed out loud with pleasure at the sight of them. They held nothing back from each other. To stand beside them was to bask in the overflow of their love.

I awoke with a start. To my dismay, dusk was settling around me once again. I'd slept the entire day away. I gathered up the coffee cup and hurried back toward the house. It was a long walk and darkness was falling. Since I'd set out so early, I hadn't even considered needing a flashlight, and the grounds were without any lighting. Unfamiliar with the landscape, I had to hurry or risk getting lost.

Mixed with the sense of having squandered a valuable day was a secondary feeling of bitter disappointment. I had been so certain I would find Mary at the tree. Had I slept through our meeting? I thought not. It was more likely that she simply had not come. That she would not come.

Tears are a rare thing for me, but as I hurried along the path back to Ravenwood, I felt them building. I knew it was a combination of disappointment, disorientation and desperation. The dreams of Mary and Charles were still with me, highlighting my own loss. It had been foolish desperation that had brought me to Ravenwood in quest of a ghost. Maybe Dr. Stoler was right. Maybe I'd never accepted Frank's death.

Rain that I hadn't even noticed blowing in began to fall softly. It mixed with the tears on my face as I hurried along the unfamiliar path. My cotton sweater was soon clinging to me. Half blinded, I failed to see the horse and rider step out of the trees and directly into my path. When I finally registered man and beast, my shrill cry of fear unsettled the horse and he danced forward.

I had one glimpse of a superb rider controlling the magnificent animal before I had to throw myself off the trail and out of the horse's path. In that one brief glance I saw a man with his face completely hidden by a hat. I had time to notice no more before I landed facedown in a leafy azalea. Before I could move from the clutches of the shrub, I felt the cold bite of steel against the back of my neck. My face was pinned into the azalea.

"What are you—?" I began indignantly.

"Make another move and you'll die."

Chapter Two

The pressure of the knife or whatever blade he held against my neck made me give up any ideas of resistance. Roughly he pulled me out of the shrub. When his hand grasped my breast, he stopped suddenly.

"You're a woman!" He spun me around to face him.

The light had completely faded from the day. The gray mist of rain and gathering darkness concealed most of his features, but I could see that he was dressed in the uniform of a Confederate officer. The weapon he'd used to pin me to the ground was his sword. For a second I was so taken aback, I couldn't think of anything to say.

Once I found my tongue, I had no lack of questions. "What are you doing at Ravenwood? Who are you? Where did you come from? Why are you dressed in those clothes?"

He didn't answer, but a slight grin played across his face. "And I could ask you the same," he said in a drawl.

The hand that had pawed me suddenly lifted me by the elbow with a gentle support. "The lighting was poor. There are stragglers from both armies on these grounds, and I've developed a fondness for the residents of Ravenwood. Whenever I have some spare time, I ride through here to patrol."

I had been frightened before, but it was nothing compared to what I experienced now. "Wha-what armies?" His dress. His speech. It was as if I'd stepped into a nightmare.

"What armies?" He laughed. "The Confederate and the enemy, of course. What did you think, the Trojans and the Greeks?"

"Oh, Lord." The words escaped me on a sigh. I was too afraid to scream. It occurred to me that the man and horse standing before me were figments of my deteriorating imagination. If I could conjure up Frank, why not a Confederate soldier and horse? I decided to play for time and test him. "What year is this?"

"Eighteen sixty-three. April. Have you lost your senses tumbling around in the bushes?"

His hand was still beneath my elbow, and for good reason. My knees threatened to give. In an instant he had his hands about my waist, offering support. "You're rather tall for a woman and strangely dressed. I thought you were a boy."

"I don't feel very well," I answered as I stumbled forward. Thank goodness he was on the tall side, for a man, or I might have crushed him on the spot. In a moment I had my spine re-engaged and I stood on my own. I had gone to sleep in 1993 and awakened . . . in the midst of the Civil War? It was not possible. It was . . . insane. But the man beside me was flesh and blood. A very solid man with firm muscle. The horse smelled of horse. Even the delicate scent of the paper-whites was all around me. If this was a dream, or a nightmare, it was Technicolor. But after all, hadn't I come to Ravenwood in search of a ghost?

For the first time I noticed the silence. The night was hushed, as if it waited for a burst of fire or a volley of cannon. "Where is the Union army? Why aren't they shooting?"

"Several battalions have dug in at the low ground not two miles from here. We're expecting reinforcements any day."

He spoke with such matter-of-factness, and absolutely no fear. I didn't completely accept what might have happened to me, but I felt a sudden rush of pity for this man. He had no concept of the future, of the futility of the battle about to be fought. How could I tell him that those reinforcements would never come? That the siege of Vicksburg was one of the most torturous events of a long and bloody war. That his army, his men, were doomed to starvation and death, along with many of the residents of the town. I was overwhelmed with what I knew and could not tell.

"You're looking ill. Let me walk you back to Ravenwood. I'm sure that we can find something to bolster your spirits."

I hesitated. What would I find at the plantation? Would Canna Quinn be mourning the death of his daughter, Mary? What would he make of my sudden and unexpected appearance? What had happened to the mini van I'd rented? How could I wake myself from this nightmare?

"My name is Nathan Cates, lieutenant colonel in the Seventh Confederate Cavalry."

How should I respond? I decided on a simple name. "Emma Devlin."

He hesitated, as if he waited for more. "Are you a relative of the Quinns?"

"No. A guest."

Nathan captured the reins of his horse and we started back to the house. Several minutes passed in silence. I sensed that the man beside me struggled to say something. I was completely disoriented and unable to decide what I believed. Silence was my only choice.

"Miss Devlin, I've taken a vow this summer, and I'm about to break it. I think this has gone far enough."

He'd lost me completely, but it sounded sinister. "What vow? What are you talking about?"

"I took this . . . job, and it's a matter of honor with me to fulfill my obligations. But I can see that I'm distressing you, so I think I'd better tell you the truth."

With his words, it was as if lightning had zapped behind my eyes. The costume! The strange cadence of his speech! The courtliness of his manner! "You're part of the Civil War reenactment, aren't you? You're paid to act out the role of cavalry colonel and it's against your contract to break character." I'd read all about it. With the first flush of excitement also came a bitter aftertaste of disappointment. I *had* wanted to meet a ghost. I'd been more than ready to believe it. As unreasonable as it was, I also felt anger.

"What are you doing on the grounds?" I asked.

"I didn't mean to upset you," he said.

"These are private grounds. I think you should take your horse and leave."

"Miss Devlin, please allow me to walk you back to the house. The grounds are supposed to be private, but they aren't secure. I am sorry that I've upset you. You see, I didn't expect to find anyone here, either."

He sounded genuinely contrite, and a bit of my anger passed. "You frightened me, but only a little. I didn't know if I'd woken up in the Twilight Zone or if I was in the company of some raving lunatic who was living in the past." I wasn't about to confess that I'd hoped he was a ghost.

"By your accent, I'd say you're from the South. Surely you know about the Vicksburg reenactment. It's part of the history of the town. It's one of the biggest tourist attractions. And reenactors are required to stay in character."

"I had my mind on other things." The understatement of the year. "That business with the sword at my throat, though, was pretty convincing."

He laughed out loud, an easy, slow chuckle. "Maybe I should ask for a pay raise if I'm such a great actor. Or maybe, Emma Devlin, you're ready to believe in something different in your life."

The humor of the situation struck me hard. I smiled, and that was quickly followed by a chuckle. The man had truly unsettled me. He had every right to believe I was a half-wit. All it had taken was a uniform and a half dozen comments, and I'd been ready to believe I was talking with a Confederate soldier.

"I am sorry," he said. "I brought Frisco over for a gallop around the grounds. He doesn't get a lot of exercise during the day I'm afraid, and the gardens around the plantation are incredibly beautiful."

"They are indeed." He was waiting for my explanation. "I'm staying in the house while it's closed. I'm...researching a project."

"Then you're a writer?"

His eager questions made me feel guilty of some deception. "In a way. I write for a card company, but I'm at Ravenwood on personal business." That was as much as I would give him.

"I'll see you back to the house and then be off."

He seemed to sense my desire for privacy, and I walked silently beside him. Frisco followed behind like an obedient puppy. I'd learned to ride as a child at my Aunt Charlotte's, and I liked the looks of the big chestnut gelding. The night sounds of Ravenwood closed gently around us. The chirr of crickets was a comforting noise, reminding me again of happy childhood moments.

But the silence between us had stretched too long. "How long will you be working with the reenactment?"

"On and off through the summer, I suppose. I have a teaching arrangement at Mississippi College. Then..."

I felt him shrug beside me, and without being able to see, I knew that he was smiling. He was confident of his future, whatever it might prove to be.

"You're from the South, aren't you?" My curiosity was piqued.

"I've never been able to completely curb my accent."

"And I should hope you wouldn't try. Why would you want to sound as if you came from Illinois or Idaho?"

"A good question," he said, "and one for which I don't have an answer. Are you staying at Ravenwood alone? I ask because I'll stop and check on you if you'd like."

There was no pushiness in his question, only concern. Walking through the dark with him and the horse, I felt an unaccustomed peace. "I'd like that. I am alone."

"Ravenwood is a big house. Don't let the little idiosyncrasies unsettle you."

"I'm not easily unsettled." Through the heavy green of magnolia and oak leaves I could see the night-light that had been put up near the apartment door.

"An independent woman. I like that."

"And I'd like to point out that you are a gentleman, and I like that."

We laughed together as we walked to the kitchen door and I drew the key from the pocket of my pants. "Thanks for seeing me home, Nathan Cates."

"My pleasure, Miss Devlin. And I'll be by to check on you during the next two weeks. If you hear a horse galloping about the property, you can bet it's me and Frisco."

"Did you rent him at a local stables? I thought I might like to ride while I'm here."

"No, Frisco isn't a rental, but I think I might be able to scare up a mount for you."

"No Union horses." I couldn't resist a bit of teasing.

"Any horse I bring for you to ride will neigh with a drawl," he said as he swung up into the saddle.

The light from the window caught him fully, and for the first time I realized what an attractive man he was. His legs were long and well-muscled, defined by the boots he wore. Wide shoulders supported a strong neck. His face was handsome in a rugged way, and there was a hint of sadness in his eyes. That disappeared when he smiled down at me.

"Not to alarm you, Miss Devlin, but be on the lookout for ghosts. There's a rumor that Ravenwood is haunted."

"What a charming idea, Mr. Cates, a haunted plantation house."

"Most ghosts are harmless, Emma Devlin. Many of them are simply too sad to rest. But there are some that mean you harm."

His words struck me like a cold blade along my spine. He was playing with me in a light, bantering way, and he had no idea how close to my heart he'd hit.

"I'll be careful only to consort with the good-natured ones," I answered, and unlocked my door. "Good night, Mr. Cates."

Before I locked the door I watched the night swallow up horse and rider. I'd spent the day dreaming about Mary Quinn and met a strange history teacher who doubled as an actor. For a woman who'd done nothing all day, I was exhausted—and starved. Too hungry to wait for something to cook, I made a peanut butter and jelly sandwich and took it up the stairs to the bedroom. I was suffering from an odd aftershock of meeting Nathan Cates. I was bone weary and yet I felt as if a tiny electrical pulse was running through me.

Thinking back through the meeting, I was surprised to recall that once I spoke with him, I had absolutely no fear of him. I'd never been a person who made instant friends. My mother, who has a list of complaints a mile long about me, said it was because I was sarcastic and smart-mouthed. Before people got a chance to like me, I drove them away, she said.

Frank had defended me by saying that I weeded out the wimps. At the memory of those lively debates, I couldn't help but smile. The smile faded as I thought about my reasons for being at Ravenwood. I'd spent a dreamless night my first night here. Would I see Frank tonight?

I finished the last bite of my sandwich and took the plate back downstairs. I made sure the doors and windows were locked before I abandoned the kitchen for the bedroom and a hot bath. A tiny rule I'd made for myself was that I would not think of Frank before I went to bed. If it was my subconscious acting up, I didn't want to invite a visit from the man I loved accusing me of betrayal. I picked up my book, spun the coral mosquito netting about my bed and settled down for the night.

About eleven, my eyes grew heavy and I gave up my book. Outside the open window, the night was alive with small creatures. With a smile I surrendered to childhood images and sleep.

The brush of the mosquito netting across my face woke me. Waking up in an unfamiliar place can be unsettling, and I forced myself to remain calm. A gust of April wind must have blown through the open window with enough force to billow the netting over the bed. It was a strange sensation, like waking up in the folds of an elaborate gown. There was a coral glow around the bed. I was pushing my way clear to the surface of material when I saw Frank.

Standing at the foot of the bed, he watched me closely.

"Frank." I wanted to reach out to him, to hold his hand, to touch his face. But I could not. The chill of the grave held me back. No matter how much I didn't want it to be true, Frank Devlin was dead. Though he stood before me, handsome in the pink and coral light of dawn that had begun to chase the darkness from the room, I knew he was no longer of my world.

"The past is never dead, Emma."

"I know that, Frank. I miss you terribly."

"I have suffered at the hands of those I loved."

His words were so sad, so horrible. Tears threatened to choke me, but I fought them back. "Not me, Frank. Never me. I could not have loved you more. You know that. I still love you."

"I am betrayed, Emma. Betrayed." His right hand came up and his finger pointed directly at me. "Emma..."

As in the past three times, he faded away. In a few seconds, the room was empty except for me.

"Frank." I spoke his name, expecting no answer. My tears were bitter, bitter. Frank's ghost was gone, but the specter of insanity completely filled my mind. Was I mad? Maybe the smartest thing to do would be to commit myself to an institution. Each time Frank visited, the pain was more unbearable. Each time his accusations were the same, and my ability to understand them no better.

Hugging my pillow, I cried until I had no more tears. Then I washed my face and went downstairs. I put on a pot of very strong coffee and thought about my options. I'd promised myself two weeks at Ravenwood. I would give myself that much time and no more. What I needed was a plan to find Mary Quinn. Walking to the oak hadn't worked. Perhaps by sitting in Mary's own room I might encourage contact with her. I had the coffee dripping when I ran back upstairs to change into a pair of stirrup pants and a long-sleeve blouse. God bless the creator of heavy knit. It didn't wrinkle, held its shape and was as comfortable as a second skin. I crowded my mind with these trivialities, grasping desperately at the ordinary. Beneath everything I did, the question remained: was I losing my mind?

My fingers were working the last button when I heard the knock on the door. No one had a key to the gates, and I couldn't imagine who might be on the premises. I ran down the stairs and peeked through the curtains in the kitchen door.

Nathan Cates was standing on the doorstep with a bulging grocery bag. Frisco stood patiently tied to a tree beside a buckskin mare. My mind blanked at the sight. I didn't know what to do. Nathan was dressed in his uniform, undoubtedly on the way to work at the reenactment. He'd taken me up on my request for a ride.

He knocked again, and I couldn't hesitate any longer. I'd thank him and tell him I didn't feel like riding. I didn't feel like living, if the truth were known. I opened the door. "Nathan."

"Good morning, Emma Devlin." He brushed through the door and took the grocery bag to the kitchen table. "I wasn't sure if you'd brought provisions, so I picked up a few things for you. Then I thought I couldn't take you out for a morning ride without breakfast. I hear that Southern girls are given to fits of fainting, and I suspect it might be because they don't start the day with a healthy meal. So I brought some bacon, eggs, grits and the makings of biscuits."

"Biscuits?" I was overwhelmed. In the morning light his eyes were sky blue against the gray of his uniform. The mustache I'd seen hints of the night before was full and blond, and there was a curved scar on his right cheek.

"Don't you like biscuits?" he asked.

"I like biscuits from the breakfast buffet at a number of places. But I don't make them." I didn't feel like company. I couldn't eat if my life depended on it. Yet there was something about Nathan that soothed me. I needed to be alone, to think. But I didn't want him to go.

"I make excellent biscuits. My grandmother taught me." With a quickness and skill I'd never seen in a man before, Nathan made breakfast. As he worked, he talked about Ravenwood and the peculiarities of the house. He knew much more about it than I did. His voice was deep, reliable. It seemed only a few minutes before he put a plate of bacon, eggs, grits and biscuits before me. He took a seat opposite.

Although I thought food would choke me, I ate with surprising appetite. Nathan kept up the conversation with cheerful ease. It wasn't until he'd cleared the table and poured us both another cup of coffee that he stopped talking for a long moment.

"Would you like to tell me why you've been crying this morning?" he asked finally.

I did not want to tell him. I had no intention of doing so, but the words poured out. I told him everything. Every single detail of my madness. And he listened. He didn't interrupt. He didn't question me. At some point, he reached across the table and picked up my hand. When I finished, he gave it a long squeeze.

"I know the first thing that's crossed your mind is that you're going insane. Well, you aren't."

For the first time that morning, I smiled. "How can you be so certain?"

"As a historian, I guess you could say that I believe in ghosts, or at least messages and inspirations from the spirit world. And having known you for all of two hours, at the maximum, I get the impression that you aren't the least bit unhinged."

I suppose it was his confidence—in himself and in me— that was so comforting. I needed a vote of confidence, even from a stranger. "Thanks, Nathan. Thanks for listening, and thanks for not treating me like a budding lunatic."

"Since you came to Ravenwood to see Mary Quinn, have you seen her?"

I shook my head. "I was hoping today might be the day."

For the first time worry crossed Nathan's face. "It's none of my business, you know." He stood and paced the kitchen. "I probably shouldn't say this at all."

"Say what?"

"Emma, is it possible that your husband's death wasn't completely accidental?"

The idea shocked any response from me. Frank, deliberately murdered? "Absolutely not. Frank didn't have any real enemies. He was a man of integrity, of honor. People respected him. They looked up to him."

Nathan crossed the room and stood behind me, his hands on my shoulders in a gentling motion. "Easy, Emma, easy. I didn't mean to imply that he was murdered because he was a bad man. Don't you know that sometimes people are killed because they're good? Especially men of integrity and honor. They can gum up the works for dishonest people.''

"Who would want Frank dead?''

He squeezed my tense shoulders and then released me. "I'm afraid that's a question only you can answer. But the way I'm looking at this is that Frank feels wronged. He's defied the odds and returned to tell you, the woman he trusts, that he's been betrayed. If he isn't accusing you . . .''

"Then he's looking to me to help him.'' A distinct chill touched my back and rolled down my entire body.

"If not to help him, then at least to understand.''

I was captured by the idea. I had not betrayed Frank. Not in any word or gesture during our marriage or since his death. Was it possible that he was seeking my help to find someone who had?

"What should I do?'' I looked across the room to the sink where Nathan had begun to wash the dishes. He wiped his hands on a dish towel as he took my measure.

"It depends. Remember, this is just a theory.''

"It makes more sense than anything I've thought up. Unless, of course, I want to believe I'm going crazy.''

"Did you examine the police report of Frank's death?''

I shook my head. "There didn't seem to be a reason to. I mean, it was a robbery attempt and Frank tried to help a woman they were abusing. The robbers were crazy, and when Frank gave them trouble, they killed him.''

"It sounds logical, but it may not be. If there's anything to my theory, then the police reports are the place to start. Did they identify the killers?''

"No.'' I sighed. "I don't even know that they tried all that hard. After the first few weeks, I didn't push it. Frank was dead and there was nothing that would bring him back. Revenge, or justice, if that's a better word, was my last thought. I guess I just wanted to survive.''

"Enough time has passed now, Emma. Maybe justice is necessary. For Frank.''

I looked up into the blue eyes of a man who was virtually a stranger. "I loved him so much. I still do."

Nathan smiled. "I know. And I'll bet Frank knows that, too." Dropping the dish towel on the table, he took his seat opposite me again. "Promise me that you'll heed this warning, Emma. If we're on to something here, if there's something to be found about Frank's death, it could be very dangerous. If someone had good enough reason to kill your husband, they wouldn't hesitate to kill you."

Chapter Three

If Nathan's unexpected theory gave me a rope to cling to in the free-fall of my life, then the morning ride we shared gave me the energy to pursue his idea. The buckskin mare, Lucinda, was as good and solid as any horse could be. My rusty horsemanship improved after a few miles, and when we returned to Ravenwood, I actually felt as if I wanted to live.

Nathan left on Frisco, with Lucinda following behind. Duty called, and his reenactment forces were awaiting his command. My own duties called me, and I took a cross-stitch hoop to Mary Quinn's bedroom to see if she might honor me with a visit.

The cross-stitch was an attempt to learn patience, never a strong suit in my character. In one of her often-repeated lectures my mother warned that if I went to hell I'd harangue Satan to light the fires faster. There was some truth to what she said. After the first three minutes I'd pricked my finger twice. Blood had gotten on the pristine whiteness of the cloth and I was ready to pitch the entire thing out the window. So much for demurely conjuring up Mary Quinn. What I did accomplish was a lot of thinking. And I made a decision. Jackson was only an hour away, at the most. I'd drive over there and look at the police reports.

By one o'clock, I was standing at Sergeant Benjamin Vesley's desk. Once again my brother the lawyer had pulled some strings for me. Sergeant Vesley hadn't handled the original case, but he said he'd look up the reports for me and go over them. He talked about unsolved crimes and the shame of it and how the human race was going to hell. He was a man who would have made a wonderful grandfather, but constant exposure to the worst of human nature had made him tired and weary. He was not hopeful that the police report would yield anything.

He left me alone at his desk with the papers. I think he sensed the difficulty I was experiencing. I read the statements of the officers, the evidence of the fingerprints, the procedural reports. The words "died instantly" had once brought me some comfort. Now they were cold and meant only a permanent separation.

The statements of the two investigating officers were exactly as I'd expected. The woman Frank had tried to assist was incoherent. She didn't see or remember anything except that the robbers were hurting her and a man had tried to help and they had killed him.

There were photos of the store that showed the outline of Frank's body. The blood had not been removed. The eyewitness account of the other customer in the store was also filled with shock and horror and no specifics.

Robert Mason's report was the longest. I saved it for last. I had been in the liquor store once since the shooting. I'd gone to show Robert I didn't blame him. We had both stood there and cried like babies in front of several customers. Emotionally, it was too hard on us both, so I stopped going there.

Robert's report was clear and detailed. He described the men. He heard the one in the leather jacket referred to as Diamond. I found a scratch pad on Sergeant Vesley's desk and began to make notes. Diamond had dark hair pulled back at the nape of his neck in a ponytail. Though he wore a ski mask, his eyes were visible. They were an intense blue. The other robber was younger, with a smaller frame. Diamond had shot Frank. It was Robert's feeling that they might have been under the influence of some type of drug.

After he covered the details of what was said and done, Robert made a special point about the gun. It was a .357 revolver. I had to read this part of the report twice because I didn't fully understand. "No robber in his right mind comes in with a piece like that. It was an antique. These guys acted like professionals, but the killer had this cowboy six-shooter."

Robert had been in the army and knew a lot about guns. He'd tried to get me to take shooting lessons and buy one for protection in the house. Since the information about the gun was the only thing I'd learned new, I wrote it all down verbatim. The ballistics report was beyond my comprehension, and I didn't need to read the autopsy to determine the cause of death. I stacked up the reports and went to thank Sergeant Vesley. He was waiting for me with a cup of coffee and a kindly smile.

"It's been two years," he said. "Why now?"

"I don't know." I couldn't tell him I was being haunted. "Maybe it's the last step in putting it all behind me."

"I hope so, Mrs. Devlin. I'd hate to see you turn into one of those people who avoid life by burying themselves in the details of death."

"Thank you, Sergeant."

Since I was downtown, I decided to stop by the liquor store and talk with Robert. The store had changed. Burglar bars had been installed over the windows and doors, and there was a buzzer system to announce the arrival of customers. Even through the bars and glass I could see that Robert had changed as much as I. Threads of gray ran through his hair. He was older, more cautious. He buzzed me in with a wary look.

"Emma!"

Before I knew what had happened, I was engulfed in a bear hug. "I've been thinking about you for the past month. I'd just wake up in the middle of the night with this uneasy feeling. Martha said I should call and check on you, but I didn't want to resurrect any bad memories."

"You wouldn't have, Robert. I've been thinking about you, too. I wanted to talk to you."

He went to the front door, locked it, flipped the sign to Closed and pulled the shade. "What can I do for you?" He signaled me into the storage room where he kept a small office complete with an extra chair.

"I just read the police report on Frank's death. You were adamant about the type of gun the killer used."

Robert's dark gaze locked with mine. He twisted the right side of his mustache. "What are you up to, Emma?"

"There are things about Frank's death that trouble me. I wanted to check them out, to draw my own conclusions. Then, maybe..."

"You can get on with your life." He nodded. "There are things that trouble me, too."

"What was it about the gun?"

"Wait a minute and I'll show you." He left the room and returned in a moment with a pistol. He snapped a piece from the handle and held it out. "This is a clip. Automatic. Shoots very fast. The night Frank was killed, the killer had a revolver. You know, the gun with a round cylinder that rotates to put the bullet in the chamber. Reloading with a revolver is much harder than with an automatic. In an automatic, the bullet is already in position and it moves up through spring action. Most criminals just carry pre-loaded clips. When one is empty, they pop it out and put in another clip."

What he said made sense, to an extent. "Maybe that was the only gun he had."

"I just don't understand it. It was a really fine gun. A Smith & Wesson, blue steel, hand-carved grip. An antique.

Killers like those punks wouldn't carry a piece because of its aesthetic value or the history of it. He could have sold that piece and made enough to buy several automatics. Most times killers drop the piece anyway. They want something cheap."

He had a point. "Was there anything else? What about the man with the gun? Did he have a diamond in his ear, or any type of jewelry that might tell why he was called Diamond?"

"He was wearing that mask. I couldn't see anything." Robert took a breath. "Emma, I've thought about it over and over again. I should have been able to stop it. I should have..."

I went to him and put my hands on his shoulders. "Stop it, Robert. There wasn't anything that you or I could have done. Frank, either. I've thought about it, too. I wondered why he couldn't let them take the woman, why he had to try to step in. And the answer is, that was the kind of man he was. Neither of us would have cared for him as much had he been any different."

"What are you going to do?"

"Keep thinking this through."

"What are you looking for, Emma? The police said they never got any kind of lead. I called them every day for almost a year."

"I'm thinking that there may have been more here than just a simple robbery-murder. I don't know how or why, but maybe those robbers were in *this* store on *that* night for a specific reason. You could help me by thinking along those lines."

"You're saying it was a setup, specifically to kill Frank?"

Robert's eyes were wide with shock. It did sound preposterous. Robberies happened all the time. People got killed because they were in the wrong place at the wrong time. That was easier to believe than deliberate murder.

"I'm not saying that it's true. I'm just saying that I'm thinking about the possibilities."

"Why, Emma? Why? Who would do such a thing?"

"I don't have a clue. As I said, I'm just looking and thinking. Maybe you could talk to the other store owners in this neighborhood. See what kind of robberies they've had. See how many turned violent. That kind of thing. Frank was on the floor. He was defenseless. They could have knocked him unconscious or wounded him. They didn't have to kill him."

Robert nodded. "I'll canvass the neighborhood. Want me to call you?"

"No, I'll call you. I'm going to be hard to catch these next few days."

"Emma, have you uncovered something?"

Robert's hand on my shoulder was strong, supportive. "No. Nothing like that. It's just a feeling."

"I know what you mean. For the past few weeks, I've been thinking more and more about it."

"I'll be in touch, Robert."

I pulled up the shade and flipped the sign to Open as I went out. Although I'd learned nothing, I felt a kernel of hope growing larger and larger. Robert was feeling something, too.

On the spur of the moment I decided to check out the woman who'd been in the liquor store that night. I had her address from her statement, and I thought Laree Emrick might have some new details to add.

The neighborhood was off Northside Drive, a good distance from downtown. I couldn't help but wonder what she was doing in Robert's store when she could have shopped in her own neighborhood. I knew I had no right to blame her for anything, yet my entire life might be different if she'd gone to another store that night. Might be different. If Frank was deliberately murdered, then Laree Emrick had not even really played a role in the sequence of events.

The house was freshly painted and the yard immaculate. I could hear dogs barking inside when I rang the bell. Laree Emrick was a petite woman with curly brown hair. She opened the door with a smile and an order for two cocker spaniels to quit barking.

"I'm Emma Devlin, Mrs. Emrick. You were in the liquor store the night my husband was killed."

There was no way to soften the words. She blanched and stepped back, but she opened the door for me.

"I've always felt it was my fault," she said slowly as she led the way to the living room. "If I hadn't cried . . . I'll bet you hate me, don't you?"

"No. Not at all." And I didn't. I had thought at one time that I might, but it was ridiculous. She was as much a victim as Frank, or me. "Please don't think that I've come here to start any kind of trouble. It's just that I have to settle this in my own mind. I want to be sure that Frank's death was . . . the worst kind of accident."

"I don't remember much." She motioned me onto the sofa and she took a seat in a wing chair. "To be honest, I've tried very hard to forget it all."

"Maybe we could both forget if we finally examine that night."

"You sound like my husband." She sighed and began to talk. Her story was much the same as the statement she'd given the police. She was downtown at an antique store and decided to buy a bottle of wine for dinner. It was happenstance that she went into Robert's store. The men came in. She did as they said and they started to abuse her. Frank intervened and they killed him. She remembered none of the conversation, none of the details.

"Did it ever cross your mind that those men would have killed my husband no matter what he did?"

She looked up at me. "I don't know." She rubbed her hand across her forehead. "You know, there was another customer in the store. The robbers ignored him completely.

Now that you mention it, maybe they did seem to watch
your husband more.''

"Are you certain, Mrs. Emrick?" I felt a thrill of hope
growing.

"I told my husband it was like a train racing downhill.
There wasn't any stopping it once the killers walked in the
door." She hesitated. "Yes, I'm certain. They paid more
attention to your husband than anyone else, or anything.
Even the money. You know, they never demanded more
money. They just took what was in the cash register."

"Thank you, Laree." I took my leave. My visit had upset her, but I had another tiny straw of evidence. If it was
not real evidence, then at least it was mortar to help build
the wall of my new theory.

I thought about going to my home, but as soon as I had
the idea I gave it up. I wanted to discuss my ideas with
someone. I could have called my brothers or my mother, but
it wasn't them I wanted to see. My brothers would be skep-
tical, to say the least. Mom would hover and worry. She was
already concerned about me, and I didn't want her to know
I was spending my time playing amateur detective. No one
could have hated what happened to Frank more than my
family. But they'd gone on. For them, it was over. And like
most survivors of tragedy, they didn't want to be dragged
back to the abyss.

I took the interstate to Vicksburg. Nathan Cates was the
man I wanted to talk to. He'd share my sense of accom-
plishment. I didn't examine my feelings in this, I simply accepted them. It seemed that I'd done nothing but probe at
myself for the past five weeks. Nathan Cates's interest in my
problems was a luxury I was simply going to enjoy.

Ravenwood seemed too empty when I drove through the
gates. It was silly, but I was disappointed when I didn't see
Frisco tied to the camellia near the drive. I hadn't invited
Nathan to return, so I shouldn't have expected him. I had a

sudden inspiration and got back in the van and drove to the battlefield.

Instead of the activities I'd expected, the Vicksburg National Military Park was quiet. I had to remember that it was April, still a month before the siege of Vicksburg actually began. The height of reenactment fever would come in the later months, along with the tropical heat. There was a cluster of young soldiers near some roughly constructed shelters. They carried old rifles and pistols and wore their Johnny Reb caps at jaunty angles. At first glance, they might have stepped out of the pages of history. Of course I knew them for what they were, hired actors who played the role of Confederate soldiers to entertain tourists.

"How are you boys today?" I asked.

"Just fine, ma'am," one of them answered in a long drawl. "The Yanks are giving us a little peace and quiet for a change. We're hoping our replacements will be in soon." He looked at me and grinned. "I haven't been home in over a year. My wife's gonna forget what I look like."

He looked hardly old enough to be out of school, and I smiled back at him. He was a wonderful actor. "I'm looking for a Lt. Col. Nathan Cates, of the Seventh Cavalry. Where might he be?"

The boy took off his hat and scratched his head. "No cavalry around here, that I know. That'll come later in the summer when we reenact—" He blushed to the roots of his hair at his slip.

Ignoring his faux pas, I continued. "I met Colonel Cates yesterday. I'm sure he was in this area. May I look around?"

"Just watch out for stray bullets," he said, recovered. "Hate to see a pretty woman like you get wounded."

"I'll use great care," I assured him as I headed back for my van.

A paved road, a favorite of bicyclers and joggers, curves around the park and provides challenging hills and some of the most beautiful scenery in the Hill City. The scars of the

Civil War have healed, at least the evidence of metal and fire that once devastated the earth. Green grass covers the hillsides where thousands of men died. The remaining weapons of war have been silenced and are now polished and painted for display.

The entire park is filled with monuments, some enormous and grand, others small and austere. These are the reminders of the high cost of that bloody conflict. Although I'd lived in Mississippi all of my life, I'd never visited the memorial. War and death, there was plenty of it in today's world. I had no curiosity to probe the wounds of the past. As I drove around the park, I found myself stopping to read the monuments. The cost of taking Vicksburg was high. Thousands of men, gray and blue. Most of the deaths were not easy ones.

What I hadn't expected was the beauty and the solitude of the park. Fragments of history courses I'd taken in high school and college came back to me. The siege of Vicksburg was one of the most gruesome ordeals of the war. Located on the banks of the Mississippi River on high bluffs, the city was crucial for the South's survival, and just as necessary for the North to take. Once the siege began, one side had to lose. Some six weeks later, Vicksburg surrendered, after the civilians had been driven into caves dug into the bluffs. They ate rats, and many died of starvation and disease.

As I drove along the scenic parkway, I came upon Shirley House, the only structure that had managed to survive the battle. At one time it was used as a Union headquarters, surrounded by trenches—called saps—where soldiers lived, digging their way to wherever they had to go.

Beside the house was the Illinois Monument, a magnificent domelike structure with a skylight and the names of hundreds of soldiers who died so far from home engraved on every wall. I waited there, trying to shake the feeling that at any moment I would hear the sound of cannon and the cries of wounded horses. Thank God I had not lived in that time.

My own loss, no doubt as violent, had changed me forever. But I had not lost my home and my family and my way of life. My ancestors were of stronger stock to have survived such a war and kept enough faith to raise families, to risk loving again.

The afternoon was waning, and I had not located Nathan. There had been no signs of cavalry, as the young soldier had pointed out. Apparently they were bivouacked away from the park. It hadn't occurred to me, but perhaps Nathan did not constantly ride his horse. The idea that he was out coaching young recruits in the dialogue and dialect of the 1860 South tickled me. I hadn't known him long, but I was willing to bet he was a good teacher.

I drove back to the front gate and stopped to talk with the park rangers. When I asked about a cavalry colonel, the ranger was friendly, but not very helpful. The reenactment forces were so numerous, the park made no efforts to manage them. He did not have a list of the participants in the battle. As he explained, some of the units were volunteers, history buffs who went around the country acting out roles at different battlefields. Others were like Nathan, professional historians and scholars paid for their work. I went back to Ravenwood hoping that Nathan would take an evening ride through the estate. He would see my mini van and stop. I felt good about the progress I had made in looking into Frank's death, but I wanted a sensible sounding board.

Maybe the tragedy of the battlefield had caught a ride home with me, but when I turned in the gate at the plantation, I had a sudden poignant sensation of Mary Quinn's life. It must have been a fairy tale before the war. I could imagine the old plantation running at full blast, the house ablaze with lights and laughter. From all I'd read, the Quinns were a happy family with a love of parties and feasts. Before the war.

It was foolish of me, but I couldn't resist looking around the ground for Frisco's hoofprints. There was no sign that Nathan or his horse had paid a visit to me while I'd been out.

Since I couldn't find him at the battlefield, I decided to call Mississippi College where he worked as a professor. It took forever for the secretary to answer the phone. When I asked for Nathan Cates, the young girl explained that she was a work-study student and that she didn't have an extension listed for a Dr. Cates. A pleasant young woman, she apologized and said that the regular secretary would be back the next day.

Since I had no other plans for the evening, I decided to make my version of chicken alfredo. Cooking is an act that many Southern women turn to in times of anxiety or periods of waiting. Frank and I had once spent our evenings bantering in the kitchen as we explored cuisines from around the world. There was nothing he wouldn't attempt. I'd lost my interest in cooking after his death, and my desire to work in the kitchen surprised me. I even chilled a bottle of white wine I'd brought along. Just for the fun of it I'd cater dinner to myself in the big old dining room. While the pasta cooked, I hurried over to the old house and set up two candelabras. Anything worth doing was worth doing well.

When the meal was prepared, I sat at the elegant table in the main dining room. There was seating for at least twenty, and the candles glowed against the burnished mahogany of the lovely table.

I was halfway through the meal when I remembered the oven. I'd left a small portion of bread in it to warm. There was little chance trouble would occur, but I couldn't enjoy the rest of my meal if I was worried about burning the bread. Feeling as if I should excuse myself, I left the table and hurried to the kitchen. I could see where servants would have worked up a sweat carrying dishes back and forth for three large meals a day. The bread was very toasted, but there was no damage. I turned off the oven and went back to my meal.

I had just settled my napkin into place when I saw the yellow rose beside my plate. The chill that ran up my body was indescribable. The front doors were locked, and I'd used the back one. The gates to the plantation were also locked. No one could have slipped into the house without my knowing it—except a ghost. Mary Quinn! She'd left me a message to let me know that she hadn't abandoned me, that she was considering my plight. Perhaps it was even a sign of approval that I had taken some action on my own.

Should I finish dinner and wait for her to make her appearance, or should I attempt to find her? The sound of footsteps on the second floor ended my questions. Instead of the light footsteps of a teenage girl, the tread was heavy. Ominous. Anticipation turned to fear. Old houses attracted all kinds of weirdos. I'd been gone from Ravenwood all day. Anyone could be hiding in it.

My thoughts halted as I took a sudden gulp of air. The footsteps were coming down the stairs.

Chapter Four

The footsteps continued toward the dining room. The lighting was poor, only half a dozen candles in two candelabras. There was a chance I could slip into a corner and then make a run out the door once the intruder was in the room. Of course, my chance for success was about as good as a snowball's survival in hell. Basically, I was trapped like a rat.

Without making a sound, I left the table and pressed myself into the darkest corner of the room. Heavy draperies hung at the windows, and I shrouded my body in those. Of all the childhood games I'd played, I'd hated only hide-and-seek. I couldn't stand the torment of waiting for the hand on my shoulder, the moment of capture. Even when it was only Shane pursuing me, it frightened me. Sometimes, when I couldn't stand the torture of waiting, I'd hear Shane coming closer and closer and I'd scream, "Here I am! Here I am!"

This was a million times worse. My heart hammered loud enough to wake the dead. The possibilities of danger were endless. The owner of the footsteps that came closer and closer could be anyone—an escapee from prison, a robber, a fiend. Unexpected violence had visited me once. I knew I was not immune.

"Emma?"

I almost didn't hear the sound of my name over the frantic jackhammer of my heart.

"Emma?"

I couldn't believe it. The voice belonged to Nathan Cates. I peeked out from behind the draperies.

"Emma! I frightened you."

He strode toward me with a chagrined expression.

"I knocked. The door was open. I thought you'd gone to Mary's room. I left the rose..." He took in the situation. "You thought Mary had visited, didn't you?"

Feeling extremely foolish, I nodded as I gave up the questionable protection of the draperies and stepped forward. "I went to turn the oven off. I came back and saw the rose." I shrugged. "You could say I'm gullible. I mean, I believed I'd been transported back to the Civil War when I met you."

Nathan's laughter was deep. "You've had a hard few days, Emma Devlin. You came to Ravenwood wanting to believe in something more powerful than yourself. You're not gullible. You're desperate."

"I thought Mary had left the rose, and then when I heard the heavy footsteps upstairs, I rushed into believing the worst." It was a funny situation, but I wasn't laughing. "I guess I am desperate. I've opened my mind to too many possibilities. Ghosts, robbers..." The tears were inexplicably close. "The fact that my husband may have been deliberately murdered."

Nathan's arm around my shoulders was a comforting pressure. "I'm sorry, Emma. It's a hard thing to accept."

"It might explain Frank's... return. But, God, I don't want to believe it! To lose him by accident is horrible enough. If he was deliberately taken, well, that makes it worse. And it makes me want to strike back."

Nathan led me to the table and seated me. He took the chair to my right. In the light of the candles, his expression was intense. "Tell me what you found."

At first it was hard to begin, but once I started, the details spilled out of me. Nathan asked several questions and then returned to my description of the gun.

"An antique... An odd choice. Was there any more information on the type of gun?"

"You mean, the ballistics report?"

Nathan nodded. "What did it say?"

I shook my head. "It was pretty technical. They never found the murder weapon, so there wasn't a lot to go on." Against all of my willpower, my voice faltered. "He died instantly."

Nathan grasped my hand. "We need to find out if those two killers were identified by anyone else in other robberies."

"I've asked Robert to check the neighborhood. There've been other robberies, but as far as I know, no one else has been shot in cold blood."

"That isn't evidence, but it's another little thing that stands out. It's a break in the pattern."

His grip on my fingers was warm, secure. I knew I should withdraw my hand, but I didn't. It was such a luxury to listen to Nathan, to accept his generous help.

"Most robbers won't kill. If they're making a career out of robbery, they don't want a murder charge against them. It turns up the heat. People will tolerate being robbed, but they won't accept being afraid for their lives."

"I've never thought of it that way."

"Either these killers were beyond thinking, or they were not thieves."

"Robert said they may have been hopped up on something."

"Hopped up?"

"Taking drugs, high on PCP, crack, amphetamines, or any number of things."

"Drug abusers, opium addicts, hemp smokers..." Nathan toyed with my knife, "There's always a drug for each era. I don't know about these two killers, though. From what you've said, they don't seem to be irrational.''

"I know.'' Why hadn't I thought these things before? If my mind had worked sooner, I might have stood a chance of catching the killers. Now, two years had passed.

As if he read my mind, Nathan spoke softly. "Emma, it's hard to think of things that are not in your nature. To deliberately kill goes against your grain.''

"I'm not a child, Nathan. It's just that I can't imagine who would want to harm him. Or why. We didn't have a great amount of money.''

"His business?''

"I still own fifty percent of Micro-Tech. Nothing has changed, except the company makes a little more money now than it did before. And Benny, Frank's partner, said it will begin to earn more and more.''

"What did your husband do?'' Nathan leaned back in his chair.

The remainder of my dinner had grown cold and I pushed the plate to the side of the table. "Frank and Benny formed Micro-Tech about eight years ago, just before we married. Frank had the business background. He would go into a business, assess its data base needs, including the idiosyncrasies of each business, and then tell them he could put together a computer system that would increase their efficiency and productivity. The company is successful because Frank could tailor each system on paper, and Benny could make it work on computer.''

I couldn't suppress my sigh. "They were a great team. Frank knew business inside and out, and he enjoyed working with people. Benny is the typical computer whiz. Glasses, hair on end, nervous around women. Sort of the Clark Kent type, you know. Once you get past the shyness he's a very nice man, and with a woman's advice in wardrobe, he could be very handsome. Frank and I tried again and again to play cupid for Benny. He's so bright. And he was very attached to Frank.''

Frank's murder had almost destroyed Benny. He hid it from a lot of people, but Benny had been on the verge of a total collapse. But he'd pulled through it. Micro-Tech had nearly gone under, and it was the precarious situation of the business that had finally gotten Benny out of his depression and working again. I told all of this to Nathan with a minimum of emotion.

"When Frank went into these businesses, did he examine their books?'' he asked.

"He had to. The systems were individually created. That's what made them so special. Frank learned the business and then streamlined it.''

Nathan got up and paced the large dining room. His footsteps echoed on the hardwood floor. "Emma, what if he found something in one of those businesses?''

"Something illegal?''

"Exactly. If he found that something was going on, what would he have done?''

"He'd report it.''

"You're certain? What if they offered him money?''

I felt my back stiffen at the implication. "You didn't know Frank. He never did a dishonest thing in his life.'' I paused for effect. "Never.''

Nathan returned to the table. He lifted my hand again, but I withdrew it. I knew it was foolish to expect him to understand what kind of man Frank had been. But even the implication of bribery or wrongdoing stung.

"My theory is growing stronger.'' He put his hands flat on the table. "What if Frank found something in a company, something illegal? They tried to bribe him to remain silent, and he refused.''

His words seemed to dance in the candlelight. In the last few weeks of his life, Frank had been a little edgy. Maybe disappointed was a better word. I couldn't remember what accounts he was working on, but he usually enjoyed talking about his day. I remembered that he'd been unusually silent. "Maybe," I conceded.

"If they couldn't buy his silence, maybe they had to find a more permanent way of obtaining it."

"Oh, Nathan! No!" I couldn't help it. I felt a terrible rage and grief and sense of betrayal. Had someone killed my husband because he was too honest?

"It's okay, Emma." In a flash, Nathan was at my side. His hands on my shoulders offered support, friendship. He gave me a reassuring squeeze. "The one good thing about this is that after two years, their guard will be down. They won't expect us to come hunting for them now."

"Us?" I couldn't believe he was so willing to help me. "Why are you doing this, Nathan? Why are you helping me? You don't even know me."

He returned to his seat at the table. His eyes were unwavering, but the tension had left his face.

"You're a beautiful woman, Emma. You deserve to be free of the past. There's something about you and your story, about your love for Frank, that makes me want to help. It's as simple as that."

Looking into his blue eyes, I almost believed him. But as I was learning, things were never that simple. "And nothing else?"

"I believe in certain things. They may sound old-fashioned and outmoded to you."

"What things?"

"Oh, love and honor and all of that, a certain behavior, a basic kindness toward my fellow creatures, human and animal." He smiled. "Since I'm giving you my humanitarian speech, I should say that only humans can change the history of the world. I've studied it, and some changes need to be made. I heard a quote once, and I'll tell it to you. 'An act of kindness is the mark of a generous heart.' I think you have a generous heart, Emma Devlin."

"And you, too, Nathan Cates."

His smile was tender. "Perhaps neither of us is suited for such a harsh world. But you'll survive and make it a better place. Now I think you've had enough for one day. I'll help with this and then be gone. I've an early meeting at the college in the morning."

He rose from the table and began clearing the dishes away. In only moments we had the main house locked up tight and were back in the kitchen. "I didn't notice Frisco, or a car. How did you get here?"

"I walked. Even Frisco has to have a night off every now and then."

We laughed and chatted about the day's news until the kitchen was spotless. "It looks like you're a good cook," he noted.

"If you're feeling especially brave, how about dinner tomorrow night? I'll make my special Confederate cavalryman meal."

"I didn't realize you'd had practice with other Confederate cavalrymen."

His teasing was warm and very welcome. After the day I'd had, I needed to end this one on a light note. "Well, only a few, and none as interesting as you."

"In that case, I accept."

"I'll surprise you with my historical cooking skills."

"I'll bring some wine. I happen to know of a great wine cellar, and the owner won't mind if I treat you to a bottle. In fact, he won't be needing it, and he'd heartily approve of a beautiful woman enjoying it."

I was reluctant to see him go, but I knew he'd already spent his time generously with me. He had two jobs and who knew what other responsibilities. How had I been lucky enough that he'd taken me under his wing to shelter for a few weeks?

As I climbed the stairs to my room, I silently begged Frank not to accuse me on this night. A word of encouragement would have been nice. Very nice. But what I really needed was a long, deep, uninterrupted sleep. How long it had been since I'd had one?

My dreams that night were of pounding hooves and sudden confusion. They were not nightmares, but there was a certain frantic energy to them that didn't wake me but left me with a residue of anxiety. I awoke thinking of Mary Quinn. With the war raging all around her, her last years must have been filled with dreadful nights. At least she had been spared the worst of the siege.

Judging by the coral glow in the room, it was later than I'd expected to sleep. I pushed back the mosquito netting and padded downstairs in my slippers to make coffee. How would I spend the day? Writing verses for cards was out of the question. I had no ability to concentrate on such a task. I'd begun to work at the knot of Frank's murder, and I couldn't let it go. But what to do next?

I decided a trip to Frank's family might prove valuable. It would mean another drive to Jackson, but there was nothing at Ravenwood to hold me there. I hadn't given up hopes of meeting Mary Quinn, but I'd begun to realize that my mother had been right on target in assessing at least one part of my character—I am impatient. Given a choice between waiting and acting, I'll take action anytime. If I went to Jackson, I'd be back at Ravenwood in the late afternoon with time to spare to rendezvous with Mary, if she felt inclined, and to make dinner for Nathan. Besides, there were a few things I wanted to get from my house for the dinner. Since I'd boasted of my skills, I wanted to be sure I could carry through, even in the outdated kitchen of Ravenwood.

As I drove to Jackson, I tried to organize my thoughts. Frank had been very close to his brother, James. There was a good chance if something had been troubling Frank, he would have taken it to James.

The barracuda in that particular tank was James's wife. Marla Devlin was someone I'd never liked. She'd made her interest in Frank very clear, on more than one occasion. I'd been tempted to tell her husband about her behavior, but Frank had talked me out of it. He'd pointed out that for all of Marla's faults, James loved her deeply. I could only keep my fingers crossed that I'd find James at work—and Marla out shopping, as usual.

James Devlin's business, a sporting goods store in one of the bigger malls, had been a good solid business for years. A former Olympic contender in the four hundred meter, James knew sports, and he knew quality products. He was handsome, popular, and always available to help local kids' teams with free coaching or a sponsorship. In physical coloring, he was the exact opposite of Frank. James was blond, clean-shaven, with blue eyes.

Marla wasn't in evidence. Since she never waited on any female customers, I'd developed the theory that she "helped out" in the store because it gave her an opportunity to meet men who spent a lot of time taking care of their bodies. What she did once she met them, I didn't really want to know.

"Emma!" James greeted me with a warm smile and a hug. "Decide to take up jogging and buy new shoes?" I knew how it hurt him to see me. I reminded him of Frank. Obviously, James had decided to bluster past the sadness.

"Not on your life." I groaned and patted my hips. "My old joints would revolt and quit on me."

"Marla could show you some different fitness routines—"

"Thanks, but no thanks." I cut him off with a smile. "You know I'm a hopeless slug. Always was, always will be."

"But Frank loved you anyway." James gave me another hug. "And so do we," he whispered in my ear.

For a split second, I thought I might cry, but I lifted my chin and stepped back from him. "I need your help," I said softly. "I may be losing my mind, but I have something I must pursue."

"What?" James motioned to two stools behind the cash register. "Business probably won't pick up until around lunch, so we'll be able to talk. You sound pretty serious."

"There's no easy way to say this, James. Your brother may have been deliberately murdered."

The color drained from his face. "What are you saying?"

"I've been looking into it. There are some things that don't add up. Not big things, but little things. The more I dig, the more I find."

"Why are you doing this, Emma?"

The skin around his eyes had remained white. His expression was pained.

"Don't you realize that if you drag all of this out again, it's going to tear everyone up all over again?"

I'd expected some resistance from James, but not this. "But what if it's true? Whoever did it deserves to pay."

"How could it be true? He was in a liquor store robbery. He was killed by a crazed robber. That's the end of it. He's dead, Emma. This won't bring him back! Marla's right. You've spent the past two years dwelling on this and it has twisted you."

It was hard to check my anger, but I did. "I didn't want to start this. I resisted it. But I had no choice."

"What are you talking about?" James stood and began pacing the store. "You certainly have a choice. Stop all of this right now!"

"I can't. In the weeks before Frank died, did he mention anything about his work?"

"You think Benny Yeager did something to Frank? The man almost lost it after Frank died."

"Not Benny. I know Frank's death hit him almost as hard as it did me, and the Devlin clan." I softened my voice, pushing my impatience down. "But Frank worked with a lot of other people. Other businesses. You know as well as I do that if he found something illegal, he would have tried to report it. Maybe someone wanted to stop him."

James walked across the store to the counter and leaned on it with both hands. "This is insane, Emma. You're losing your grip completely. Frank and Benny designed computer systems and programs to help businesses. They weren't spies or CIA agents, or even IRS agents. They didn't uncover illegal schemes."

"I'm not asking you to believe me, James. I'm only asking you to tell me if Frank mentioned anything to you about being troubled at work. You were close. He might have confided in you."

"And not you, Emma?"

James spoke with a cruelty I'd never seen in him before. "Maybe not." Tears burned my eyes. "I'm sorry I troubled you." I rose to leave when James's hand on my shoulder stopped me.

"I'm sorry, Em. I didn't mean that."

"Forget it, James. I shouldn't have come here with suspicions." I twisted free of his grip. I had to get out of that shop. With my luck, Marla would walk in at any second.

"Emma, Frank did mention one thing. I thought it was strange at the time, too, but I never put a sinister twist on it."

His words made me pause. I turned back to face him. "What?"

"About a week before he was killed, he asked me if I'd ever taken a state bid on athletic equipment, like for a school."

"And?" I prompted. James didn't want to talk about this and I didn't understand why.

"I told him Marla took care of the larger contracts and such, and I wasn't up to speed on all the details. He wanted to know something about state laws with bidding and cost overruns and stuff like that. He did seem tense. He kept rubbing his neck, as if he was having trouble again.''

Frank had injured his neck in a car accident once, and whenever he was under stress, the old injury aggravated him. He would unconsciously rub his neck whenever he felt the muscles begin to knot.

"Did he mention any businesses or contracts in particular?"

James shook his head. "Not to me. Maybe Marla. I don't know if he pursued this with her or not. Like I said, she's the one with all the details in that area. She does all of the big contracts.'' James smiled. "She's done well, lately, too. Devlin's Sportsplex has picked up some nice work with several of the high schools and colleges. Marla has a real knack for sales."

I might have to talk with Marla later, but not today. The near clash with James had taken a toll. Marla would run over me like a cement truck, and if she knew anything, she wouldn't tell me out of spite. Because Frank had rebuffed her advances, she hated both of us. The old saying that hell hath no fury like a woman scorned was made for Marla. I didn't feel like taking a blast of sulfuric flames.

"I've got another appointment now, James. Maybe I'll catch Marla later."

"She should be back." He frowned. "She should've been back."

"It was good to see you." I leaned forward to give him a hug. Whatever passed between us, I didn't want to lose my connection with James. Frank had loved him so much. It would be like losing another little bit of Frank.

"Take care, Emma. Please try to let this go."

"I'll try," I promised.

"Well, well, if it isn't our long-lost sister."

I broke away from James guiltily. It was a brotherly hug, and only Marla would have made it seem otherwise. "Hello, Marla. I didn't hear you come in."

"Obviously. Nor did my husband."

She looked stunning, as usual. Her apricot sweater and skirt were perfect with her dark hair's amber highlights. It was a dye job, and an exceptional one. Her olive complexion was flawless, and her apricot nails were at least a half-inch long and flawlessly manicured. She was so damn ... immaculate.

"Emma was asking some questions about state bids and contracts."

I couldn't be certain, but it looked as if a flicker of apprehension touched Marla's eyes.

"What about state bids?" Her voice gave nothing away.

"Does the lowest bidder always get the contract?" I was floundering. I didn't know what I needed to ask, but I had to think of something.

"Not always. A lot depends on quality as well as quantity and price." She shrugged. "Then, of course, it's the governing body's subjective opinion at times."

"Are state bids public record?"

"What are you driving at, Emma?"

This time Marla was distinctly ill-at-ease. I'd touched some sore spot without even intending to do so.

"I'm trying to learn how the government conducts business."

"Take a course from the Small Business Development Center."

"Marla!" Shock rang in James's voice.

I was saved by the entrance of three teenage boys determined to find the perfect running shoe. James went to wait on them after giving Marla a stern look.

"What are you up to, Emma?" Marla was smiling as she talked, but not with her eyes.

"I told you. I'm trying to learn something."

"James may think you're an innocent. I know better. You're up to something. Let me warn you. If you tamper with me, you'll pay."

"Is that a threat, Marla?" I was more angry than afraid.

"You're damn right it is. Leave things alone. Don't go poking your nose where it won't do any good."

Chapter Five

With a grocery bag of special ingredients, my favorite Eugene Walter cookbook, *Delectable Dishes from Termite Hall,* and my cast-iron skillet on the back seat of the mini van, I was ready to head back to Vicksburg. The encounters with James and Marla plagued me. There was something off center with Marla. I'd asked a simple question, and she'd badly overreacted.

Almost as if she had something to hide.

Jackson was only minutes behind me when I realized that Marla's behavior resembled nothing more than guilt. My questions about state bidding laws had made her feel guilty. Why? What did she know? On the spur of the moment, I took the exit for Mississippi College. Nathan had said he had an early meeting at the school. There was a chance I might catch him, and he would be able to refer me to some sources to check about bidding laws.

The college campus was tranquil. It is a small institution that boasts a law school and an old name. The history department was easy to locate, and I hurried to the reception area. I was glad to see an older woman at the desk instead of the young girl I'd spoken with the day before.

"I'm looking for Nathan Cates," I explained.

"Is he a student?" The older woman reached for a student directory. "You'll probably be able to find him faster if you go to the registrar."

"He's a professor." At her blank look, I added, "A history professor here. Nathan Cates. C-A-T-E-S."

"We don't have a Cates here," she said slowly.

"But he teaches history..." I forced myself to stop. The woman wasn't being obstinate, she simply had no idea who Nathan was. "Could you check your faculty listings? Maybe he's new," I suggested. "Maybe he's been hired under political science or something else?"

She brightened at that thought and pulled out another directory. "I know almost everyone in arts and sciences," she explained. "I've been here nearly twenty years, but he could be new or temporary."

Her finger traced the column of names, going through the C's one by one. "Could it be a K?" she asked.

"Try it." I had the strongest sense of someone staring at me, but when I glanced over my shoulder, there was no one there.

The secretary completed the list of K's, to no avail. She gave me a sympathetic look. "Are you certain he said he worked here? I can show you in to see the dean, if you'd like."

"No. It's personal. Would you do one last favor for me and call payroll? If he's on this campus, anyplace, they'll have a listing for him."

"Folks want their pay," she agreed as she punched in the extension. It took only a moment for her to obtain a negative reply. Nathan Cates did not now, nor had he ever worked for the college.

"I'm sorry, dear," she said as she replaced the receiver. "I know you're disappointed, but you're a smart one to come here and check him out. My daughter had something similar happen to her. She wasted six months on a man who wouldn't know the truth if it bit him on the ankle. This day and age men can't be trusted.''

"Thanks for all your trouble." My voice sounded hollow, the echo of something in my chest. I'd trusted Nathan so completely, so foolishly, a stranger in costume who rode up on a horse. But why had he lied to me? Why had he shown any interest in me whatsoever? None of it made sense. The drive back to Vicksburg was a torment.

Ravenwood was as beautiful as ever, and twice as empty. I felt time slipping away from me. I had a head full of suspicions, but I was really no closer to solving my dilemma with Frank than I had been before I came here. If anything, I was only more confused.

When I unloaded the van at the apartment, I was faced with another decision. Should I make dinner and pretend nothing was wrong until I sprang my discoveries on Nathan? Or should I meet him at the door and tell him I knew he was a liar? I wanted to do the latter, but I made myself begin the preparations for the meal. I wanted to know why he'd done it. Chances were I'd never learn the truth, but I was going to attempt it. So far, I had nothing but questions, and I was sick of it.

I'd settled on a simple menu of pork chops, stuffed okra and a grits casserole topped with black-eyed peas. Cornbread on the side with some fresh collards and dewberry cobbler for dessert. I'd noticed the berries growing lush and sweet along one of the paths around the plantation. The briars that protected the berries could be annoying, but I'd learned picking expertise as a child.

I took a plastic bucket from the kitchen and set out to get the berries. I needed the fresh air and the sunshine. My encounter at the college had upset me even more than I was willing to admit. I kept picturing Nathan, so concerned for me, so interested in my troubles. So compassionate. And such a liar. An act of betrayal.

Nathan was the first person I'd let close to me in two years. That made his act doubly bitter. It was just another lesson that vulnerability was a luxury I couldn't afford.

In only fifteen minutes I had my bucket brimming with enough berries for a large cobbler and more to spare. I set it aside and decided to take a hurried walk to the old oak. My hopes of a visitation from Mary grew dimmer with each day that passed, but I couldn't allow myself to give up. If I had enough faith, she'd come. I had to believe it.

As before, the tree exuded some unexplainable comfort. I took a seat on the same old root and let my thoughts wander. Did they still perform shock treatments on mental patients? The question popped into my mind and made me shudder. If I didn't solve the riddle of Frank's return, would I end up in a sterile room with bars on the windows and my family as my only visitors? I guess maybe I wanted to feel sorry for myself, because I was doing a damn good job of it.

The first strains of "Dixie," clearly whistled, startled me out of my self-pity. Someone was coming down the path, whistling as if they didn't have a care in the world.

I stood, prepared to confront the whistler. Ravenwood was like a bus station, it seemed. Even when it was closed, people came and went at their whims. But perhaps this was the groundskeeper and it was I who was intruding on his work.

It was Nathan who rounded the curve and swept off his cavalry hat with a bow and a grin.

"I thought you'd be slaving away in the kitchen," he said.

"Soon," I replied, turning so that he could see only my profile. I couldn't look him in the eye. I was too angry, too hurt. If I was going to play this cool, I couldn't blow it by letting my anger show.

"I found some delicious berries already picked in the path," he said, coming up to stand beside me. "I couldn't believe my good luck. But I only ate half of them because I didn't want to spoil my appetite for dinner.''

"Half..." I realized he was teasing me and stopped.

"Are you okay, Emma?" He turned me to face him and I knew it was pointless to pretend.

"I stopped by the college, Nathan. No one had ever heard of you before. You aren't on the payroll and the history department secretary who's been there forever didn't know your name."

Instead of a denial, laughter came from his lips. "So, you're investigating me, too? Sounds like you've been bitten by the detective bug."

"No, I wanted to ask you something about state bidding laws. I thought you could recommend some research sources." I was annoyed at his easy dismissal. He was still smiling and acting as if I were a child. "It isn't amusing."

"No," he agreed, reluctantly letting the laughter fade from his eyes. "And I'm sorry, Emma. It's just that it isn't such a mystery. I'm on a grant. National Endowment for the Humanities. I'm not on payroll or employment records at the college because I'm being paid by the federal government."

"Oh." My cheeks burned with a flush of shame. I'd accused him of deception of the worst kind. All I'd managed to accomplish was to show my ignorance and ingratitude.

"I was very lucky to get the grant," he said softly. "I should have explained it all properly, but I was afraid you'd think I was swaggering, or else be bored by the trivia of university life."

I held up both hands. "Don't apologize to me. I'm the one who owes you an apology. Nathan, I feel terrible." The tiniest smile touched my lips. "And I also feel much better. The thought that you'd lied was giving me a lot of trouble."

"Betrayal is a terrible act, isn't it?"

"Yes." Betrayed was the exact word that Frank used. Sadness swept over me. "It must be horrible to feel betrayed by someone you love." I turned away from him and leaned against the rough bark of the tree. There was a carving with the initials C.W. and M.Q. It almost broke my heart.

"Let's go back to Ravenwood," Nathan suggested, taking my arm. "I didn't eat your berries, but some smart creature may find them and haul them away."

"I picked them for a cobbler." My arm rested lightly in Nathan's. He had a strange courtliness that I enjoyed, an ability to make me feel more alive than I'd felt in years. Walking beside him in his cavalry uniform, I could almost imagine what it would have been like to stroll the grounds of Ravenwood with a Confederate soldier.

"How did you know cobbler was my favorite dessert?"

"Really?" His response was part of his wonderful gallantry. If I'd mentioned gallberry pie, he would have answered the same. "And I suppose stuffed okra is another favorite?"

"I don't believe I've had the pleasure. But it sounds promising."

I laughed out loud. There was no tripping this man. He'd been trained by someone with a strong sense of propriety and upbringing. "I'd love to meet your mother."

"And she'd love to meet you, Miss Emma."

I laughed again. When we finally got to the kitchen, he left me to finish the preparations for dinner. He had errands to run, and I wanted some time to prepare the meal and then take a shower. I'd mentioned only briefly my concerns about state bidding. Nathan had pointed out that the next logical step would be to look at the last accounts Frank managed. If there was a state contract among his clients, then it might be the best clue yet.

It would mean another trip to Jackson, but at least this time I didn't have the specter of Marla hanging over me. It would be good to see Benny. At least six months had passed since our last visit—a board meeting for the directors of Micro-Tech. I decided to call Benny and set up an appointment for lunch. I didn't want to tell him exactly what I was doing. Frank's death had upset him too much, as James had so brutally reminded me. I didn't want to open old wounds unless absolutely necessary.

My mind busy with thoughts of the next day, I began the preparations for the meal.

As he delighted over the stuffed okra, Nathan told me what he'd learned about bid laws, but it wasn't heartening. The laws were complicated and varied from governing body to governing body. Although they were designed to give all bidders a fair shake, they didn't always work.

Nathan approved of my decision to check the accounts at Micro-Tech the next day. We agreed to meet for dinner at a local riverside restaurant the next evening, and Nathan left. Once again I climbed the stairs to my bedroom and co-cooned myself in the coral swirls of the bed. But sleep wouldn't visit me. It wasn't bad dreams of Frank that kept me awake. I realized for the first time in a long while how lonely I was. The perceived deception of a man I'd known only a few days had hurt me deeply. Was it because I had no old friends? When Frank died, I cut myself off from most of our social group. It was too raw, too painful to be with them. I kept in touch, but I realized it had been in a very distant way. Except when my family thrust themselves upon me and forced me to acknowledge them, I'd spent the past two years alone.

Nathan Cates had finally broken through that barrier.

I asked myself why, but my mind veered away from that question. I wasn't ready to answer, and that in itself made me concerned. Nathan had touched me. He had warmed a place in me that was frozen and hard. As the land around me at Ravenwood, I was beginning to feel the warmth of spring and a new cycle of life. Sleep surrounded me on that thought and I drifted away.

The next morning I was in the middle of Jackson traffic before I realized I hadn't called Benny. Well, he wouldn't be upset to see me. We'd always had a great fondness for one another. Instead of telling him what I was doing, I'd decided to show an interest in the workings of the company. Benny had frequently asked me to attend more meetings and to take an active role in the business. Although I held Frank's fifty percent of the stock, I had pushed all of the responsibility onto Benny. Maybe it was time that I grew up and tried to help.

Micro-Tech is only a block from the capitol. Frank had picked up the old building on George Street for a great price, and he and Benny had remodeled it completely. It was a blend of art deco and high tech design, and for the first time in two years, I smiled as I looked at it. Frank's personality was all over it. He'd loved the bright colors and lines of art deco, and Benny had supplied the high tech complements. No two men had ever shared a more compatible partnership. I parked in front of the office and was getting out of the mini van when Benny stepped out the front door to greet me.

"Emma! It's wonderful to see you!"

I hugged him with all of my strength. "Were you standing in the door waiting for me?" I teased. "Maybe you have ESP, Benny."

"Actually, I was rushing out to buy some stamps." He took my arm and led me toward the door. "I didn't believe it was you, at first, but who else could be so beautiful so early in the morning."

"My goodness." I was overwhelmed. Benny was usually so shy and bashful. "You've learned the art of flattery. Have you been taking lessons?"

Benny flushed. "I guess I'm just glad to see you." He looked at the floor. "Really glad. I've been afraid you'd find Micro-Tech too painful a reminder and decide to sell your stock.''

"Benny." I gave him another hug. "I wouldn't do that. This business was Frank's life. I'd never let it go."

He looked up and smiled, the same shy old smile that I remembered so well. "That's a relief. I guess I'm just a worrier. At night, I wake up thinking about these things."

"Well, that's one worry you can forget. I'm in Micro-Tech until you decide you want to buy me out. Besides, you've been doing such a great job, why would I want to sell? Our profits were up last quarter."

"And should be again this one." Benny brightened. "Let me show you."

"What about those stamps?"

"I forgot." He brushed back his unruly hair. "I'll make a dash to the post office and be right back. What if I pick up some pastries and coffee?"

"I was counting on that. I didn't bother with breakfast and unless you want to hear my stomach growling all morning, I'd better feed it something."

"Back in thirty!" Benny said as he dashed out the front door. "Beth will take good care of you."

Beth, the secretary-receptionist, chatted a moment before I excused myself. She was new at Micro-Tech, and I thought Benny had done a good job of hiring her. She was neat, friendly and not overly nosy.

I hadn't expected it to be so easy to get some time alone. Benny almost lived at Micro-Tech. Taking full advantage of my opportunity, I went to Frank's old office and closed the door. Everything was just as Frank had left it. There was a picture of me in a straw hat, laughing, on Frank's desk. The calendar still showed the year he was killed. Only the janitor had been in the room. Swallowing my tears, I took the key to Frank's desk out of my pocket and found his daily appointment book. I slipped it into my purse for study later and then keyed in his computer.

I'd never spent a great deal of time learning how to op-
erate a computer, but I had some knowledge because I used
one for my own work. My fingers were clumsy on the keyboard. Nerves. I was beginning to think I'd never even get
to the opening menu of Frank's files when I finally mas-
tered my fingers. Most systems work on some password or
code or series of numbers. To gain access, I'd have to think
like Frank. What word would have tickled his dry humor,
or caught his attention enough to be granted the honor of
being assigned as a code word? He liked unusual words and
Indian names. I tried several of those, beginning with
"wombat." No luck. I tried Devlin; FAD, his initials; Ken-
nedy, his favorite president; and even martini, his favorite
drink. My scalp was beginning to tingle with exasperation
when I finally typed in Emma. The screen shifted to blue
and the menu was visible.

The files were extensive, and since I was unfamiliar with
them, I read through them twice. Nothing jumped out at me
in a grand revelation. In fact, it looked hopeless. I could
spend two weeks culling through the files and probably
wouldn't understand a single thing. Why had I expected to
find what I was looking for underlined and boldfaced? I
checked my watch. Benny would be back in a few minutes.
Maybe the easiest thing to do would be to come straight out
and ask him what Frank had been working on.

No, then I'd have to tell him why I was interested, and
even though he looked happy and stable, I knew how close
to the edge he'd come once before. If I had more evidence,
I'd tell him. But I only had a few suspicions and some things
that didn't match up. It wouldn't be fair to upset him without stronger proof.

I went over the files again. I tried all the combinations I
knew for access to a calendar. Frank and Benny were ge-
niuses at inventing efficient programs—and ones that I
couldn't open. I took a deep breath and read the screen

again. It had to be easy. Micro-Tech's unwritten motto was that any moron could use their systems.

It hit me like a cement block—date. I typed it in and was rewarded with a reshuffling of all entries on the screen. Seconds later, I had what I wanted. Scrolling down to the last entries, I took out a piece of paper and began to write down the companies Frank had visited in the last few months of his life. There were dozens, and I scribbled as if Satan were breathing down my back. One looked no more promising—or sinister—than any of the others. There were music companies, dry cleaners, asphalt and cement companies, building supplies, pool and patio shops, banks. That struck me with some interest. If there had been dirty dealings at one of the businesses, a bank would be a good place since they handled so much money. I had three dozen names before I cleared the screen and went to the safe.

It was curiosity more than anything else that made me twist the dial. Frank never kept anything at the office. Our important papers were in a safe-deposit box in the bank. The office safe had been more of a joke between him and Benny. They said they kept their lunches there. And the gun that Frank had bought and never used. It occurred to me that even if he'd had the weapon on him the night he was murdered, it wouldn't have made a difference. Robert Mason kept a gun. He hadn't used it because there hadn't been time. The killers had been too volatile.

The dial spun beneath my fingers. Left, right, left. When I pulled the handle, nothing happened. I tried again. I knew the combination by heart. It was our wedding date. The safe refused to open. I had to be doing something wrong. Settling back on my heels, I went at it again.

"Emma! What are you doing?"

I almost screamed at the unexpected sound of Benny's voice. "I've lost my touch with Frank's old safe. I can't seem to make it open."

"Checking to see what I have for lunch?" Benny teased as he settled down beside me. He gave the knob a few twirls and the safe popped open.

"I guess I was hoping that I'd find something personal of Frank's. Some last note or remark." I shrugged as I pulled out a few papers and a strange velvet sack I'd never seen before. When the safe was empty, I carried the contents to Frank's desk.

The papers were insurance premiums on Micro-Tech and a few records about titles and deeds for the company. I handed them back to Benny.

"Frank asked me to keep this for you until you came looking for it," Benny said, pointing to the sack. "I wanted to tell you, but he made me promise."

"What is it?" I touched the blue velvet and drew back my hand. I hadn't bargained for finding any personal secrets, especially not ones cloaked in blue velvet. It could only contain jewelry.

"Open it, Emma. Frank spent a lot of time picking it out. He was going to give it to you as your anniversary present."

Benny's voice sounded choked. I couldn't look at him. I was afraid we'd both break down and cry. Very carefully, I opened the sack and poured the pearl necklace onto the desk. It was opera length, each pearl luminescent against the polished mahogany.

"It's beautiful," I whispered.

"Frank said it would be gorgeous against your skin, with your dark hair. He was going to pretend that he hadn't gotten a present, and then bring you down here the next day for a surprise party." Benny choked. After a moment he cleared his throat and continued. "He told me that he wanted you to find your surprise when you came to this office. He made me promise that I wouldn't say a word. Then the accident happened and, well, I didn't know what to do. Weeks passed, then months. Then I didn't know how to give it to you." His face was white with tension. "I'm so sorry. I just couldn't think about any of it."

It was almost too much. The wave of pain that washed over me was like a fist slamming again and again. I clutched the pearls like a lifeline. In a few moments I was able to put them away and look up at Benny with a smile.

"He was a wonderful husband," I said.

"And partner." Benny reached across the desk and patted my hand. His own was shaking. "How about that coffee?"

We both needed some distance from the intense emotions, and I followed Benny into the coffee room. Beth joined us for a cup and a pastry, and Benny talked about the new directions Micro-Tech was taking.

It was wonderful to watch Benny's enthusiasm. And although Beth was very discreet, I could see that she was charmed by Benny. I could only hope that he'd see it one day soon. She was a delightful young woman with poise and a real sweetness that I thought would be just right for him. I had to smile at the idea that I still wasn't able to stop playing cupid for the computer whiz.

"You look terrific, Emma," Benny said as I picked up my purse to leave. Beth had returned to her desk and we had a few moments alone. "I hope this is a sign you'll be coming by here more often."

"I'd like to, Benny. I think I can now, without too much pain, for both of us. I'd intended to take you to lunch, and I'd still like to if you have a clear schedule."

Benny's face fell. "I can't. I'm having lunch with a prospective new client. Big account, too. But I'd rather eat with you."

"Duty before pleasure," I quipped. "No time for fun when there's money to be made."

"Frank always warned me that underneath that beautiful exterior lurked Simon Legree."

"Since we can't make lunch, maybe you could come over for dinner one night soon. Bring Beth if she'd like to come."

"Beth?" Benny looked puzzled.

"She's a delightful young woman. I enjoy her company."

"Yes, she's a sweet girl." Benny hesitated. "You know she worked for a company that Frank took on as an account. When he found some discrepancies in their books, they fired Beth and accused her of embezzlement. Frank never believed the charges, and he mentioned that he'd like to hire her." Benny sighed. "After he died, I did. It was sort of like a wish fulfilled."

Like Frank, I couldn't believe Beth was capable of stealing, but it did cast a new light on the situation. "Well, bring her over if you'd like." I was in no position to offer advice to anyone.

"Emma, I have to ask you this." He looked down at his feet. "Have you ever felt there was more to Frank's death than just a stroke of bad luck?"

My breath escaped in a small rush.

"I didn't mean to upset you!" He steadied my elbow and tried to steer me toward a chair.

I got a grip on my emotions and convinced him I was fine. "That would be a bitter pill, wouldn't it?" I asked. "No one disliked Frank enough to kill him."

"I know that. It's just that...sometimes, when I think about it... Well, I just wanted to ask. To see what you thought."

I opened my mouth to tell him, but I hesitated. Of all the people who had loved Frank, Benny was the most vulnerable. Even more than I. "Don't think about it, Benny."

"I guess we have to move forward instead of always looking back. It's just that, well, lately I've had the feeling that someone is following me. I know it sounds paranoid and all, but when I work late up here, I could swear someone's watching every move I make. I was hoping maybe you'd hired a detective or something.''

"No, I haven't hired anyone." I tried to sound light, but what he said troubled me greatly. If someone was watching Benny, would they try to hurt him? "But you know it's never a bad idea to be on guard. Violence can strike anyone, even well-intentioned people like us.''

Benny took his glasses off and cleaned them. Without the thick lenses, his eyes were a crystal blue. "I must be getting paranoid in my old age, and I was worried for you." He walked with me out the front door and to my van. "I'd die if anything happened to you, Emma.''

"No need to worry, Benny, I'm healthy as a horse.''

"And I want you to stay that way.''

He gave me a kiss on the cheek as he held open my door. "To the future, Emma. A happy one for both of us," he said before he slammed the door. As I pulled away, he stood on the sidewalk watching me. I suddenly realized that in the past two years, Benny had been as lonely as I had.

Chapter Six

Sitting in the Riverview waiting for Nathan to arrive, I had the strangest sensation that I was living two entirely different lives. Outside the picture window by my table, the Mississippi River curved slowly through the twilight toward New Orleans. There were several houseboats docked on the Louisiana side where the bank is strangely flat. The Vicksburg side is high cliffs, a vantage point the South protected during the four years of the Civil War. While my mind played with the past, I watched two tugs churn upriver pushing large flatbeds loaded with blue plastic shipping containers. What was it about this town that made the past so suddenly alive for me?

Perhaps it was the Mississippi, home of Huck and Tom and the U.S.S. *Cairo* and so much more. I was an inland girl, born in the middle of the state where only the Pearl River offered commerce. The Pearl is a dirt road in contrast to the Mississippi's super highway.

"What thoughts are amusing you?"

I looked up to find Nathan standing next to my table. For the first time he was dressed casually in jeans and a cotton pullover of peacock blue. His eyes were complimented by the shade.

"The river," I said, nodding out the window. "It endures. And I feel so... temporary."

"Love endures, Emma. If you truly love someone, that never changes." His knees brushed against mine as he took a seat. "Like the river, the course shifts over time, but it never disappears."

"Have you ever loved like that, Nathan?" It was a very forward question, but it seemed so right to ask.

"Once." His smile was sad. "But she died. She was trying to save our daughter. A house fire." He looked toward the muddy swirl of the river. "They both died."

I felt his pain as if it were my own. It was no wonder that he understood my love for Frank. I reached across the table and captured his hand. There were no words, so I simply held his hand until I felt his fingers curl around mine.

When he looked back at me, some of the sadness had left his eyes. "We endure, Emma, because we can love. That's our gift to the world."

Whether by blessing or curse, the waiter appeared with the bottle of wine I'd ordered and two glasses. The moment passed between Nathan and me, but I was left strangely shaken. The emotions he generated were so strong, so turbulent.

He turned the conversation to my discoveries for the day. After dinner we went over the list of names I'd made and I got out Frank's appointment book. We settled on three companies to check: South Trust Savings and Loan, Wilson Asphalt and Cleveland Electrical Engineers. Frank had met with officials at all three companies shortly before his death. He'd met with them repeatedly. It wasn't a smoking gun, but it did bear looking into. Nathan tried to help me frame several leading questions to ask officials at each of the companies, but my grasp of the intricacies of business was a serious drawback.

"Come with me," I finally said. "Drive over to Jackson with me tomorrow. We'll go in as a team. You can make sure I ask the right questions."

For a minute I thought he was going to refuse. It wasn't fair of me to ask him. He was, after all, working two jobs.

"Okay," he agreed. "But give me a day to get my suit pressed and some loose ends tied up. If we're going to do this, we might as well do it properly. And you need to call and make appointments for us. We can't just drop in."

"Good idea." I felt my excitement rise. Nathan gave me confidence in myself. If there was anything to Frank's death, we'd find it.

Since we'd both driven to the restaurant, we parted in the parking lot. Nathan walked me to my van. While we'd dined, night had fallen and the sky was thick with stars. It was one of those beautiful spring nights when the air smells fresh and clean. A boat on the river sounded a mournful horn.

"You're a brave woman," Nathan said apropos of nothing.

"Hardly. Remember that I was dragged into this. I'm the one who's being visited by a ghost."

"You could have ignored it. Or believed yourself insane. Both of those roads would have been easier."

I'd never thought of insanity as an easier route, but in a weird kind of way it made sense. I would have put control in someone else's hands.

Wind gusted through the parking lot. Nathan reached across the short distance that separated us and brushed my hair from my face. I'd chosen to wear it loose rather than tied back. His fingers lingered on my cheek, then slowly traveled to the back of my head. I knew he was going to kiss me. I wanted him to.

He drew me close to him and I put my arms on his shoulders. I was pressed full-length against him, against the solid masculinity of his chest and body. His kiss blocked out the rest of the world.

When we finally broke apart, we were both breathing raggedly. "I've wanted to kiss you from the first moment I saw you," he said. "This isn't what I bargained for."

There was wry humor in his voice, and I shared it. I hadn't come to Ravenwood for a romantic encounter. The kiss had deeply unsettled me, but there was also a pure joy singing in my veins. Nathan's kiss had stirred me in a way I thought would never happen again.

"You bring a lot of emotions to the surface, Emma. I feel things for you, with you, that I haven't in a long, long time."

"I was thinking the same thing." I touched his cheek, rasping the slight stubble with my nails. "I need some time to think about all of this." I traced one side of his mustache.

"We're virtual strangers."

"In many ways," I agreed. "Yet I feel that I know you."

He kissed me lightly on the lips. "I'm going to be busy tomorrow, but I'll be at your door early Thursday."

"Will you make biscuits for me again?"

"Anything to make you smile," he said as he opened the van door and held it for me.

When I was seated, he bent down and kissed me again. "Thursday, Emma," he said as he closed the door and walked away. He seemed to disappear into the darkness.

That night I thought a lot about Nathan. So many things about him were extraordinary. His concern for me, first of all. There was something a bit unnatural about it. Wonderful, but unnatural.

And what about me? I'd become dependent on a man I hardly knew. It was an unnerving thought, and tinged with guilt. I went to bed expecting a visit from Frank. Though none came, I still couldn't shake a sense of foreboding.

I spent the next day in the gardens at Ravenwood. A pair of old gloves and a basket of tools had been left under the kitchen counter, and I made myself at home working among the flower beds beside the apartment. The formal gardens I walked in and enjoyed—and left for the professional gardeners. But I thought I could do no harm in the smaller beds where a few weeds had begun to show. Whatever the flowers needed, I was desperate for some physical work.

My emotions needed to be untangled and explored. I was not in love with Nathan Cates, but the possibility was there. He was a man I could love. Those thoughts shocked me, because I'd never believed that after Frank I would think along those lines. The question I needed to answer was whether or not to act on my feelings. As I dug in the rich earth, I came to my own conclusion, right or wrong.

I could not begin with Nathan until I had resolved everything with my husband. What would it do to my feelings for Nathan if I felt as if I'd abandoned or betrayed Frank? I knew that answer. It would destroy anything good we could ever hope to build between ourselves. Frank would not destroy it, I would. My guilt would.

I put the trowel and gloves back in the basket and stood, satisfied with my morning's labors. The flower bed was freshly turned and not a weed dared poke its head up through the black earth.

I showered and changed and made the calls to Jackson to set up the appointments for the next day. Then as a treat I dressed for lunch at the Vicksburg Tea Room and went sightseeing. I had the sense that Vicksburg, like me, was caught somehow between the past and present. It was a modern town with the traffic and hustle of any other small city, but there was the sense that two blocks down and just around the corner, the past was waiting. Perhaps I'd been spending too much time with a historian.

That night I read until a troubled sleep took me. Frank did not awaken me, but other images disturbed my rest. A hundred questions popped into my head. I was making notes in a steno pad when I heard Nathan's knock at the door.

I read my questions while he took off his suit jacket and made biscuits. He was a charming sight in his gray pin-striped suit pants, starched white shirt and an old pink apron with ruffles. Just the sight of him quelled some of my anxieties.

"One word and I'll burn the biscuits," he warned with a smile.

"Not on a dare," I said solemnly. "I was only going to say that pink is your color."

We bantered our way through breakfast and the drive to Jackson. By unspoken consent, we didn't talk about the kiss we'd shared, or the emotions we'd stirred.

The savings and loan was our first stop. Carlton Frazier was the vice president we'd arranged to see. A tall man with thick glasses, he took my hand in his own damp one as he indicated two seats in front of his large desk.

I introduced Nathan as a potential investor in my late husband's company. Nathan and I had decided that our best ruse would be to pretend that he was interested in buying some or all of my shares in Micro-Tech. Since South Trust was listed as a client of the computer company, we'd decided to approach the S&L for a possible loan for Nathan.

Frazier listened to my little speech with growing perplexity.

"Whatever gave you the idea that Micro-Tech had worked with South Trust?" he finally asked.

My confusion almost undid me. "But my husband and Benny Yeager did rework your computer system, didn't they?"

"South Trust has never done business with your husband or a company called Micro-Tech." Frazier stood. "Where did you get your information?"

I cast a look at Nathan. He edged forward in his chair. "Mrs. Devlin must have confused her documents," he said smoothly. "I tried to explain to her that it wouldn't matter if your bank had done business with Micro-Tech or not.

Such information wouldn't influence your decision on the loan.''

"Exactly right." Carlton Frazier settled back into his chair. He shifted his focus from Nathan to me. "I'm just curious how you came to your conclusion."

I shrugged helplessly. "I suppose Frank, my late husband, must have said something about South Trust to me. He talked about his business often, but I hardly ever understood any of it. I guess he spoke of your bank and I jumped to the conclusion." I turned to Nathan. "Have I committed some terrible business faux pas?"

Nathan patted my hand in a condescending way. "Of course not, Mrs. Devlin. Of course not. No harm done, is there, Mr. Frazier?"

"Absolutely none," Frazier answered. He smiled slightly.

"I think I need to powder my nose," I said, rising. "If you gentlemen will excuse me."

Once in the ladies' room, I gave Nathan ten minutes to work on Frazier. We'd almost dropped the ball due to my careless examination of Frank's files. But South Trust had been listed as a client, and it had been on Frank's appointment book. Unless he had personal business with the S&L, he'd met with someone at South Trust on behalf of Micro-Tech.

When I returned to Frazier's office, Frank was ready to go. He held a loan application in his left hand while he shook Frazier's hand with his right.

As soon as we were safely in the mini van, I turned expectantly to Nathan.

"Very strange," Nathan agreed. "We need to get into your husband's files."

"That can be arranged." I reached into my pocket and drew out the key to the back door. "Maybe we should stay in Jackson tonight and slip into Micro-Tech when no one's about."

Nathan nodded. "Where to now?"

"Wilson Asphalt."

"That's Steve Gray, right?"

"If I haven't managed to bungle this information, too."
I didn't have much time to mope. The asphalt company was
only five minutes from the S&L. It was a low beige building that rambled on and on, surrounded by a chain-link
fence and several signs warning of armed security guards.
It crossed my mind that it would be extremely difficult for
a thief to haul off cement or asphalt, unless they stole the
trucks. I guess my career as a scribbler gave me no idea of
the devious plots that could be developed in a criminal
mind. Anyway, who would steal cement? I started to ask
Nathan, but he was seriously studying the layout of the
buildings.

"Anything wrong?" I asked.

He shook his head. "Your husband must have been very
bright. How would a person ever learn about all these different types of businesses?"

"He loved it." I shrugged. "He wanted to be a baseball
player, until he found he had a real head for business."

"And what would you have chosen, Emma, given two
such different careers?"

"He made the decision before he knew me. And for myself, I can't say." I grinned at him. "Maybe I would have
been a detective."

"Maybe it isn't too late," he answered.

We entered Wilson Asphalt smiling, but there was an edge
to my senses that kept me alert. I'd booked the appointment only for myself, and I intended to introduce Nathan as
my business advisor. The guise I intended to use was one of
a "silly businesswoman" checking on the reputation of her
late husband's business before deciding what to do with her
shares of the stock. With any luck, Mr. Gray would offer to
let us see the system Frank had designed for Wilson Asphalt—or at least acknowledge that Frank had done business with the company.

The interior of the building was as dismal and foreboding as the outside. There were no windows, only solid walls that ran down long corridors papered in muted tones with blue carpeting on the floor. There was no sound as Nathan and I were led back through a series of corridors to Mr. Gray's office. The company president was overseeing a shipment at the moment, but he would be with us in no more than ten minutes.

The receptionist, as bland as the building, showed us into a large office with lots of certificates hanging on the walls but no windows. She closed the door firmly behind her.

"Claustrophobic, isn't it?" I asked, striving for a light note.

"Why would someone build a structure like this?" Nathan looked around as if he were truly amazed. "It's horrendous."

"Not half as bad as the people who built it," said a voice behind us.

We hadn't heard the door open, and we were both slightly embarrassed when a petite woman with a headful of bouncing curls closed the door behind her.

I was struck by the childlike quality of her face and figure, a Shirley Temple woman/child with luminous brown eyes and dimples.

"Get out of here before you both get hurt," she said in a low but urgent whisper. "I mean it." She looked at the door as if she expected it to fly open and a troop of terrorists to enter. "I don't have time to fully explain. Whatever it is you're up to, forget it and get out." She edged back to the door and put her hand on the knob.

"Why would we be up to something?" Nathan found his tongue before I could. His question was asked in a gentle, amused voice.

The woman looked at me. "You're Frank Devlin's wife, aren't you?" She didn't wait for an answer. "I saw your name on Steve's appointment book and put two and two together. Get out of here before you stir up a hornet's nest."

"You have to be a little more specific," Nathan said.

"I don't have to be anything," she snapped back. "I'm risking myself to come in here. Whatever you think you're going to dig up, forget it. Clear out before Steve Gray comes in here."

When she could see that she wasn't going to scare us into leaving, she nervously twisted her hands. "My future is at stake here. Get out before you get everyone suspicious and then I'll never be able to find out what's going on." The words rushed out of her. When we didn't budge, she let a low curse slip out. "Do whatever you want. Just don't blame me if you get hurt."

She was almost out the door when Nathan jumped up and caught her by the arm. "Wait a minute." He drew her back into the room. "What's your name?"

"Nella Colson, project director." She laughed, and it was bitter. "If you tell Gray about this, he'll see that I meet with an accident."

Even though she spoke boldly, there was a tremor in her voice. She actually believed he would kill her.

"We won't tell anyone anything, and we'll leave if you'll meet us later, to talk over some of this."

Nella looked from Nathan to me. "Okay," she finally agreed. "Seven. At Poet's. I've got to have some help from someone." She assessed me and Nathan with another long look. "I guess it's you two. Now get out of here."

I nodded. "I think I'm feeling terribly sick," I said, grasping my stomach with both hands. "Nathan, could you help me to the van before I embarrass both of us?"

"Certainly." He slipped his arm around my waist and all three of us started down the hall together. At the first corridor to the left, Nella left us, running soundlessly along the hallway until she disappeared in a turn.

"What do you make of her?" Nathan asked as I groaned theatrically.

"We'll see if she shows tonight."

"And if she doesn't?"

"I can recover from this bout of the stomach flu and we can reschedule our appointment."

"Always a plan behind that innocent face," he whispered in my ear, and his soft breath made my stomach contract seriously.

When we made it to the receptionist's desk, she took one look at me and hurriedly opened the door. She was more interested in seeing the back of us than she was in asking any questions. Stomach viruses aren't the best credentials for a guest.

Safely back on the interstate, Nathan looked at me, his eyebrows raised in question. "The electrical company?"

"Why not?"

After the intrigue at Wilson Asphalt, the session at Cleveland Electrical Engineers was anticlimactic. The president, Jeffrey Sells, proudly showed off every button and whirl Frank and Benny had designed for his company. He spoke glowingly of Micro-Tech and urged me to hold on to my stock. He said it was a grand investment for a woman on her own. He took it upon himself to lecture Nathan to give a fair price for the stock if he decided to buy it. It was one of those curious encounters where I felt flattered that a stranger would take such an interest in my welfare and angered that he didn't trust me to have a lick of sense simply because I was a woman.

The upshot was that we left knowing Micro-Tech was a great company and nothing else. Cleveland Electrical was marked off my list of suspects, for the moment at least.

We had most of the afternoon and evening to kill before our meeting with Nella Colson. If she showed. I drove us to my home, a wonderful old three-story house that my Aunt Tilly had left me when she died. It was a house that had been in our family for generations, and I'd always loved the front porch and big windows. The maintenance on a three-story wooden house in the humid South was enough to terrify anyone other than a fool or a writer. I qualified in both categories.

I gave Nathan the grand tour, even allowing him to see the third floor, which I used as my study. It would have been perfect for an artist's studio, and in truth, I dabbled in watercolors a little.

It was a most peculiar sensation, showing Nathan my home, the place that reflected me so openly and honestly. I was struck again by the things of Frank's that I'd never bothered to put away. His books, his drawings, even a pair of his sunglasses on the mantel. I'd never noticed any of those things before, but I suddenly saw where my mother had grounds to accuse me of not letting Frank go.

At Nathan's suggestion, I called Wilson Asphalt under the guise of running a credit check on Nella Colson. I found out from the bland receptionist that Ms. Colson had worked for that company for five years and earned a salary of fifty-five thousand dollars. Although I didn't dare press harder, I could tell the receptionist had no love lost for Nella Colson. She obliged by offering the fact that Ms. Colson had been passed over for promotion twice and might be leaving the company soon. She got off the phone in a hurry, to my regret. I could only assume that the subject of our conversation must have appeared on the scene.

Next I called Sergeant Vesley at the Jackson Police Department. He grumbled when I asked him to run a check on Nella Colson, but I explained she was applying for a job with me. When that failed to move him, I mentioned my brother's name and asked if he would check as a special favor. He was reluctant, but Shane was well-known among the officers. Vesley came back with a clean record for Nella. Not even a traffic violation.

"Look before you leap to any conclusions," Nathan warned me as we got ready to leave.

We went to Poet's early. We'd decided to eat there and watch for Nella Colson. The more we talked about her, the more curious it seemed. How had she known who we were or what our intentions were? No one had known of our appointment. No one. And Ms. Colson had said Steve Gray was checking us out. If it were true, why would he do so? Why wouldn't he have believed my story on face value?

As usual, we had thirty times more questions than answers. We'd just finished our meal when Nella entered the room. She spoke to the hostess and was directed to our table.

"Just remember, you can't trust every stranger, Emma. We don't know what her game is. If she has evidence of illegal behavior at Wilson Asphalt, it could be because she's involved in it. She might be trying to pump us to see what we know."

Chapter Seven

Nella took the first sip of her martini and lowered the glass to the table. "I suppose you've been asking each other why I'd want to tell you so much about Wilson Asphalt. What's in it for me?"

Nathan and I exchanged a glance. "We've wondered about it," I said.

"I left a job in New Orleans to take this one. I left a man I might have fallen in love with, because Steve Gray offered me career opportunities I hadn't been able to find in another company. And then he reneged. About five months ago I discovered that promotions at Wilson Asphalt come due to gender, not ability. I vowed then that I'd find some way to get even."

"The charges you're making are pretty serious, Ms. Colson." Nathan sipped his wine. "Revenge is a very poor system to run your life on. Wouldn't it just be simpler to cut your losses and move on?"

"Maybe so," Nella answered, her voice so still that it only made her anger more obvious. "But it isn't just revenge." Her eyes glittered. "Those bastards are trying to frame me."

Nathan's hand touched my leg under the table, effectively cutting short my response. "Now that sounds a bit melodramatic, Ms. Colson."

"Maybe it does, but it's the truth." She lifted her chin. "I've devoted my life to that company for five years. I've worked nights and weekends. I'm thirty years old and I haven't had a date in the past four years because I don't have time for social activities. And then I find out that the company I work for is corrupt. They've been accepting state funds and not delivering the goods. Someone in the state highway department is getting rich on taxpayers' money. Not only has Wilson Asphalt cheated me, it's cheated everyone in the state. It isn't just revenge, Mr. Cates. Not by a long shot. Mississippi can't afford any more crooks." Her voice dropped to a furious whisper. "And I can't afford to take the fall."

If the emotion in her face and voice was manufactured, the woman could have made a fortune in film. She was incredibly convincing, even down to her righteous fury at seeing the state cheated.

"Where are you from, Ms. Colson?" I asked softly.

"Hattiesburg. About ninety miles south of here."

I nodded. I knew the town well.

"Very close to the Free State of Jones, isn't it?" Nathan asked with a smile, referring to the Mississippi county that refused to go with the North or the South during the Civil War. Jones County had attempted to remain neutral—and had become known as the home of many a bandit and outlaw.

"Plenty of my relatives were Jones Countians," Nella said with the first hint of a smile. "Plenty of them were outlaws. And the rest were sheriffs."

We all laughed together at that, and I felt an intuitive liking for the petite woman who sat across from me. She was a live wire. She spoke with such passion, I wanted to believe her. But Nathan's words of warning came back to me. I was always too willing to trust. This was one time I had to use a degree of caution.

"Assuming we believe your motivation, why should we believe what you're telling us? And how did Micro-Tech fit into what was happening at Wilson Asphalt?" Nathan asked.

Nella pulled her chair closer to the table. She looked over both shoulders and leaned forward before she started to speak. "Wilson Asphalt puts in bids for state projects. Their estimates are always under everyone else's, so the state takes the low bid—state law. To make a big profit, Gray doesn't deliver but half the materials agreed upon, and the job foreman for the state signs off saying that all of the goods contracted for have been received."

Nathan nodded, and I followed along as best I could. "Then there must be someone who works for the state who's also involved in the fraud," I said.

"Exactly," Nella agreed.

"Any ideas?" Nathan asked.

She shook her head. "If I knew, I'd blow the whistle on them now. If I can only get some evidence, then maybe we can net all of them."

"Wouldn't it be better to call in the police, to let the professionals handle it?" I asked.

"I was hoping you two might volunteer. I couldn't believe my luck when I snooped around and found out who you were. Micro-Tech did do the setup. Maybe there are some records we can find at your company that would nail these guys. And very possibly, the people who murdered your husband."

This last was directed at me, and it almost took my breath away. Nella knew plenty about our business. "How did you know what I was trying to do?"

Nathan gave me a warning look, but it was too late. I'd already put my foot in it.

"I thought when Frank Devlin was killed that it was real convenient for Gray. See, the day Mr. Devlin was killed, he had a private conference with Gray. I don't know what went on between the two, but when Mr. Devlin left, my boss was white with fury. He was badly shaken. He made a phone call.'' Nella paused and looked over both shoulders again.

''Do you know who he called?'' I asked. It was strange, the rush of pure and total hatred I felt at that moment for a man I'd never met.

Nella shook her head. ''No. I heard him say that the fat was in the fire. He agreed to a couple of things and then put the phone down. I barely made it to another door on the corridor before he came barreling through the building. He got in his truck and drove away.''

''What about the contracts? Have you seen them?'' Nathan asked.

''I've seen the bids and the contracts. I've also talked with the drivers and delivery teams. The amount of cement and asphalt on roughly forty percent of the jobs is below the contracted amount.''

''Can you prove it?'' Nathan asked.

''Not without the paperwork.''

''Can we get the paperwork?'' I wanted revenge. Nathan could say what he wanted about the motivating factor of revenge, but it was working for me. If Steve Gray and his illegal business deals had anything to do with the death of my husband, I wanted to make him pay.

''I'll need your help. I can get into the computer system, but I can't get past the security codes on Gray's private files. Since your husband was the computer whiz, I was hoping you could get the codes. I can get us into the building when no one else is there.''

Nella smiled as she looked at Nathan and then me.

When I'd begun this attempt to resolve Frank's death, I don't think I'd ever really anticipated that we'd find anything. Looking up leads and finding little scraps of evidence had been fun. But this was solid, and I was experiencing a strange blend of emotions.

"Nella, why didn't you quit Wilson Asphalt and get on with your life?" I asked. It was what I would have done, until this moment. In the past, when I'd suspected bad treatment or wrongdoing in an employment situation or a friendship, I'd walked away from it. I'd never stood up for myself. Not really. I was curious why this young woman had decided to take the hard route, and why she'd chosen to trust us to help her.

"Why don't you forget the past and move on with your life?" she countered.

We stared at each other for half a minute before she spoke again. "The first three years, I thought I had to pay my dues. I didn't mind. During my fourth year, when I was passed over for promotion, I guess I convinced myself that it was something Steve didn't really want to do. The young man, five years younger than me—" she rolled her eyes "—was a big client's son. Maybe it was that Gray owed the man. It's a business world, after all. I know how deals get made. I'm not a Pollyanna."

"And then?" I prompted.

"The second time it happened, about five months ago, I realized that Gray promoted another guy over me because that was the way he intended to run the company. It finally penetrated my thick brain that no matter how good I was at my job, no matter how much better I was than any of the males he hired, I was never going to advance. Then I started paying more attention to a lot of things."

"And that's when the shortages on materials started to become apparent?" Nathan asked.

"That and a lot more. All of this was right under my nose, and I never even thought about it. I went out and inspected the jobs and made up the bids, and when we got the jobs, I made sure the mixtures and composites were correct." She sipped her drink again, her gaze cast down at the table. "I signed those contracts stating that the correct amount of supplies was delivered. My name is on the dotted line.''

I wanted to reach over and pat her hand, but I didn't. Instead I looked at Nathan. Nella Colson told a good story, and I could see by Nathan's face that he was as inclined to believe her as I was. But he was also warier.

''You said you could get us into Wilson Asphalt at night?''

''If we're careful. I have to tell you that Steve doesn't trust me completely now. He suspects how angry I am. I caught him going over my figures on the last two state jobs.''

Nathan leaned forward in his chair. ''Your key to the office still works?''

''Last time I checked.''

''Then if we're going to do this, we'd better act fast. Tomorrow Emma needs to make a trip to Micro-Tech to see if she can't get Benny Yeager to show her how some of their programs run. Then we'll be able to access the files at Wilson Asphalt.''

''When?'' I was amazed at the speed with which Nathan intended to act. He was always so cautious.

''Tomorrow night.''

''The sooner the better,'' Nella said slowly. ''After your visit today, I'm sure they're in a panic. Gray's smart enough not to let me see it, but he's freaking. They could destroy all the records.''

''Exactly what I'd do if I was a criminal,'' Nathan said.

''And if we're caught?'' I asked, since no one else was going to.

''It could be serious trouble,'' Nathan said as calmly as if he was ordering cream for his coffee. ''Trespassing, breaking and entering. Possibly a charge of theft or business fraud.''

''Or a bullet in the back of the head,'' Nella said. Her soft voice was a startling contrast to her brutal words. She looked at me. ''These people are ruthless, Mrs. Devlin.''

Nathan's fingers curled around my hand, warm and supporting. "We don't have to do it this way, Emma. We could hire a detective. Or even go to the police."

Nella snorted. "If Steve Gray has his hands in the pockets of the state treasury, you can be sure he has some friends in high office. Even if you were lucky enough to find a cop willing to solve this case, he'd be cut off by the people at the top. And a detective—any man who works for hire—can be bought by a higher wage."

"I didn't mind playing a bit at amateur detective," I said, trying for a strong and reassuring tone, "but corporate spying is more than I bargained for."

Nathan's face was completely composed, but Nella's fell with bitter disappointment.

"That doesn't mean, though, that I'm not game to try this. Nella's right. We can't trust this to anyone else. If the police or a hired investigator bungle it, then the evidence will disappear forever. I'll never find out who was behind Frank's death. If it was anyone."

"Are you certain?" Nathan's question, and the look in his eyes excluded everyone but me. He would do whatever I wished, whatever I felt was best for me. And he would never question my decision. His support was almost as palpable as a physical touch.

"I can't be certain this is the right thing to do. I don't know the consequences we'll face. But this is what I have to do. For my peace of mind, my sanity."

Nathan nodded. Nella stood. "Then I'll meet you guys here at nine o'clock tomorrow night. We should wait until about eleven and then try Wilson Asphalt. That'll give us a couple of hours to go over the floor plans and try to figure out the most expedient approach to this."

"What will happen to you, Nella, when it's all uncovered? Will the authorities hold you to blame, too?"

"Maybe not. I was innocent until a few months ago. Then I started planning a way to catch them, but I could never access the codes and all of the files are kept locked in a vault." She smiled. "Believe me, I tried everything whenever I had an opportunity to open that thing. Fort Knox couldn't have a better security system. It's the computers or nothing."

"Tomorrow at nine," Nathan agreed, standing as Nella left. When he sat back down, he turned to me.

"No hesitations?"

"What if one of us is injured?"

He looked long into my eyes. "There aren't any guarantees in life, Emma, except that it ends in death. We can only hope to escape as much suffering as possible, and enjoy the opportunities that are presented to us."

"Since Frank's death, I haven't enjoyed a lot."

"I know." He reached across the table and took my hand. "I sensed that about you from the very first. You've held yourself back from life. But you can't do that any longer. Believe me, you must take each day and live it. Whatever it is you're doing, live it completely."

I smiled at him, not because he was amusing but because he was so impassioned. "I've heard that all my life."

"Me, too. And it's true."

"And what should we do about us?" I asked. It was incredible that I could be so bold, but there was something about Nathan that gave me the courage. And though my heart didn't want to admit it, there was also the sense that our time was . . . limited. I didn't know how to explain what I felt, and I didn't want to examine it.

"What would you like to do?"

"When you say to live life to the fullest, are you talking about us?"

His smile was slow, but there was a sadness in his eyes that made me want to cry out. "Yes," he answered. "I am most definitely talking about us."

"Then the thing that I think we should do is pay the bill and go to my house."

The hint of a more spirited smile crept around the edges of his mouth. "And then . . ."

"If you dare to ask me what we'll do then, I'll tell you in very plain Anglo-Saxon language, and I think it might shock you to hear me say it."

He laughed out loud as he rose and eased back my chair. When he bent over me, he whispered into my hair, "I wonder, Emma Devlin, how much you'll shock me before the night is over?"

I AWOKE the next morning in Nathan's arms, and for the first time in what felt like years I knew that I had slept soundly. The beat of his heart was solid against my back and I luxuriated in the sound and feel of him. Had I shocked him? He had pretended so when I untied my gown and let it fall to my feet. If anything was true, though, it was that the intensity of our lovemaking had shocked us both. Awed might be a better word. If I had ever doubted the depth of my feelings for Nathan, I no longer did. I loved the man.

As if he read my thoughts, he reached tighter around me and drew me back against him. His lips brushed a kiss on my naked shoulder before sleep claimed him again, and I could only sigh with pleasure and satisfaction. Nathan Cates was as generous and sensitive in bed as he was in every other aspect of his life.

"Your behavior last night was shocking."

His whisper against my shoulder sent a chill of pleasure down my body.

"I thought you were asleep."

"Nope, just playing possum. It's an old Confederate trick."

"If I recall last night properly, you were full of quite a few tricks, and not all of them can be blamed on the army, Confederate or Union."

"If that's a complaint, ma'am, I'll try to do better this time."

With a quick twist, he flipped me over so that I faced him. The morning light caught softly at the golden stubble of his beard. His blue eyes were sleepily content, and for a moment I thought the sadness was completely gone.

"I love you, Nathan," I whispered softly, not daring to take my gaze off his.

"And I you." He kissed me softly and thoroughly before letting me go again.

"If I had gone hunting for love, would I have found you?"

"No." The sadness was back in his eyes. "You would not. It's because you were looking for something else that our paths crossed."

"My late husband's killer." Even saying the words aloud didn't make me feel guilty for the night I'd spent with Nathan. Frank and I had loved each other completely. Nothing that I ever shared with Nathan, or any other man, would ever destroy or diminish my love for Frank. Lying beside Nathan, I knew that Frank would only wish me the best.

"You're thinking that Frank would be happy for you, aren't you?" Nathan asked.

"How did you know?" It was uncanny how sometimes he knew exactly what I was thinking, especially when it was about Frank.

"Because my wife, Elizabeth, would have felt the same way. She would only wish that I could find someone to love, someone decent and caring. Someone like you, Emma."

"There are people who are married for fifty years, and they never know each other the way you and I do, Nathan. I can't explain it, but we do."

He raised himself up on his elbow. "We shouldn't have made love."

His words stopped me cold. It was as if I'd been physically slapped. "Why not?" Had I misunderstood what he'd said about his late wife? Was he going to feel as if he'd betrayed her with me? I couldn't stand it.

"I should be able to offer you marriage, Emma, and I can't."

"Marriage?" I was stunned.

"I love you, Emma. I'd like to offer you...the rest of my life. But that's impossible." The sadness was back in his eyes, stronger than I'd ever seen it.

"Nathan, I don't expect you to marry me. To be honest, I haven't considered it. But since you've brought the subject up, why can't you?"

His fingers stroked my face and tangled in my hair. "I could spend the rest of my life kissing you good morning," he answered.

"We don't have to be married to accomplish that." I tried for a smile and was rewarded with one.

"A long time ago I made a promise, Emma. I haven't fulfilled it yet. My stay in Vicksburg is temporary. After it's over, I don't know where I'll go."

"Nathan, when you told me to live for the day, for the moment, I believed you. I haven't asked for anything permanent. Frank and I expected to spend the rest of our lives together. We planned for that." My voice roughened as I remembered the joyous plans we'd made together with such detail and happiness. "There aren't any guarantees. I don't expect you to offer me the future."

"It's what I'd like to give you more than anything. And the one thing I can't."

Before I could say anything more, he kissed me again. In only a few seconds the tenderness turned to something more urgent, and all of our hesitations were burned away in the hunger of the moment.

I ARRIVED at Micro-Tech at lunchtime, hoping that Benny was gone. Luck was with me and I convinced Beth to allow me to use Frank's old office to conduct some personal business. I told her to take her lunch and I'd catch the telephones.

She was genuinely pleased that I'd thought about her needs, and she was at the door before I called out to her.

"Can I use these computers while you're gone? I want to type up some business letters."

"Sure." She hurried back and flipped on the one in Frank's office, assuming, almost correctly, that I didn't know diddly about computers.

"I won't mess up anyone else's files, will I?" My innocence was perfect.

"No," Beth answered matter-of-factly. "You're in luck. There's nothing in this computer now. The files are out of date." She cleared her throat. "I mean, no one has really used this computer since your husband died."

She was gone in thirty seconds, and I was left with a computer screen patiently asking for direction. In a few seconds I had the menu called up and was scrolling through to the Wilson Asphalt file. In another minute I had the file up and hurried through the accounting sheets showing all of Micro-Tech's bills to Wilson Asphalt paid in full. And that was it. The file ended.

Out of curiosity, I checked the date of the last payment. It was two days after Frank's death, a total of twenty thousand dollars for the personalized system and computers, the last of four payments.

To assuage the feeling of hopelessness, I checked out South Trust Savings and Loan. After my meeting with Carlton Frazier, I wasn't surprised to find the menu empty of any entries for the S&L. Since I was checking, I went whole hog and called up Carlton Frazier. There, just as they were in Frank's appointment book, were the four meetings Frank had set up. Beside each one I found several notations: Big Loan. Very Risky. Warning Issued. I didn't know what they meant, but I suspected that maybe Carlton Frazier had turned Frank down on a loan request thinking that Micro-Tech was too risky.

Well, Frank and Benny had shown everyone that the computer company was a money-maker. Maybe Frank's meetings with Frazier had been loan related and the bank president had decided to spare me and himself by evading my questions instead of saying he'd turned Frank down.

It didn't matter now. I sighed and was about to shut off the computer and beat a retreat before Benny got back from lunch and I had to explain myself. Just before hitting the off switch, I decided to check out Steve Gray. Just as Nella had said, Frank had met with Gray on the day he was killed. And about fifteen times before that. The meetings grew more frequent and longer toward the end. I could only wonder why it had required so much of Frank's attention. Usually after the program was sold, Benny designed it and installed it and they both trained the employees on it. It looked as if Frank had done the majority of the work at Wilson Asphalt. But he hadn't trained the employees. He hadn't lived that long.

I ran through the list of meetings with Gray, noting each one in the steno pad I'd carried in my purse. I couldn't see where the dates and times would be helpful, but it was all I had to take back to Nathan. It was better than going home empty-handed.

I was making the next-to-last entry when I stopped. This meeting was with Gray, Frank—and Carlton Frazier. The creepy sensation that maybe I'd stumbled onto something really important made my stomach knot.

From the outer office there was the sound of the front door softly closing. It was as if someone had tiptoed into the office. And then there was the sound of a lock sliding home.

Chapter Eight

Risking discovery, I flipped the switch on Frank's computer to turn it off. If it was Benny or Beth coming back from lunch I'd look like a fool if I hid under the desk. But what if it wasn't?

From the back of my mind, the mental image of a young man with a ponytail in a black leather jacket sprang forward. Diamond! Was it him walking so stealthily toward Frank's office?

Finally my survival instinct overruled my fear and I dashed to hide behind the door. When it swung open, I'd see the intruder before he saw me. What did I care if I looked like a fool?

I held myself rigid against the wall, dreading the possibility that my heartbeat would resonate off the surface and give me away. I watched helplessly as the doorknob to Frank's office twisted slowly. The door creaked as the intruder pushed it open and peered inside. Then it gradually opened wider. I had to restrain myself from leaping forward and giving my presence away. I waited as the door widened and a slender form moved into the room.

The figure that entered was beyond my wildest imagination. Amber-highlighted hair. Olive silk pantsuit. Marla Devlin crept into the room and made a beeline for the safe against the wall. The dial spun beneath her fingers and she had the safe open in only a moment.

"Damn!" She whispered viciously. "I never should have left it here for so long."

I had two choices. One was to confront Marla on the spot. The other was to slip out of Frank's office and make an escape out the back door. The latter seemed the wisest choice. I had no idea what Marla was doing at Micro-Tech, or how she'd come to have the combination to Frank's safe. She could have gotten it from James, since Frank had at one time kept family insurance papers there. But what was she after?

I didn't ponder that question long. I removed my high heels and, moving like a cat creeping through the jungle, I slid out from behind the door and into the hall. The carpet was soft against my stockinged feet, and I hurried down the corridor and to the back door, which opened with a push bar. My plan had become crystal clear and very simple. I'd go back to the front door and enter as if I'd just arrived. That way I'd catch Marla snooping without giving her the benefit of catching me.

I was turning the corner from the alley onto George Street when I was brought up sharp by the sight of Beth, Benny's receptionist, standing at the door of Micro-Tech with Carlton Frazier. They were talking intently, and Beth shook her head several times. I drew a sharp breath when Frazier grabbed the young woman's arm in a grip that even at a distance of fifteen yards I could see was brutal. Beth winced and tried to shake free. Frazier bent into her face, said something, and released her arm. Without another word, he turned away from her and stalked down the street to a burgundy Cadillac.

Beth put both hands to her eyes and leaned against the locked door of Micro-Tech. In a moment she straightened, looked up and down the street as if suddenly aware she might attract attention to herself. She tried the door, found it locked, and in a few seconds had her keys out and stepped inside the building.

As soon as Frazier pulled away from the curb, I hurried to the front door and dashed in. "I know I'm a worthless receptionist, Beth," I said breathlessly. "I had to run to the post office and get something in the mail to New York. I know I shouldn't have left the phones after I promised you but... What's wrong?" I could only pray that my acting was passable to a woman who was in an emotional state.

"It's nothing," she said, waving her hand and looking down at her desk. "Don't worry about the phones. Sometimes we have to leave them at lunch."

Her voice was defeated. I'd never seen anyone more beaten. If she was part of some nefarious plot, she was a poor participant. "Is something wrong?" I asked again. "You look upset."

"A personal matter," she managed. Then she jumped up and ran to the ladies' room crying.

I'd give Beth a chance to calm down before I tried to talk with her any more. I started back toward Frank's office and caught sight of just the edge of an olive silk jacket rounding a corner. Then I heard the metal push bar on the back door hiss softly. Marla had also chosen to take the back exit. Had she heard my voice, or had she planned all along to sneak in and out without being discovered?

What could she possibly have expected to find in Frank's safe? It hit me like a ton of bricks. The pearl necklace! Frank may well have asked Marla's advice on purchasing the jewelry. He wasn't an authority on pearls, and of all people, Marla would know everything there was to know about them. And it would be just like her to think that Benny hadn't given me the necklace in two years so perhaps he'd forgotten about it. She thought she could steal the necklace for herself!

The front door swung open and Benny's delighted gasp forced me to compose myself.

"Emma, we're going to have to put a desk in for you," Benny said as he gave me a hug. "What's going on?"

"I can't write," I said, shrugging my shoulders. "I sit down and nothing comes out. So I thought maybe I'd come here and see if I could learn a bit about Micro-Tech."

"Writer's block, huh?" Benny said with sympathy. "I don't know how you manage to come up with all those clever sayings, anyway."

"My mother says they're cynical and mean-spirited," I said. We shared a laugh.

"Your mother wants to keep you on the straight and narrow, and it's a good thing someone is trying to make you behave," he teased. "Frank used to laugh a lot about some of your misadventures."

Our eyes met, and for the first time we didn't feel overwhelmed by a sense of loss. "Frank saved my posterior plenty of times," I said. "He had a perfect right to laugh at me."

"Well, you have to admit, that tongue of yours can get out of hand."

"Freely admitted," I said. "So tell me something I can do to help here for a little while this afternoon. I mean, I really am at sixes and sevens, and if I could type or do anything, it might help me work through this block thing."

Benny scratched his head and looked at Beth's empty reception station.

"Ladies' room," I whispered.

"We can ask Beth when she returns." Benny snapped his fingers. "Wait a minute. I'm having a meeting with Marion Curry from Curry Photography at one-thirty."

"Her business has really grown," I said. "An incredible talent."

"She's the best in the South. I'd be delighted to get her account, and I think I can come up with a program that would make the business end of her work a lot easier."

"So maybe I could sit in and take notes?"

"Sure," Benny said. "We normally don't do that, but what could it hurt?"

"You don't want to be alone with the beautiful Ms. Curry?" I teased. "She's single again, you know."

"Single and safe from me," Benny said. "A woman like that wouldn't have a bit of interest in someone as boring as me. She photographs famous people, for book covers, and she used to do a lot of album covers for rock groups and stuff."

"And she isn't married to any famous people, either," I reminded him. "She keeps her business here in Jackson when she could have gone anywhere. Maybe she likes homegrown Mississippi men?"

"Maybe you're an incurable cupid," Benny said. "You can sit in on the meeting, but only if you promise not to try and set me up for dinner or something with Marion Curry."

"Okay, okay, I promise," I said.

Long blond hair blowing in the spring breeze, Marion Curry arrived right on time. The meeting was a revelation to me as I sat beside Marion and listened to Benny talk. Once behind the desk and in a professional capacity, there was nothing of the shy computer whiz in his manner. Benny was articulate, bright, and very capable.

Most of Benny's attention was focused on his client, and it was a good thing. It would have been hard to miss the jubilant expression that crossed my face when he began to talk about the different systems Micro-Tech had created. This was exactly the information I needed. I scribbled away, taking down everything I could, as Benny wooed his client. Without any interference from me, there was a definite connection between the two.

As Marion was leaving, the photographer asked Benny if he would consider posing for a calendar of single, successful men. "We did one last year and made a tubful of money, and the men we featured weren't complaining at all about the publicity." She smiled.

Benny blushed to the roots of his hair but accepted the business card she offered. "I'll think about it," he said, casting me a sheepish look.

"That's perfect," Marion said coolly. "Sort of bashful, shy, very charming. I'll expect you next week to come by and see my facilities for a new computer system, and for a sitting." She turned on her heel and walked out.

"I didn't do a thing!" I said, holding up both hands in a gesture of innocence. I was so excited myself that I was glad to have something to pin it on.

"You didn't have to. Boy, she's a powerhouse."

"I admire that kind of woman. She knows what she wants and she goes after it." I flipped my notebook shut. "That was really interesting, Benny. Shall I type up the notes for you?"

He shook his head. "Just keep them. I made some notes myself. If I have any questions, I'll ask you."

I nodded. "Maybe I should get home. I can tell it's going to take me a while to learn how Micro-Tech works."

"Emma, I don't expect you to come down here and work. Frank and I had an agreement, and I take a very healthy salary out of the company. It isn't as if I work for free."

"I want to help. Maybe I need to do this."

"Whatever you say, but don't think I expect it. I'm always delighted to have your company, and I'll teach you whatever you want to know."

"I'll never be much help on thinking up programs, or the business angle. I'll have to settle for basic skills in and around the office. And maybe just some advice."

"Sounds good. Come back tomorrow and I'll have Beth show you the filing system."

He was half teasing. It showed in his smile. "You think you can scare me off with a little secretarial work. Bah! I can even dust and make coffee."

We were laughing as we walked into the main reception area. Beth was back at her desk, her face a carefully composed mask.

"I'll see you tomorrow," I told her cheerfully.

She looked to see that Benny had returned to his own office. "Please don't tell anyone that I was upset here at work," she whispered.

"Benny isn't an ogre," I answered. "I'm certain if you need some time off, or want to talk with him about anything, he'll be happy to help you."

"I had a bad time in my other job." She spoke breathlessly. "I don't want to see it happen here. Benny was so kind to hire me. He's given me so much." Her voice choked again. "Please!"

"Certainly, Beth," I answered. My heart ached for her. Whatever Carlton Frazier had said to her had completely unstrung her. This would be interesting fodder for chewing on with Nathan and Nella.

At the thought of Nathan, I suddenly couldn't get home fast enough.

Since I hadn't bothered with lunch, Nathan made sandwiches and insisted that I eat. I was about to pop with the information I'd learned about the computer systems, but I bided my time. I wanted all of the smaller details out of the way before I sprang my surprise.

We sat side by side on the patio and I told him everything I remembered of the time I'd spent at Micro-Tech. We were both disappointed about Frank's computer files, but the visit by Marla and the exchange between Beth and Carlton Frazier were both very interesting. Unless Beth had money difficulties with the bank, then it would be safe to assume that Frazier was visiting her because of something at Micro-Tech. And he'd clearly been intimidating her.

When I'd told almost everything, I relaxed against the cushion of the couch. Nathan lifted both my feet into his lap. He teased me with a few tickles, then grew serious. "Is it possible that someone went in and partially eradicated Frank's files?"

"Yes, it could be done easily." I hadn't thought of such a thing. Beth's encounter with Carlton Frazier looked even more sinister in this light.

"How do you read Beth?"

"Well, she's young and timid. She worships Benny, but he doesn't know she's in the world. I'd say she could be coerced to do something, but she isn't a criminal type."

"And we already know Frazier's exerting some kind of pressure on her. You told me that Benny hired her . . . after Frank's death."

"Right. She'd been accused of embezzlement at her last employer and Frank had felt she was innocent. After Frank died, Benny hired her as a sort of memorial act to Frank." I held up my hands. "I know it sounds crazy, but Benny and Frank were that close. And Frank was always taking in strays of one type or another. But he was a good judge of character."

"Even with Beth?"

"I'm willing to bet she's a decent person." I thought about her frightened face. "But she could be desperate, and desperate people do things against their natures."

"How well I know."

That poignant sadness had returned to Nathan's eyes. Leaning forward, I touched his shoulder. "Are you okay?"

He nodded. "I am now." His hand slipped around my foot and he began to apply gentle pressure to it. "I've been told that certain areas of the foot correspond to each of the body parts."

The sadness had been replaced with an imp of mischief.

"Is that so? Well, I think you're making all of that up." The delightful pressure he was applying to my foot increased as the other hand began to gently massage my calf.

"I'd never make up any theories like that. But I think this muscle here—" he increased his touch on my calf "—affects the... lungs."

"You're very silly," I answered.

When his grip suddenly increased, I gasped with the sensation.

"See, it affected your lungs," he noted.

The seriousness of his expression made me laugh. "Yes, Dr. Cates, and what other grand revelations have you uncovered?"

"Well..." He lifted my foot into the air and studied it. "I believe this large toe here stimulates the gall bladder. And this one here, the spleen."

"Those are pretty safe bets. Neither can be proven or disproven, at least not sitting on the patio."

His hands massaging and rubbing my feet and lower legs were having an affect on my entire body. I felt like a contented cat, wanting to stretch and purr and rub closer.

"And this part of the foot," he said as he massaged my heel, "connects to the heart."

"You've already touched my heart," I whispered.

"Then soon you'll be completely under my power." He put my feet aside and pulled me onto his lap.

His eyes were a sunny clear blue as he looked down at me, and his mouth curved into a smile of real happiness. I kissed his lips softly. We could be happy together. There was every chance and not a single reason we couldn't.

"I love you, Nathan," I told him.

"I know, and it's the most wonderful thing that's happened to me in a long, long time."

The afternoon sun was dipping behind the oak trees that surrounded the yard. Secure in Nathan's arms, I allowed myself a moment of total bliss. The sun, the flowers, the breeze, the feel of his cotton shirt beneath my hand.

"Could I convince you that you're in my power enough to get you into the house?" he whispered.

His voice, the feel of his breath against my neck, sent shivers of anticipation all through me. "I think so," I answered carefully. "Maybe a little kiss would help."

He obliged with a passion that swept everything else from my mind. I don't remember walking into the house, or even getting upstairs. Nathan filled my thoughts.

Later, it was difficult to direct my thoughts to business. But when we were getting dressed to meet Nella, I told him about my session as a secretary for Benny and Marion Curry. This was the tidbit of information I'd saved, the one real moment of glory.

"Benny said that many of their systems work alike. Once we get into Wilson Asphalt tonight, I may have a chance at opening their computer system with what I learned today."

Nathan slowly zipped the back of my black bodysuit. "I love these gadgets." He kissed my exposed neck. "I love your hair up. I love the fact that you're absolutely brilliant."

"Did your degree in history include a doctorate in flattery?"

"I only speak the truth, ma'am."

"Nathan, what are we going to do tonight?" I added the paisley smoking jacket that would prevent me from looking like a cat burglar when we met Nella. I didn't know the first thing about dressing to break into a building, but black seemed appropriate.

Nathan was wearing a dark pullover and jeans. He flexed his legs in the new material, stretching the denim to a better fit. "We have to get inside first. Then we have a few options. I want you to go to work on the computers, and Nella is going to try the corporate vault."

"And you?"

"Surveillance and recon."

"Which means?"

"I'll keep an eye out to make sure the security guards aren't around, and if they are, I'll treat them to a temporary nap."

"You mean, hit them?" It really hadn't occurred to me that there might be violence involved.

"Emma, they aren't going to let us in just because we say pretty please. Just a tap on the chin, or head, as the case may be. Nothing worse than a headache."

He was right, of course. I was living in a fantasy world to think that we could simply walk in and snoop around. We had already inadvertently alerted Gray. Our phony little stomach flu routine had gotten us out of the building, but Gray was bound to have suspicions about why I'd made the appointment in the first place. In fact, I was surprised he hadn't already called Micro-Tech and asked questions. Perhaps his guilt prevented him.

"How much time do you think you'll need?" Nathan asked.

I had no idea. "An hour?"

"Better try for half an hour. If the security guard system works like most others, then the guard will patrol the entire premises every hour. They could have closed-circuit television, but I doubt it. Nella can answer a lot of these questions for us. Anyway, if I have to incapacitate the guard, he might have a check-in system with his buddy. Say, every half hour. That would be the maximum time."

My palms had a sweaty sensation and I stretched my fingers. Half an hour was no time at all. And I didn't really know what I was hunting for, except records of contracts with government agencies. I'd have to access a printer. It suddenly seemed hopeless.

"Do you want to go ahead with this?" Nathan asked.

"They wouldn't really shoot us, would they?" Nella's bold statement was etched in my brain.

"Doubtful, but not impossible. My theory is that hired security guards would hesitate to shoot at anyone for a break-in. But if Gray has his own men there, people who have something to risk, they might be a little more trigger-happy. If there is any trouble, give yourself up immediately."

"And you?" Nathan wasn't the type to surrender.

"Someone has to make bail for you women." He chucked me under the chin. "Don't take it too seriously. I promise, I won't get hurt. All you have to worry about is your own pretty hide."

"Nathan, I want to find out what happened to Frank. I need to find the truth."

"I know that." He kissed my nose.

"But none of this is worth risking you." I put my hands on his arms and squeezed with all of the strength I had. "I mean it. I can live with my doubts, but I don't know if I can live without you."

"We came together because you decided to try everything to resolve Frank's murder. I became part of your life because I wanted to help. There's no going back on that now, Emma. If we did, our love wouldn't amount to much, and eventually the doubts about Frank would return."

"Why must I risk one to have the other?" It wasn't fair. I knew I sounded like a petulant child, but I wanted to slam my fist down on something and demand a better choice.

"Love is a risk," Nathan answered softly. "The biggest risk of all. And you're strong enough to face it, Emma. Whatever the consequences, you'll survive."

Chapter Nine

Nella was as good as her word. She had sketches of the entire plant and a list of the guards who patrolled the premises at night. There were two guards: one inside and one out. There were cameras in the warehouse area of the facilities, but as far as Nella knew, there were none in the corporate offices.

We sipped coffee in a far corner of the restaurant, waiting for the time to pass. In the early morning hours, the guards would be least alert. Wilson Asphalt had never suffered a break-in of any type, and Nella assured us that security was lax. The guards came from a local firm that hired off-duty policemen. Many of the guards had already pulled a full shift during the day, and they found the night work at Wilson's to be complemented by a brief nap every now and then.

We laid out our plan of action. Nella and Nathan would get the doors open and then signal me. I'd be hiding behind a stack of tires outside the warehouse. Nella had assured us that we had to enter the offices through the rear. One security guard sat in a chair near the front door; the other one would be easier to evade.

Once inside, we would separate and each go to our specific task. Mine was breaking into the computer files on Wilson Asphalt and government contracts. Nella had given me some specific incidents, but I was to get everything I could—with a look at Wilson Asphalt's relationship with Micro-Tech, of course.

We made the drive in the mini van and parked in a used-car lot a mile down the service road from the company. How strange for the salespeople to find an extra car among their inventory if we didn't return for it. That thought made me chuckle under my breath.

"Something funny?" Nathan asked. He was guiding both Nella and me from shadow to shadow toward Wilson's. If he'd learned this surveillance stuff from studying to be a reenactment colonel, he'd certainly been an apt pupil.

"I was just entertaining a few melodramatic conclusions to this evening."

Nella snorted. "Don't underestimate Gray. He's a ruthless man where a buck is involved. When it may be his future, I don't know where he'd stop. He practically had a vice president from the S&L quaking in his shoes this morning."

"Frazier?" Nathan and I asked simultaneously.

"Yeah. You know him?"

"There's a chance he might be connected with Frank's death in some way, but we haven't a clue how," I said.

"He always seemed like a decent enough guy." Nella was panting. We'd stopped for a moment behind a frenzy of signs touting the Hilltop Motel. Outlined in vivid neon of all colors were diving girls, palm trees, televisions blinking blue and green and a tangle of connecting neon tubing that gave it all a surrealistic touch. It heightened the feeling I was having that reality had been left far behind.

I tuned back in on the conversation. "Frazier may be a decent guy," Nathan told Nella.

"Could be coincidence," I added. "Any idea what he was talking with Gray about?"

"Money, I assume. South Trust has loaned Gray some money in the past. I was never privy to the details."

Nathan signaled us to move again, and we dashed along the sides of buildings. Wilson Asphalt was only a hundred yards away, and I felt the first real misgivings. It was a kind of fear I'd never experienced before.

"Emma?"

Nathan sensed my hesitation and his warm hand caressed my shoulder. "I'm fine," I assured him.

"It's not too late. You call it."

"Let's go." And in the darkness I gave them a grin of assurance that I certainly didn't feel.

We covered the last hundred yards in a running crouch. Nella had a key to the padlocked chain-link fence, and we let ourselves in as silently as possible. We left the gate closed but unlocked for a hasty getaway. Inside, strange shapes and dark shadows leapt out at me. Only the security of Nathan's strong presence leading the way kept one foot moving in front of the other. The tires were just where Nella had said they would be, and I waited while the two of them moved on.

Nella's key opened a metal door into the main building, and Nella and I hurried in and pressed ourselves against the wall. Nathan took a quick look around the exterior to find the placement of the guard. I kept my eyes closed and tried to visualize his agile body moving through the shadows...safely. Just when I couldn't stand it any longer, he slid through the door.

With a wave of his hand, he indicated that we were to remain where we were while he took care of the guards. My ears strained for the sound of a thud or a crash, but there was nothing. A few minutes later there was only the darker shadow of Nathan at the end of the corridor gesturing us toward him.

"Be quick," he warned as Nella and I split and went our separate ways.

My work was in the main offices. Wilson Asphalt had a computer network with twenty-two stations. Many of them were used by contract writers to develop plans and designs. What I wanted were the computers with the files on money. My assumption was that those files would be locked in the computers used by Gray or his direct underlings—and separate from the network. Nella had said Gray was smart enough to leave all incriminating evidence in someone else's files, so I turned right in the corridor and made my way first to the number one supervisor's desk.

The main office was quiet. Too quiet. Nella and Nathan had disappeared completely. I inched forward, knowing that time was crucial yet afraid to move too fast. When I first looked in the cubicle where the guard was supposed to sit, I thought it was empty. Then I saw the guard, his body slumped on his desk. My heart lurched. My first impulse was to rush to him and try to help him, to make sure he was alive.

"He isn't hurt," Nathan assured me. I turned to find him at my side. "He'll wake up with a headache. That's all. Now get busy. We haven't time to waste."

Before I could slip away, Nathan picked up a strand of hair that had fallen from my knot. It took all of my will-power to move away from him and back to the task at hand.

While listening to Benny I'd learned what I hoped would be the password to the computer's main menu. My first attempt was a bust. Gray wasn't so obvious he'd use his middle name, which I'd picked up from some of the checks he'd written Micro-Tech. My second effort—digits from his social security number—was also no good. In talking with Marion Curry, Benny had given me one more clue. I typed in P.A.S.S.W.O.R.D. The main menu items flooded the screen. Benny had said that while setting up a network, he and Frank always used the word "password" as the password. The client was then supposed to change the password to a secret word that was significant only to them. I wondered how many other people simply used the code established by Micro-Tech.

I scanned the files as rapidly as I could. There were several state contracts and, once I had the printer ready to work, I set about printing out the information. The contracts were lengthy, and since I wasn't certain what was important and what wasn't, I had to print out the entire thing.

I saw Nella coasting through the dark office toward me. "I can't even begin to open the vault. Want to try?"

"Sure." What could it hurt? "Just make sure this thing keeps printing. If it stops, come and get me."

I retraced my steps to the corridor and took a right into an office that had a solid metal door. Nella had a key to that door, but not to the vault. It was like something from a bank. It would certainly make our lives easier if we opened the door and found Gray's files. Though I worked with the combination dial and lever, I could make no progress. I was ready to give it up when I heard Nella softly call my name.

"Guard!" she whispered.

I searched the small space of the vault room and tried to find some place to hide. The room was bare. There wasn't even a table or desk to duck under.

Before I could even think of another plan, the full blast of a heavy-duty flashlight caught me in the face. I was blinded like a rabbit in the road.

"Hey! What's going on here?" the guard asked.

I threw my hands up to ward off the light. "It isn't what you think," I tried. I could hear him pull out his radio and flick it on.

"Jimmy, this is Henry. I've found a little—"

There was a thud and a low groan as the man crumpled to the floor. His flashlight thunked down after him, striking hard and then going out.

"Get what you have and we've got to go," Nathan said.

"Nella!" I whispered urgently.

There was the rattle of another door opening fast, then a loud, high-pitched scream.

"Get out of here!" Nathan pushed me toward the corridor. "Go out the front. I made sure it was open for us. Run!"

I didn't wait for a second invitation. My best bet was to get out of the building and wait for Nathan and Nella. I was almost at the front door when I heard Nella's cry.

"No! My God! No!"

I turned and moved in the direction of Nella's voice. It sounded as if she was in one of the back offices. Strong arms grabbed me and pulled me against a hard chest, frightening the breath out of me.

"Don't look, Emma," Nathan's voice commanded.

But it was too late. Carlton Frazier was slumped back in the chair in front of the desk. The bullet hole in his forehead was neat. Only a trickle of blood had escaped. His open eyes were glazed, and the back of his head was a mess. There was no doubt he was dead. Nella stood beside him, arms hugging herself.

"He was dead when I came in here," Nella whispered. "I heard the guard coming and I ran in here to hide."

"We have to get out," Nathan urged again.

Nella moved toward the body and slipped a manila folder out of his hands. "It's my file," she said. She held it out to me.

I could tell she was in a state of shock, so I took the file from her and gently moved her toward the door. "Let's go, Nella. Now!"

I had my arm around her and we were at the door when I heard the shot and felt Nella sag against me. She didn't even scream. She just leaned hard into me and began to crumple to the floor.

"Get down!" Nathan yelled as he came up behind me fast and threw himself on top of me. Bullets began to ricochet off the metal doors and thud into the walls behind us.

I couldn't believe it was happening. Nella had told us that we might be killed, and when I'd heard her say it, the words had chilled me, but I hadn't really believed them. As a bullet bit deep into the carpet and wood near my face, I knew how correct Nella had been.

Up against the wall, Nathan was checking Nella's wound. "We have to get her to a hospital. Fast," he said. "I'll distract them. You make a break for the back door. Get the van and get back here fast."

"How are you going to get Nella out?"

"I will," he promised. "Just take care of yourself. Emma," he grabbed my arm. "You know I love you."

Nathan lunged sideways and rolled down the hall, darting into another room. In a moment he was back in the corridor and this time he made his way to the front of the building. The shots were ringing wildly through the offices, and I could only pray the police would come at any minute. I'd rather be arrested any day than shot.

I rolled out into the corridor as I'd seen Nathan do. No one fired at me so I made a dash to the back door. One guard was tied against the wall. That meant Nathan had only one man to confront. And Nathan was smart. But there was Nella to worry about, also.

That thought put wings on my feet and I ran down the side road to the van in Olympic time. In a moment I had the van aimed for Wilson Asphalt.

Before I had a chance to turn the van around, Nathan appeared at the side door. He opened it and put Nella in as gently as he could. Then he hopped in the front seat beside me. "Drive, Emma, like you've never driven before."

I put the accelerator to the floor and the van slewed in the gravel until the wheels caught traction and we lurched down the service road. Behind us, everything was strangely quiet.

"Who do you think tried to kill us?" I asked when we'd pulled onto the interstate. I headed for the closest hospital. In the rearview mirror, I could see Nella breathing, but her face had a deathly pallor. She couldn't die. She couldn't. It would be my fault. She wouldn't be doing any of this if it hadn't been for me.

"I couldn't see their faces." He lifted the manila folder. "What's this?"

I stared at it blankly for a few seconds. "Nella's file, I think. She handed it to me and I guess I never put it down." I felt my stomach drop. "But I didn't get anything else. Not a contract and I didn't even check on Wilson's connection with Micro-Tech."

"Well, you didn't get killed, either," Nathan offered. He tangled his fingers in my hair, loosening the bun. "We're still here, and there's always another chance."

"The eternal optimist. Did you learn that from studying history?" I was trying too hard to keep it light. My disappointment was bitter, and the shock waves of what had happened were beginning to rock me.

Nathan's laugh was tinged with sadness. "No, I learned other things from the past. But for the present, I'm going to check on Nella while you drive."

He gave me a progress report from the back of the van. Nella faded in and out of consciousness, and Nathan made no real effort to bring her around. He said the pain would be intense and she might as well avoid as much of it as possible.

I knew the drive to the hospital as well as I knew my own name, but it seemed to take forever. In the insignificant 2:00 a.m. traffic, we seemed to crawl forward, as if the interstate was the proverbial tar baby. When we finally arrived at Mercy's emergency room, Nathan carried Nella in and didn't waste a moment obtaining attention.

Since I was left to answer the questions on the clipboarded emergency form, I muddled through them as well as I could. I listed her wounds as accidental and prayed that the police wouldn't arrive and connect Nella with the gunfight at Wilson Asphalt. Or with Carlton Frazier's death.

Emergency rooms are places where the best and worst of mankind are on display. I was being treated to a rare inside look at two women who'd been in a "cutting" over a man, who'd also been cut, when Nathan reappeared at my side. I had the clipboard with all of the questions about Nella at my side.

Nathan slipped the questionnaire from the board and folded it into his jeans' pocket. He took my arm as he started toward the exit.

"What...?"

He shushed me until we were outside. "No point in hanging around. I stayed with Nella until the doctor examined her. She's fine. She also knows she's in a precarious position. She knows how to handle it."

"We can't leave her." I looked back over my shoulder as Nathan led me away.

"We can't help her," he said. "If we stay, it'll just be bad on all of us. Especially me, Emma."

I hadn't considered his position. No doubt his funding would be withdrawn if he were arrested for breaking and entering, not to mention murder.

"I'm not thinking about my career," he said. "But we can do Nella more good on the outside. Besides, she can stonewall them for several days. If she gets in too much trouble, we'll tell the truth then." He held up Nella's keys to Wilson Asphalt.

"We're not going back there, are we?" I couldn't believe it. We'd nearly been killed.

"Not tonight, but we have to eventually. Or at least, I have to."

"This doesn't really even involve you, Nathan." I was so tired I could barely get the key in the ignition of the van. All I wanted was to get home and get into a bed.

"Everything that involves you, involves me," he assured me. "Don't think about it anymore. We'll come back later today to check on Nella."

AFTER FOUR HOURS' sleep, I felt better than I expected. Nathan had kept the television on, hoping for news of Carlton Frazier's death. There was nothing. Not the first report. A brief mention of the "gunplay" at Wilson Asphalt gave the impression that a break-in attempt had been stopped by local security guards.

"What about Frazier's body?" I asked Nathan. I was sipping my second cup of coffee. My nerves were mercifully numb. Somehow I'd managed to block the picture of Frazier, dead at the desk, out of my mind for the time being.

"They must have moved the body," he answered, his forehead wrinkled as he thought it over. "They didn't want anyone to know he was killed at Wilson Asphalt."

"It's almost like a nightmare. Maybe we dreamed it."

"Nella would feel differently with a hole in her shoulder. She has evidence that it was real."

"I wonder what story she told the doctors."

"Get dressed and we'll find out," Nathan suggested. "Maybe we could take her something to eat."

"Good idea." I went up to my bedroom for a quick shower and a change into slacks and a sweater. Half of my brain still seemed to be asleep. The events of the night before had become slightly fuzzy.

As I was brushing out my hair, I remembered Nella's file. Nathan had tossed it on the bedside table, and I started to leaf through it. Why was Frazier holding Nella's file? That was one for the books.

Her résumé was neat—and impressive. It was at the bottom of the page that I saw her references. At first I thought I'd misread, but I hadn't. Marla Devlin was one of her references to Wilson Asphalt. I flipped further into the file and found the letter of recommendation Marla had written. A glowing letter.

It stated their long-term acquaintanceship and the fact that they'd attended the same private school in New Orleans. So, Nella Colson wasn't everything she appeared to be—she was much more.

I took the file to Nathan and showed him. His expression never changed as he read the damning material. When he looked at me, he asked simply, "What do you believe? Do you doubt Nella?"

That took the wind out of my sails. Did I? I didn't want to, but I did doubt her. I nodded yes.

"Then let's ask her about this."

On the drive to the hospital, we talked about the events that had happened. I couldn't help but wonder if Nella had set us up and been accidentally injured herself. I doubted her, but I couldn't believe that she would try to kill Nathan or me. Was there some other twisted game she played? I couldn't forget that it was the mere mention of government contracts that had made Marla Devlin blanche.

Nella had been put in a room on the fifth floor of the hospital, and Nathan and I walked rapidly down the seamless hospital corridor. We found Room 511 and knocked. When there was no answer, I went in first. The rumpled bed was empty. I stepped back outside, thinking perhaps Nella was in the bathroom and needed a few moments of privacy. My own experiences with hospitals and those ridiculous gowns left me with a lot of desire to give others their privacy.

After a decent interval, I knocked again.

No answer.

I eased open the door. The bed was the same, empty. There was no indication that anyone was in the room. I motioned Nathan inside and we made a hurried search. The bathroom was empty and there was no sign of Nella or her clothes. She had vanished.

For all of my doubts about Nella's motives, I was suddenly afraid that someone had kidnapped her. Maybe she had been innocent in last night's events. Perhaps she'd been as thoroughly set up as we had.

"Should we report her missing?" I asked.

"No." Nathan moved me toward the door. "Let's get out of here."

"But what if she's in danger?"

"I didn't say we weren't going to look for her. We just don't want to be caught here visiting when the patient has disappeared."

As we started out the door, a piece of crumpled paper under the bed caught my eye. I retrieved it and dashed back to Nathan's side as we strolled out into the corridor and back to the elevators.

"What is it?" he asked.

I smoothed the paper and stared at the address printed on it. It was an address I recognized.

"It's a tag from my brother-in-law's athletic shop. It would seem that Nella bought something from my in-laws."

"Then we should pay her a little visit there," Nathan answered, and his grin wasn't exactly friendly.

Chapter Ten

I left Nathan in the parked van about two blocks from James and Marla's house. Nella's disappearance had disturbed me deeply. Bodies—alive and dead—were disappearing into thin air.

As far as I knew, Carlton Frazier's death had not been reported, or at least the police were keeping the media silent. Since I knew a couple of reporters in town, I found that unlikely. They weren't the sort of people I'd call easily manageable.

Walking down a sidewalk lined with dogwoods and tallows, I wondered about that fact. Nathan and I had kept an ear open for any hint of the murder. Our conclusion was that the police had not found the body. So who had removed it? And what about Nella? Was she friend or foe? As important as those questions were, I had no inkling what the answers might be.

I was hoping Nella Colson would be able to answer at least one of them.

James and Marla's home was an older residence that they had spent considerable time and effort restoring. It was in an established neighborhood where lawns were kept immaculate and children played outdoors without fear. There were always watchful parents on the street, but there was also the sound of laughter and bicycles and wagons. The familiar pang of knowing that I would never have Frank's child struck me, and I suddenly wondered why Marla and James remained childless. I knew it wasn't by choice where James was concerned. He loved children and made it abundantly clear. Could it be that Marla had been unwilling? Or one of them unable? Perhaps there was more to the root of Marla's behavior than I'd considered before.

The ten yards of sidewalk that led to the wide front porch of the house was bordered by impatiens and ornamental cabbages. Marla had a gardener, I knew. Her nails were too perfect to allow for much digging around in the dirt. With that sarcastic thought in mind, I walked across the porch and rang the bell.

The chimes echoed in the house. After three minutes, I rang again. There was no answer. I checked my watch because Nathan had an appointment at the college. But I wasn't willing to give up my search for Nella.

I hadn't thought to call the sporting goods store. James was most certainly at work. And Marla? Who could tell? I didn't really want to see either of them. I wanted Nella Colson. I wanted to squeeze the truth out of her.

I pressed the bell for the third time and waited without results. My fingers curled around the doorknob and I turned it. The door opened. Inside, the house was very still and quiet. It was possible that no one was home.

The need for some solid answers pushed me forward. Tiptoeing like a common criminal, I went upstairs. I knew the layout of the house. James and Marla's bedroom was a jumbled mess, as if they'd gotten out of bed late and hurried off to work. Nothing unusual there.

It was the guest rooms I wanted to check. If Nella wasn't there, surely there was some evidence she might have been.

There were three extra bedrooms, two up and one down. Neither of the upstairs rooms yielded a clue. I hurried downstairs and went into the pretty pink room that fed off a back hallway.

At last, evidence of use! The bed was rumpled. Most convincing of all, there was a used bandage in the waste can. Nella had been here. Where she'd gone was anybody's guess, but she'd been in Marla's house. My suspicions grew.

I left the bedroom after a thorough search. There wasn't any way to tell where Nella might have gone. I was getting ready to leave when I noticed the door to James's study was slightly ajar. Nella could have heard me come in and hidden away in the darkly paneled room.

I eased the door open and took a moment to adjust to the dimness. The room was the only place in the entire house where light and sunshine didn't rule. James, yielding to his belief that studies should be dark and somber places, had had the entire room paneled in dark wood.

The windows were shuttered with wooden blinds, and even though I knew James loved the room to be dark, he most often kept the blinds open. Today they were closed. My heart picked up a few beats. Someone had deliberately closed the light out. Why else but to hide?

I considered calling Nella's name to let her know I had found her. Instead, I stepped into the room and boldly closed the door. She was twenty pounds lighter than me— barely bigger than a child—and she was wounded. How deadly could she possibly be?

My hand eased up the wall and I flipped on the light. My eyes registered the big desk with clutter spilling out over the floor. Books had been pulled from the neat shelves. And a pair of feet stuck out from behind the desk. A man's feet.

I knew it was James. But why? The lightning-fork question seared into my brain. Why James? Before the bitterness and grief could rise up in my heart, I rushed forward to make sure there was nothing I could do to help James Devlin.

He was dead. Shot in the chest. The telephone was on the floor beside him. His outstretched hand made it look as if he'd been trying to call someone. I should have called and warned him, I thought as the tears welled in my eyes.

I must have stood there for at least three minutes just staring at the chaos around James. Books on sailing were scattered beside him. I recognized a book on boat building that Frank had given him two years before. I think I picked up the book. I really don't remember. When I finally came to my senses, I knew I had to get Nathan. What should we do? The police had to be called. Anonymously? And where the hell was Marla?

If she had anything to do with James's death, I vowed that I'd make her pay a dear price.

Emotions swirled around me. Perhaps my meddling had been responsible for James's death. If I hadn't started prying into the past, would he be alive today? I stumbled out of the study and down the hall. I didn't want to think anymore, not until I had Nathan beside me. I knew the automatic response the human body could make to survive. I turned mine on, ordering myself to walk. Forward. Walk. Walk. Door.

I was out on the porch, trying to decide whether it was important to close the front door or not. It seemed a monumental decision. The squeal of tires drew my attention to the street. It was such a nice street. No one drove that way on this street, not even the teenage boys. The old cut-glass knob was still in my hand as I turned to look out among the dogwoods and green, green tallows. I clearly thought how beautiful the trees in the fall when the tallow leaves turned such vibrant shades of yellow and red. James and Frank had planted those trees together. The dogwoods had been there—"White for spring," Frank had said. "Let's add a little fireworks for fall." And they had laughed as they dug the holes on a cold February day.

Bittersweet. The memory was so sharp and painful that I cried out. My heel caught on a rough spot on the porch and I stumbled, dropping to my knees. Flashing through the new green of the trees was a dark burgundy shape. Above my head, the glass on the door and shards of wood flew in all directions. Slow motion. Bullets sprayed around me, and I heard the sound of repeated firing. Instinctively I rolled down the porch and allowed my body to fall limp among the blooming azaleas. My mind was filled with the smell of spring dirt as silence returned to the street.

I felt my body shake with suppressed sobs. My arms had tiny cuts where the shattered glass from the door had blasted into me.

"Emma!" Nathan's voice called to me and I heard his footsteps running down the sidewalk.

"Emma!"

I wanted to lie in the dirt forever. I wanted to yield to the pain of James's death. James, Frank, two good men killed without warning or reason. It was pointless to continue. I was beaten.

"Emma?" Nathan's arms lifted me from the shrubs. "Emma." He spoke my name softly and pulled me against his chest. With almost no effort, he lifted me. "Don't think. Don't talk."

His voice was like a familiar litany, soothing and comforting. The rhythm of his stride was like a rocking chair. I was safe. Nothing could hurt me as long as I stayed in Nathan's arms and never opened my eyes.

The shadows of the trees danced on top of my closed eyelids. Dark, light. Dark, light.

"Nathan." I couldn't slip into a mindless vacuum.

"Easy, Emma. Don't talk now. We're almost to the van."

"James is dead in the house." His grip on me tightened, but for a moment he didn't say anything. He continued to walk, carrying me like his own fully grown child. The noises on the street penetrated the careful wall I was trying to construct. There was a shrill of childish laughter and a mother's voice calling out the name of her son. There was panic in the mother's voice. She feared for her son. She'd heard the gunfire and she was trying to make her little boy get inside and be safe.

The tears started and I couldn't stop them. "He was dead at his desk. The room was torn up. Nella had been there, I'm certain. But the house was empty." I spoke in a choppy way because I couldn't breathe, talk and cry all at the same time.

Nathan eased me into the driver's side of the van and then went around to the passenger side to slip in beside me.

"Drive, Emma. It'll do you good to think about driving."

In some insane way, he was right. My hands went to the ignition and the wheel, and as we eased into the street, I knew that concentrating on some specific task, something real, would keep me from slowly unraveling. "Where should I go?" I asked.

"To the college."

I nodded. What did it matter? All that really mattered was that I had a destination. I drove.

"We're going to have to stop and call the police," Nathan said after we'd made our way through the worst of the downtown traffic. Interstate 20 rolled beneath the wheels of the van. "Clinton will be fine. We'll call from the school."

"Okay." I would have agreed to anything.

"What about Marla?" he asked. "What are you going to do?"

What indeed?

When I didn't answer, Nathan reached to the stick shift and took my hand. "I know you haven't thought about this, but it's important, Em. Did you see the car that shot at you?"

"Yes." There was the vivid burgundy lacing through the green trees. Burgundy Caddy. The same kind of car that Carlton Frazier had driven. The pieces clicked.

"Those people could have killed a child on the street." Nathan tightened his grip on my hand. "They were determined to kill you, but it didn't matter who got in the way. I saw the car speed by the van, and then when it got even with the house, a man's arms came out the passenger window and I saw the gun. He was blasting away before I could move."

"I don't know how he missed me."

"Emma, this is getting too dangerous." Nathan frowned. "I feel that I've encouraged you to do this, and now I'm not certain I can protect you."

"You want me to stop?" I took my eyes off the road long enough to really look at him. "I can't."

He sighed. "I suppose I knew that."

I exited at Clinton and drove onto the campus. It was a refuge, a place where violence would not erupt. But was any place safe from the mad acts of determined men?

Nathan made the call to the police. Someone had already reported the drive-by shooting, and the police had obviously found James. They made an effort to obtain Nathan's name and whereabouts, but he deftly sidestepped them and hung up. As he talked, I sat on the step of the van and battled the ebb and flow of nausea. I couldn't begin to think of what to do next. It was overwhelming. Somehow, though, Marla was going to have to be told. I weighed several courses of action. At last, whether it was cowardly or wise, I decided to let the police handle it. I didn't want Marla to know I'd been in her house. That was the bottom line. If Nella knew I was on her trail, I might never find her. There was nothing I could do for James now. And Marla wouldn't benefit from my sorrow or sympathy. The idea that I'd found James might only infuriate her.

When Nathan returned to sit beside me, I told him what I'd decided.

"I have an idea," he said. "This is going to sound strange, but I want you to come to a lecture."

It was as if he spoke a foreign language. "Lecture?"

"Here, on campus." He looked at his watch. "I'm due to give one in about thirty minutes. I can cancel if you want, but you need some time to adjust. The shock has been tremendous. Come and sit in. It's an auditorium. The room will be dark. It'll give you an hour away from everything you've been through.''

The idea was crazier than anything I'd ever heard, yet I knew it was the thing I should do. The recent events had to settle. There were clues hidden in everything, and if I pressed too hard, I'd shut them out. I had to let things sink in. The important clues would rise to the top.

I nodded my agreement.

"Good," Nathan whispered. "Good."

THE STUDENTS filed out, talking among themselves about the presentation on Vicksburg under siege Nathan had just given. I was still sitting, dazed and disoriented. My mind shifted from the horror of the present to the nightmare of the past that Nathan had described with such force. His vivid descriptions had brought the past alive in my mind, and it was a tragic and brutal past. There seemed no respite from violence, at least not in the past or present. Not for the Devlin family, who had lost two brothers in tragic deaths. Yet I had Nathan, a man I had grown to trust.

I wasn't aware of Nathan standing beside me until he cleared his throat. When he offered his arm, I accepted and stood. Together, the last stragglers, we left the auditorium.

"The next move is up to you, Emma," he said as we stepped into the fading day.

"We need to tail Marla." I hadn't planned on that answer. In fact, Marla had not crossed my mind for an entire hour. But it was the right thing to do. I knew it as surely as I knew my own name.

"Exactly," Nathan said. "She'll either lead us to Nella Colson, or to someone else we need to find."

"Want to hazard a guess?" The anger was hard in my voice.

"Steve Gray would be my popular choice," Nathan said as he stopped beneath an old oak and turned me so that he could put both hands on my shoulders.

"Do you think Gray and Marla are involved?"

"It has crossed my mind once or twice." Nathan sighed. "I don't know your sister-in-law, but even if she is involved in this, I don't think she knew how far it would go. Not her brother-in-law's murder, and now her husband's. No amount of profit or gain could be worth such a price."

"Who knows if Marla values her loved ones the same way we do?" I asked the question rhetorically, but it scared me to think that I might be right. There were people who valued nothing except a dollar. I wondered how much Diamond had been paid to kill my husband in cold blood.

"Why don't we go back to Vicksburg tonight?" Nathan suggested. "The police are going to be looking for you. They'll have some questions. It might be easier if you're rested."

"Okay." I felt a need to return to Ravenwood, as if it had become a central focus for my emotions. I had to smile at the ludicrous idea that I was more in control of my life when I was living in an antebellum mansion than in my own home. "I'll retreat to Vicksburg," I said, only half kidding. "The South may have lost the war at Vicksburg, but I've found a haven."

Nathan smiled. "It's only a temporary retreat, ma'am. We'll take on the enemy again tomorrow."

We spent the evening talking about Mary Quinn and Vicksburg. Nathan knew that I suffered, and only once when I was thinking that James might be alive if it wasn't for me did he mention anything that had happened during the day.

"None of this is your fault, Emma. You didn't ask these people to enter your life. Neither did Frank. When violence visits you, there are two solutions. To become a victim or to fight back. You've chosen the latter road. You've simply decided not to be a victim."

He stayed with me in the cozy apartment, and somehow we made it through the night.

The next morning we were back in Jackson early enough to follow Marla to her lawyer, to the funeral home and to a house I didn't know. Of course I didn't know all of her friends, but I was startled to see her ring the doorbell and then push an envelope through the letter slot. She didn't even wait to see if anyone was home.

From there, she went straight to Sportsplex. A black wreath was hanging on the front door, and I had to fight hard to keep back the tears. Marla went inside and locked the door. She didn't put out the Open sign. Apparently she had some business in the back of the shop.

"I can't believe she's working," I told Nathan. "She hated working in the store. I'd give anything to know what she's up to."

"We may have our chance," Nathan said, nodding to a silver pickup that drove to the side of the building and parked. "Recognize him?"

"No." I didn't.

"Steve Gray. I saw his picture in his office the night we broke in."

"Gray! You were right." I hadn't wanted to believe that Marla was involved with such a man. How could she when she'd had a husband as loving and devoted as James? My hand reached for the door handle. I wanted to go inside and confront her.

"Hold on, Em," Nathan said, restraining me by grabbing the arm nearest him.

"She's a witch! She doesn't even have the decency to wait until James is in the ground."

"Judging by the look on Mr. Gray's face, this isn't a loving visit."

I looked up. He was at the door, knocking loudly. His face was knotted with some negative emotion, but I couldn't be certain if it was anger, worry or fear. All three, I hoped. And maybe a touch of stomach flu thrown in.

Gray looked furtively in both directions as the door opened. He stepped inside.

"It could be business," Nathan said.

He was trying to cheer me up, but it wasn't working. "Yeah, he's teaching her the fine art of defrauding the state on contracts."

"That could be it."

"I suppose they couldn't put business off until after her husband's funeral?"

"Not if something's gone wrong."

"We can only hope."

"Should we follow Gray or Marla?" Nathan asked.

"Marla, I think. I'm assuming Gray has a business to run and that he'll go back to Wilson Asphalt. I wish we could ask him about Nella."

"You're still hoping Marla will lead us to the elusive Ms. Colson, aren't you?"

"Nella's the one person I'd like most to talk with on this day. For some reason, I think I could wiggle the truth out of her."

"I'll bet you could," Nathan answered. "Well, we're about to let one fish go to catch another."

Gray came out of the building as if his pants were on fire. He almost ran to his truck, cranked up the motor and drove away.

"If that was a romantic encounter, it was a quick one," Nathan commented.

"He did look angry. But it could be that Marla's putting some kind of pressure on him to get rid of his wife and marry her. Maybe we should follow him." It was hard watching him drive away while we sat and waited to see if Marla would do anything else.

"Better decide quickly. Which one?" Nathan was craning his neck to see which way Gray went on the interstate.

"Marla." As a child taking tests in school I'd developed a theory. "Always go with your first choice."

He settled back into his seat. "I don't think we'll have long to wait."

We didn't. Marla was out in the next five minutes. She went home, changed clothes and drove to Amanda Devlin's house, which made me feel sad and uncomfortable. I knew Frank's mother would be beyond grief. Her boys had both been so special to her. To me. I wanted to go inside and confront Marla with what I thought she was up to. But it would hurt Amanda more than anyone else.

"She's here for the rest of the day," I finally said. "I'll come back later this evening. I'll bet the Devlins and my family have been looking everywhere for me." My emotions were so raw that I felt my throat close with unshed tears. "I wish there was something I could do. There ought to be something."

"Want to go home for an hour or two?"

"Yes, but not to rest. Nella's file is there. I want to take a look. I think now it's time to call her family to see if they've heard from her."

"Good thinking," Nathan agreed. "You know, you might have made a good detective after all."

At home, my inspection of Nella's file told me that she was from New Orleans. The story she'd told us was undoubtedly a blend of carefully woven fact and fiction. I dialed her parents with a large amount of trepidation. I didn't want to worry them, but on the other hand, I hoped they'd be able to flush Nella out of the woodwork.

When I asked to speak to Nella Colson, there was a pause.

"Nella lives in Jackson," Mr. Colson answered.

"I'm having some difficulty finding her," I explained. "She isn't going to work . . ." I let my voice drift away.

"That fool girl!" Mr. Colson exploded. "I told her to quit that job and come home. I told her no job was worth getting hurt."

"Is there somewhere I might be able to find her?" I asked. "I've been worried about her myself. There have been some . . . difficulties at Wilson Asphalt."

"Nella's a headstrong girl. She was digging into things that were better left untouched."

I wanted to tell Mr. Colson that I was certain his daughter was okay, but suddenly I wasn't. I'd assumed that she'd left Marla's house voluntarily. That she'd left before James was killed. That maybe the killers had been looking for Nella. Now I wasn't so sure. Maybe Nella had been taken.

"We've been worried sick about her," Mr. Colson said. "She calls us every other night. Her mother's been sick. She hasn't called for three nights."

"If you hear from her, tell her Emma Devlin called," I said. "And, Mr. Colson, I wouldn't repeat any of this to anyone else. Especially not a stranger."

"Who are you?" he asked.

"If I can help Nella, I will." I hung up before he could ask any more questions.

Chapter Eleven

Amanda Devlin's house was unbearable. James's mother was broken by her grief and there was no consoling her. The rest of the Devlin clan had gathered to offer what comfort they could, but James Devlin was a man who would be sorely missed. Just like his brother.

To take my mind off my own pain, I watched Marla. Her grief for James seemed genuine. She seemed sincerely shocked by the violence that had taken place in her home.

"I don't understand it," she said to more than one person, a perplexed look crossing her face. "James never did anything to anyone. I don't understand it."

It wasn't unexpected when the police arrived. They questioned Mrs. Devlin and Marla, and finally me. It had not gone unnoticed by the authorities that two brothers in the same family had died violent deaths.

I was always taught to respect authority figures, and it was hard for me to lie to the two officers, but I did. Nathan and I had already discussed what I should do when questioned, and we'd agreed that a pretense of total innocence was the best ploy. We'd tipped our hand already, and we had to be extremely careful.

My own mother insisted that I spend some time with her. She was concerned that James's death would reopen the always fragile scar of Frank's murder. I did my best to assure

her that I was okay, but she knew me too well. Her gentle
hand stroked my hair and offered the comfort of a mother.
That was nearly my undoing. But I managed to hold together and leave. The resolve that I would help to bring the
guilty parties to justice was the only comfort I knew I'd find.
Except for Nathan.

My love for him grew with each hour we spent together.
There were times when he seemed troubled by the rapid
bond that flourished between us, but our need for each
other was stronger than any reservations. I knew he wanted
to offer me something permanent, something honorable. I
wanted it, but even without it I couldn't deny myself the
lifeline of his love. The events of my life had made me a firm
believer in the present. The future was far beyond my control.

I went to James's funeral alone. I had found a corner and
prepared myself to endure when I heard my name called. To
my surprise, Sergeant Vesley was standing beside my chair.
"Terribly sorry," he whispered as he took a seat.

I must have looked at him in a peculiar way, because he
went on to explain that James had given uniforms and
equipment to a boys' club ball team that Vesley coached.

"James Devlin was a kind and generous man," he said.

"He was," I agreed.

"Lots of strange happenings in Jackson this week," he
added. He was looking toward the front of the chapel,
watching the mourners find seats and settle in for the service. His gaze seemed to follow Marla.

"Is that so?"

"We've got a missing person's report on a senior vice
president at a savings and loan. And just this morning there
was a report filed on a young woman; she's missing, too."
He shook his head. "Now, we get a lot of missing teenagers
and the like, but not professional people. Unless maybe they
took off together—a man-woman thing."

"I hardly think so." I spoke before I thought. It was just the knowledge that Carlton Frazier was dead that made me sound so certain, and I realized my mistake immediately.

"You don't think so?" he asked.

When he looked at me I noticed that he was far shrewder than I'd first assumed. He'd tricked me with that question, and I'd taken the bait like a starving bass. "Of course, that's just female intuition," I said. "Whenever there's a chance, people always assume there's a . . . romantic element. That often isn't true."

"Well, that's what the woman's parents said when they called in and reported her missing. They insisted she wasn't involved with anyone. Trouble is, they didn't have much to go on, really. They said she hadn't called home in several days. And the place where she worked was all shot up a few nights ago. She hasn't been to work."

"Yes, I remember hearing that on the news." I could feel sweat beginning to gather at the small of my back. Sergeant Vesley was treading on dangerous ground for me.

"We found a small trace of blood at Wilson Asphalt. In two places."

"Blood?"

"Strange thing, though, it wasn't the same type. You don't have to be Dick Tracy to figure out two different people were bleeding. But the security guards were vague about what happened. They said no one was hit."

"I see." I was afraid to say anything else at all. This guy wasn't Dick Tracy. He was more Columbo. Bumbling and sweet—and never missing a clue.

"Have you ever done business with South Trust Savings and Loan?"

"Me?" I tried to sound confused. "My husband took care of all our banking business. Since his death I haven't had to do anything."

"You've been one lucky lady," he answered. "My wife hates banking or insurance or income tax, any of that kind of stuff. She says that's why God made men, to tend to the details." He chuckled at his own joke. "There's just one other thing."

"What is that?"

"The young woman who's missing. She's the same one you called to check her background. Nella Victoria Colson. Isn't that strange?"

"Nella Colson!" I tried to force shock into my voice. "How terrible."

"Why would you want to hire a construction project director to work for you, Ms. Devlin? I can't see how you'd need someone like Ms. Colson to help you write greeting cards."

He had me trapped squarely. "Ms. Colson was unhappy in her job, Sergeant Vesley. I was only offering a temporary solution."

"Then you don't know anything about her disappearance?"

"I've been looking for her myself." That was no lie.

"You know, the bullets at your brother-in-law's home were a little odd, too. The bullet that killed James Devlin was fired from the same gun as the ones that were shot into the front of the house."

I didn't say anything. The minister had taken his place at the altar. There was the sound of low crying and the smell of chrysanthemums. It was an odor that had haunted me for weeks after Frank's death.

"The unusual thing is that Mr. Devlin had been dead for at least four hours before the house was shot up. Now why would the people who killed a man return to the scene and shoot up the front of his house?"

"I don't know." I wanted to break from the room and run, but I knew I was trapped. Sergeant Vesley was simply baiting me.

"I don't, either. But if you think of anything that might explain it, I'd like to know."

"I'll be sure and contact you, Sergeant."

He started to leave but then hesitated and touched my arm. "Ms. Devlin, there are some mean people out there. Take care of yourself. And if you hear from Ms. Colson, please notify me. Her folks are worried to death. And we're a little curious about a report of a young woman suffering from a gunshot wound who checked into a hospital and then checked out—without giving her real name."

"I'll call you if I hear anything from Ms. Colson," I assured him, taking a deep breath when he finally left the room. Out of the corner of my eye I watched him leave the chapel. He'd made a special trip to talk to me. He'd wanted me to know that he suspected I had a hand in part of what had happened. Sergeant Vesley wasn't the kind of man who believed in coincidence.

The cemetery was a painful place. James was buried not far from Frank. Too many Devlins laid to rest. As soon as the service was complete, I went to Marla's car and waited for her.

As Nathan and I had discussed, I asked Marla to give me a lift home after the funeral. I wanted a few minutes to talk with her privately about Nella Colson. If it came to it, we could tail her again, but I wanted immediate action.

Marla was reluctant to give me the ride, but she could hardly refuse. My house was directly on her way home, and she'd shunned every effort by her friends and relatives for company and support. She'd said she wanted to go home and be alone.

"I wish there was something I could do," I said as we drove out from beneath the shade of the trees and into the traffic.

"Me, too."

She didn't elaborate, and I thought she meant it. There might even have been a hint of tears in her voice.

"Do you have any idea why someone would kill James?"

"You don't think the police have covered this ground thoroughly enough?" she snapped. "If you're going to interrogate me, I'll put you off here. You can get a taxi home."

My own anger ignited, but I held it back. "When I lost Frank, everyone thought it was an accident, Marla. Whoever killed James did it deliberately. Your home wasn't robbed. And the killers came back and sprayed the house with bullets. That's a little hard to ignore."

"I'd like to know who's responsible for this." She ground out the words. "Whoever it is, they'll pay!"

"Do you think Frank's and James's deaths are related?"

Her head whipped around so she could stare at me. "It's been two years, Emma. Don't you think you could let it go? It gives me the creeps when you act so weird." She turned her attention back to the road, and just in time before she barreled through a red light. She stomped on the brake and almost sent the car into a skid.

There were other questions I wanted to ask, but I delayed, giving her a moment to compose herself. How far should I push her? I'd never considered that Marla would injure herself, but her driving was reckless, as if she didn't care what happened to her. Was it guilt that rode her so hard?

"James never did anything to anyone."

She spoke so quietly that I had to look at her to be certain she was talking.

"Those bastards killed him, without a qualm."

"Who, Marla?"

She stared at me and I could see a tear leaking down her cheek, tracing its way over her perfect makeup. "Don't you think if I knew for certain I'd kill them?"

"Who do you think it is?"

She drove on, acting as if she hadn't heard my question. When we were only three blocks from my house I decided to try again. "Where is Nella Colson?"

The question was effective. She jerked the steering wheel and narrowly missed colliding with a little red Honda. The driver hit her horn and shook a fist out her open window.

"How did you know about Nella?"

I shrugged. "She said you were friends."

"Little Nella, the girl most likely to succeed." There was bitterness in Marla's voice. "That was what she was voted in high school. Well, the only thing she's succeeded in doing is messing up her life real good. And mine, as well."

"Where is she, Marla? I have to talk to her."

"I do, too. When you find her, let me know. And ask her if my husband was alive before she left the house." She pulled her car to the curb in front of my house. "Or ask her if she killed him."

"You think Nella killed James?" The idea had occurred to me, but I'd dismissed it almost instantly. Nella lacked that edge, the ability to kill. Or at least, I thought she did. The truth was, I hardly knew the woman.

"Why did you help her escape from the hospital?"

"I didn't. But when she called me from a pay phone, I picked her up and brought her to my house. James never said a word. She was a friend of mine, so she was welcome." Marla's voice cracked and she leaned her head against her hands on the steering wheel. "Get out of my car," she said. "Get out now."

"Marla..." I wanted to say something to comfort her, but I didn't know what.

"You don't think I deserved James, do you?"

"I never said that."

"You didn't have to. I know Frank told you I made advances toward him." She waited. When I didn't say anything, she continued. "I had to do something to get James's attention. There were weeks when he didn't know I was alive."

I didn't want to hear this. None of it. Maybe I'd been harsh in judging Marla in the past. Maybe there had been a reason for her flirtations—and more—with other men. Right at that moment, though, I didn't want to hear it.

"I'm sorry, Marla. It wasn't my place to judge. And I tried not to, except when Frank was involved."

She shook her head. "Just get out of my car and let me go home."

I opened the door slowly, not certain if she should be left on her own. "What are you going to do?"

"Go home, take a bath, make a drink and go to bed."

"I'll come by and check on you later."

"Don't bother, Emma. Hypocrisy doesn't suit you."

"I wasn't being a hypocrite, Marla. I'm worried about you."

"Don't." She waved her hand. "I've learned to take care of myself."

On the curb, I hesitated. "Do you have any idea where Nella might have gone?"

I thought she was going to slam the car into gear and drive away with the door open. Her hands gripped the wheel until her knuckles were white. "Why do you want to know?"

"If Nella didn't have anything to do with James's death, then it's possible that the people who killed him were looking for her."

"So? I should be worried for my friend who skipped out and left my husband dead?"

"What if they took her, Marla? What if she didn't leave voluntarily?"

That got her attention. "Hell! I hadn't thought of that."

"If you can think of any place she might be, I'd like to look for her. If she's okay, then I can talk to her. Maybe she knows something."

Marla considered for a minute. "There are a couple of places I can check."

"Tell me and I'll do it." I wanted the names myself. Marla's tears seemed like the real item, but I wasn't completely convinced.

When she looked up again, she smiled. "No, I think I'll take care of this myself."

"Marla?" I wanted to ask her about Steve Gray. What was their connection? But I restrained myself. To give too much away now could prove a disadvantage. I wasn't sure enough of Marla's true feelings.

"Don't worry about me, Emma. I can take care of myself." With that she did crank the motor. As she started to pull away I had no recourse but to slam the car door shut so it wouldn't bang after her. I stood on the curb and watched her drive away.

As soon as she was gone, Nathan came down the front steps. His arm went around me. "There was just a news bulletin on the television. They found Carlton Frazier's body in the Pearl River. He was weighted with heavy chains."

"How awful." It was a grisly image and one I rebelled against. I knew he was dead before he was put in the river, but still . . .

"Sergeant Vesley just called here and wanted to know if you'd made it home from the funeral yet."

"I'll bet he did." I filled Nathan in on the sergeant's questioning as we walked into the house.

"Call him, but don't give anything away," Nathan whispered.

In a moment I had Vesley on the telephone. He was his usual stumbling self, until he got to the questions he was interested in. "Ms. Devlin, what business did you have with Mr. Frazier when you visited South Trust Savings and Loan?"

Vesley was a thorough man, dang his soul. "A loan, Sergeant. Was I his only appointment that day?"

He chuckled. "No, but you do seem to turn up a lot lately. Did he give you a loan?"

"No, it wasn't for me. But I didn't shoot him because he turned my friend down." The minute the words were out of my mouth I saw Nathan's face draw into a frown. I knew then that the news reports had not said that Frazier had been shot. It was left to make it look like a drowning—a trick the police often used to trap criminals. And I'd just sprung the trap around my own slender ankle.

"Ms. Devlin, I'd appreciate it if you didn't leave town any time soon. If you do, please notify the police department."

"Isn't it odd that I go to the police to find help solving my husband's murder from two years ago and I wind up being a suspect in another killing?" My heart was pounding but I couldn't stop myself. "If I were more appreciative of irony, I'm sure I'd enjoy this situation."

"I'm sorry, Ms. Devlin, but I wouldn't be doing my job if I wasn't a bit suspicious. I'm sure that in time we'll unearth the real culprit. Until then . . ."

"I'll remain in Jackson," I finished for him.

"I should have warned you," Nathan said as soon as I hung up the phone. "They only said his body was recovered."

"I should have been smart enough to think this through before I opened my big mouth." I sank into a chair. All day long I'd fought the terrible sense of grief I felt at James's death. Now I was overwhelmed by bone weariness. I had no tears to cry. I was dry, completely empty inside. "What should we do?"

"Why don't you tail Marla?" Nathan suggested.

"And you?" I was surprised that he had suggested we split up. I suddenly realized that he might have some duties to perform. "Do you need to go back to Vicksburg?"

"Not today, but tomorrow." Worry creased his forehead. "I have to go back for a day or two. Then I'll return."

I nodded my agreement. "What about this evening?"

"You follow Marla."

There it was again, but he had no companion piece of information to tell me what he intended to do. "And you?"

"I'm going back to Wilson Asphalt."

"No." The word popped out of my mouth, sure proof of what my mother calls my impetuous nature.

"We have to get the goods on those people and they won't be expecting a sneak attack tonight. It's the best possible time. You've gotten the computer codes, at least partially. You can tell me and I'll get in there."

"I only got into the contracts. That won't be proof without the sign-off sheets and a survey of the sites where the cement and asphalt were used. I also didn't get far enough to tell what Wilson had to do with Micro-Tech." As I talked I realized that if Nathan went back, I'd have to go with him.

"Tell me how to get the information. I can."

"Not as quickly as I can."

"No." This time it was Nathan who issued the one word denial.

"You need me."

"You could get killed." He walked toward me, his blue gaze never leaving my face.

"I suppose you're invincible?"

He smiled. "Not really, but I'm better trained at escaping injury than you."

"History professors aren't exactly authorities on warfare simply because they study it." I sounded as stubborn as a mule—and just as determined.

"I've had a bit more training than what comes out of books."

That part was true. He seemed to know how to take care of himself in sticky situations. "You aren't going without me." So, I was a quick learner.

"Emma, you could get killed."

"Nice try, Nathan. I'm going if you're going. This is my problem to begin with. I can't let you get yourself killed while I sit home and cross-stitch."

A genuine smile touched his lips. "I hardly see you doing anything so...wifely...as cross-stitch."

I was tempted to fib, but didn't. "I gave it a try once. I managed to use my finger for a pincushion. I'd probably do more damage to myself waiting for you. Besides, if you leave me, I'll come after you and probably blow the entire thing."

"What about Marla?" he asked.

A brainstorm struck me and I felt as if a light bulb had gone off in my head. Why hadn't I thought of this before? I cleared my throat. "You've never had the pleasure of meeting me before, but my name is Marla Devlin."

Nathan's face shifted to amazement. "You sound... sultry, like a woman with something on her mind."

"That's usually the way Marla talks." Although she'd lost her sexy swagger today at the funeral.

"What's your plan?"

I couldn't help the fact that my face split into a grin. "We'll call Steve Gray and pretend that I'm Marla. She can ask him to meet her some place out of the way. That way we'll at least make sure that he isn't around when we break into Wilson Asphalt."

Nathan was beaming. "Excellent idea, Emma. Maybe he'll take his goons with him."

"We have to get in and get out." I suddenly realized that I was afraid to go back to Wilson Asphalt. Nathan had consented to my plan but his next words made it obvious that he was still concerned.

"Emma, this time if they catch us, they're going to kill us."

Chapter Twelve

As a precaution, I made a late visit to Marla's. True to her word, she was in bed, her sleep heavily laced with vodka tonics. One of her friends was spending the night with her and I stayed long enough to see that she was sound asleep—and that the telephones were unplugged. My excuse was that the news media would drive her crazy, but I didn't want Steve Gray calling her and endangering me and Nathan.

I rehearsed my best Marla voice on the way to Wilson Asphalt. We'd decided to "case the joint" before going any further. Although we approached from a different direction, the drill was the same. We found a spot between parked vehicles at a truck rental facility where we could watch both the back and front of Wilson Asphalt. The building and grounds looked dead as a cemetery, and all of the stacks of culverts and materials didn't help. It looked like some graveyard for mastadons. I wouldn't have admitted it out loud, but I was afraid of the place. Afraid of what might happen to Nathan, or me, once we forced another entrance.

Nathan was settled back on his haunches like a cowboy by a campfire. I tried the same pose, and after fifteen minutes I knew the circulation to my lower legs had been destroyed. I heard his soft chuckle as I shifted for the fifteenth time.

"You've got a lot of heart, but you aren't much of a spy. Too fidgety."

"My personal theory is that men are able to store all of their blood in their stomachs. That way their legs don't cramp." I eased my bottom down to the pavement and stretched out my legs with a sigh.

"Emma, I could take you back to the car." We'd returned the van to the rental agency and were using my sedan.

I shook my head. "You won't get rid of me that easily."

"Then come here." His arms circled me and drew me back against him. His chest was as solid as a wall, and my body responded with a wiggle of contentment. "Now keep an eye on the front," he whispered in my ear.

That small touch of his breath on my sensitive neck reminded me how much I'd rather be at home with him. But we'd made our choices for the night, or they had been made for us by a set of circumstances we couldn't alter or ignore. I put my concentration on picking up every detail possible about what was happening at Wilson Asphalt.

Nathan checked his watch. We'd decided to watch for an hour. By then we should have a good idea if the routine had been varied since the "break-in."

"Nathan," I whispered, nodding to the street. A lone vehicle was coming. It moved slowly, lumbering along the service road. In front of Wilson Asphalt, it stopped, the big motor of the pickup idling at a deep rumble. After a few seconds it turned into the front lot at Wilson's and stopped. The lights and motor were cut and a tall man got out.

"Well, well," Nathan whispered. "Maybe our luck has just taken a turn for the good."

"That's Steve Gray!" I hissed. "How could that possibly be good luck?"

"Exactly. We know where he is, so you can call him, and there's also the chance that he might leave in such a hurry that he gets careless."

"Do you think he killed Carlton Frazier?"

Nathan hesitated. "I don't know. Evidence seems to point to that conclusion, but that same evidence would indicate that Nella killed James Devlin. I'm not willing to convict someone just because they were, or could have been, at the scene of the crime. Or because it happened on their property."

I nodded. I wasn't certain what I felt. Too many things had happened, but I believed that whoever had killed Frazier had also killed James. The burgundy Cadillac was the link there. Frazier's car. Or at least I had assumed it was Frazier's car. It could have been someone else's. Possibilities cluttered my brain. Too bad I didn't have a license plate number.

"Emma, do you think you can sneak back to that convenience store down the street?"

"Sure." I'd give anything to be able to get up and move around. "If my legs aren't paralyzed."

"I think they'll recover." Nathan reached around me and applied a gentle massage to my thighs. "Later we'll make sure they're fine."

"Ah, the good Dr. Cates," I said, unable to stop the emotions he could so easily stir.

"If you can pretend you're Marla and call Gray, I can watch to make sure he leaves immediately."

My breath was suddenly a bit short. Performer's nerves. I'd never pretended to be anyone else in my life. Now it was vitally important that I do a convincing job.

"Be careful," Nathan whispered as he helped me to my feet. He gave my rump a solid pat. "I don't think there's been any permanent damage there. Feels fine."

"Thanks." I gave him the widest grin I could muster. "I'll be right back."

Crouching low so that I could hide among the vehicles, I started back down the road toward the small convenience store that was less than a mile away. I'd memorized the

numbers to Gray's home and the office, and I had a pock-
etful of quarters.

The night air was cool, but not cold. Still, by the time I
got to the pay phone my lungs burned. My hands were
trembling as I fumbled first with the receiver of the phone
and then with the quarters. At last I slotted one in and dialed
Wilson Asphalt. Gray answered on the second ring, and his
voice was curt.

"Steve?" I put as much winsomeness in my voice as I
knew how. "Where have you been? I've been trying to find
you."

"What do you want?"

I couldn't tell if his voice held anger or fear. I remembered his face the day he'd stood at the door of the sporting
goods store waiting for Marla to let him in. He certainly
didn't sound like an anxious lover. Maybe I had misjudged
Marla and her relationship with Gray.

"I'm in trouble."

"So what's new?"

He was ruthless, and afraid. Now I could read him a bit
better. Marla had something on him. Business or personal,
I couldn't deduce, but he was a man who disliked having
someone else hold the upper hand. I could well imagine that
Marla would not be reluctant to crack the whip over him.

"What's new is that you'd better help me get out of it,
or..." Or what? I didn't know what to threaten him with so
I let it hang.

"Or you'll go to the police? I hardly think so. You've got
as much to lose as I have."

His breath was short. Anger or fear? Once again I
couldn't be certain, but I played it for fear.

"I've already lost more than you'll ever know. Meet me
at the reservoir. You know that little cove on the north
shore? Just off Twin Lane." It was a place where teenagers
rendezvoused back when I was in high school. I'd been over
there only a few months before, doing some sketches, and I

knew that it was private and secluded. Steve Gray could wait to meet me there until hell froze over. It was also a good forty-five minutes from town.

"I'm not meeting you anywhere. Every time I see you, I get in deeper and deeper."

"Be there, or be prepared to face the results." I hung up, satisfied that he'd taken the bait.

Using the shadows and walls of buildings, I made my way slowly back to Nathan. The one thing I didn't want to do was find myself headlighted in the glare of Gray's truck lights.

Nathan was exactly where I'd left him, and it didn't look as if he'd budged an inch. Only when he grabbed me, pulled me down beside him and gave me a quick kiss did I realize his excitement. "Excellent work. He took off like someone had set fire to his tail feathers. And he took one of the guards with him. He must be afraid of an ambush."

"I wonder what poor Marla knows that would make him so worried?"

"That's a question we can deal with tomorrow," Nathan answered. "Now let's get this done while we have a chance."

With Nella's keys, we made our entrance through the front door. The offices were strangely quiet. Gray had obviously taken the inside guard with him, and if Nathan and I had a scrap of luck, we could get what we needed and get out before anyone discovered us.

I went directly to the computer in Gray's office. It was an eerie feeling, going back where we'd found Carlton Frazier dead, but I had no time to be squeamish. When I hit the combination of switches, the computer blipped on. In a matter of seconds I used the password to get through the security code to obtain the list of contracts. Scrolling through the listings, I selected three to print out and keyed in the commands. The printer whirred into life.

I shifted gears and returned to the main office to open another computer file to check on any listings with Micro-

Tech. The schedule of payments as there, easily accessible, and it matched the amounts and dates that I'd found in Frank's system. There were several additional dates where Benny had come in and trained the staff on use of the computers. It looked very much in order.

There had to be more. I hunted through the remaining list of expenditures and found nothing. Suddenly I realized that the noise of the printer had ceased. Those contracts were pages long. Maybe the paper had become jammed. Hurrying back to Gray's office, I bent over the printer. There was only one page. When I looked at it, I knew that our quest was over. "You're too late." Those were the only words on the page.

Gray had left the listings but blanked the files, leaving only brief messages. I tried another, just to be certain. In only a few moments the printer chattered out another message. "Curiosity killed the cat."

Gray wanted us to know his intentions. I tore off both pages, killed the printer and computer and went to find Nathan. It wouldn't do any good to hunt further. Now that Gray knew what we were after, he wouldn't have left any evidence behind. His files were gone. And if we wanted them, we'd have to figure out where he'd taken them.

Wordlessly I handed the pages to Nathan when I found him guarding the front door.

"Damn!" He slipped his hand around my arm and we started to leave. He, too, knew that it was futile to hunt any longer. We'd known Gray would move fast, but he'd surprised us with his efficiency. No wonder he'd been able to get away with crooked contracts for so many years. The man knew how to take care of himself.

When we'd made it back to the car, Nathan shook his head. "That was too easy," he said. "It was almost as if they left the front door open for us. Gray wanted us to find the files blank."

"He had to know what we were after." I wanted to kick myself. "Since I left that contract in the printer."

Nathan picked up my hand and held it. "You aren't exactly a veteran of attempts on your life, Emma. That contract was the last thing on your mind, and rightfully so."

"I might as well have left a note saying, 'Hey, Steve Gray, we're looking into your state contracts. Better cover your tracks.'"

"Remember, we only have Nella's word that Gray's contracts have been less than aboveboard. And Nella hasn't exactly proven to be the world's most reliable source."

I sighed. That was truer than I wanted to believe. "I wonder where she is?" I couldn't help but have a nagging sense that Nella had not left Marla's house under her own power. As much as I tried, though, I couldn't remember a single detail that would have indicated a sign of a struggle, except in the study where James was found. And that looked as if someone had been hunting for something specific.

"Where to?" I finally asked.

"How about your sister-in-law's."

"Marla's? Why?"

"We may have put her in a very precarious position. If she's involved in some of his schemes, he may decide he wants her out of the way."

"Yes, there are already three dead people. Why not make it four?"

"Or even six, if he can get us."

Or seven, if he'd already gotten Nella. I didn't say it out loud because I was too afraid I'd make it true.

I drove to the beautiful street where a short time before someone had tried to kill me. We had a clear view of Marla's house. Looking at it, I felt the memories of a life that I'd once lived overwhelm me. I'd never cared for Marla, and neither had Frank, but we'd visited her and James often. The two brothers were close, and we wives tolerated each other.

"Taking a trip to the past?" Nathan asked softly.

I nodded, suddenly too choked up to talk. His arms encircled me and pulled me back against him so that I was cradled like a child.

"Travel can expose some unusual sights, beautiful and painful, especially a trip to the past."

He always seemed to know exactly what I was thinking and feeling. It was one of the things about Nathan that I adored. And he wasn't upset or afraid of my past. I bore the scars of tragedy, and Nathan wasn't afraid to look at them. Maybe it was because he had his own scars. We'd both suffered extreme loss. Maybe that was why we understood each other so well.

"I've never been much of a traveler," I finally managed to say. "Trips, even to the past, are hard on me."

"Travel broadens the mind," he answered, tightening his arms around me until I felt cocooned in safety. "Wander far and wide, just be careful. No dark alleys without a light at the end."

I chuckled softly. How well he put it. "It seems that my travels are populated by ghosts."

"Only on this trip, Emma. You have many travels to make. In the future, you'll find companions of flesh and blood. Boon companions. I'm certain of it."

"Can I hold you to that, Mr. Cates?"

"I'll swear it on a stack of Bibles."

I snuggled deeper into him. My nerves had settled considerably, and I felt sleep tugging at my eyelids. I had to fight it. If Nathan and I were going to sit watch over Marla, I couldn't fall asleep on the job.

"And what about your travels? Where will you go?" I asked. Nathan had made it clear he had something to finish, but he never gave any details. Fighting sleep, my normal reticence in questioning him was weakened.

"Oh, here and there."

He was deliberately making light of my question. "Will your companions be boon?" There were so many things I wanted to ask, but his reserve kept me at bay.

"Emma Devlin, I couldn't ask for a better companion than you. For travel or for life." He kissed the top of my head. "Now sleep. You're fighting it like a tiger, but it's one battle you'd do well to lose."

"That isn't fair. You can't sleep if I sleep. Who'll watch Marla?"

"I'll take the first shift," he said. "That's how soldiers do it, one at a time, four-hour shifts."

"You'll wake me?"

"In plenty of time."

I was too tired to fight any longer. I sank into a deep sleep supported by Nathan's quiet strength.

"THE NIGHT PASSED without incidents," Nathan reported when he shook me awake just after dawn.

I was chagrined. I'd slept through the entire night, and Nathan hadn't gotten a wink. "You promised to wake me. You said four-hour shifts."

"Emma, you only slept about four hours. We were up rather late, if you'll recall."

There was a twisted grin on his face, and I couldn't help but smile as I tried to rub the sleep from my eyes and put some order in my tangled hair. "Nothing happened?"

"Four cars drove by. One young lady came home very, very late from a date and her father met her at the door with words of disapproval."

"Poor kid."

"Poor kid!" Nathan was insulted. "She came home at three o'clock in the morning. I'd save my sympathy for her parents."

Nathan was the perfect picture of fatherly outrage. I leaned over and gave him a kiss. "You're going to make a wonderful father some day. I'm afraid you'll terrorize any young men who will ever dare to try and date your daughters, but I think that may be a good thing."

Nathan laughed, but not before the flare of sadness touched his eyes. I remembered too late that he had already buried a daughter, a child who would never grow up to date.

"I'm sorry," I whispered, touching his face with my hand. The line of his jaw was so sure, so solid.

"If you have daughters who look like you, then you'll need a terrifying man to keep the boys at bay," he said. "Why don't we head home for a shower and some breakfast?"

"And Marla?"

"We need to think of a plan to get her out of town for several days. I considered several possiblities last night. We'll talk about them over breakfast." He paused. "I have to go back to Vicksburg today, Emma. I can't put it off any longer."

"I understand." He'd been more than generous with his time, but the idea that he was leaving made my heart plunge. "Everything here will be fine."

"I'll be back no later than tomorrow. Can you stay out of trouble that long?"

Delight made me want to spin and twirl. He was only going to take care of some business. He was coming back. "Without you to keep me in line, I don't know how I'll manage. Funny, but until I met you I'd never broken into a building, been shot at, or used a false identity. I'm not certain if I can stay out of trouble or not."

Nathan was still laughing when we pulled up at the house.

The plan we decided on was a ticket to a spa in West Palm Beach for Marla. She had a friend there she loved to visit, and a week in a health spa would be something she couldn't turn down. I'd somehow convince her that James had wanted her to have it and had mentioned it to me. I didn't think Marla would put up too much resistance at the idea.

She had never been one to question where her presents came from.

Nathan insisted on renting his own car to go to Vicksburg, so I dropped him at a rental office with the promise that I'd behave and stay out of trouble for the next twenty-four hours. He'd suggested that I even rent a hotel room and hide out. I told him I'd consider it, and we agreed to meet the next day for lunch at the Mayflower Café downtown.

I left him standing in the lot, waving. The loneliness that jolted through me made me tighten my grip on the wheel. I was like a teenager with a crush—addicted to Nathan's love. I forced a rueful grin as I drove toward Marla's. How had my feelings for that man developed so suddenly?

My sister-in-law was up—and feeling the effects of whatever sleeping pills she'd taken along with a few drinks. I'd never seen Marla look less than ravishing. But with her tumbled hair, bleary eyes and unhappy expression, she looked more human. She also looked as though she'd been crying.

I made a pot of coffee for us while she sat at the counter in the kitchen and held her head. Her friend had left early, the mother of small children with responsibilities of her own. I couldn't help but believe that Marla was glad even for my company. She didn't want to be alone, and I didn't blame her.

As we sipped our coffee, I broached the subject of a trip, a surprise. Her first reaction was suspicion, and then delight. At the idea of a week in a spa and a visit with her Florida friend, she brightened considerably.

Then she collapsed. "I can't leave the business."

I'd never thought Marla would put a practical issue before her own pleasure, and it startled me. "Leave it closed. People will understand."

She shook her head. "I can't. There are some business deals in the works. I can't walk away from them."

"Surely they can wait."

"No." She buried her head in her hands. "They can't."

"Think about it, Marla. The visit would be good for you."

"No doubt about that. I need to get out of this town." She glanced toward the hallway that led to the study. Something close to panic was in her voice.

"Why, Marla? What's wrong?"

She shook her head and buried her face over her steaming cup of coffee. "You wouldn't understand," she finally mumbled. "You're such a goody two-shoes you'd never understand."

I saw a huge teardrop plop on the table beside her coffee cup. Were they real or crocodile tears?

"Try me, Marla, I might be better at understanding than you think."

She sniffled. "I despise your moral superiority. I won't be judged by you."

I bit my bottom lip. Was there any truth in what she said? I had judged her, and found her not very likable. "I haven't approved of some of the things you've done, that's true. But if you're in trouble, I'll try to help. At least take the ticket and get out of town. Don't tell anyone where you're going. That way you'll be safe."

Marla's head snapped up. "Safe? Why wouldn't I be safe?"

I'd done it again—put my foot in my big mouth. "Well, someone came into your home and killed your husband. Maybe they'll try to come back."

"Why would they do that?"

"A good question, Marla. Knowing Nella Colson might not be healthy."

"When I get my hands on Nella ..." Marla didn't finish the sentence. "I'll take that ticket," she said. "But you have to promise you won't tell anyone where I am. Not a single soul."

"You have my word, Marla. I'll make all the arrangements under another name. I'll buy the ticket with cash. You just make sure your friend will be there to look out for you."

"And what about you?" Marla asked. "Who's going to look out for you, Emma? I don't think you realize that by poking your nose into this business you've put yourself in a lot of danger."

"I only wanted to know that Frank's death was an accident. It would seem that I've uncovered a lot of other things."

"Leave the return date on the ticket open-ended. I might decide not to come back." Marla wiped the smudges of makeup from beneath her eyes in a defiant gesture. "And if I were you, I'd buy myself a ticket in the opposite direction. I'd get out while I was still alive."

Chapter Thirteen

Before I went home, I made the arrangements for Marla's "vacation." She was booked out on a one o'clock flight to West Palm Beach with a seven-day stay at Chez Palace, a swanky resort designed to sweat, pamper and scare the weight and wrinkles away. I'd used the assumed name Jasmine Rose. All in all, it was going to be to my advantage to get her out of my way.

The police had already searched James's study, but I wanted to get back into the house to re-examine the guest room. Marla denied knowing anything about Nella's whereabouts, but Marla and the truth were often strangers. Even if Marla were telling the truth, there might be a clue in the house that she'd overlooked.

Bills had stacked up, so I decided to run home and take care of a few necessities before I did anything else. Since it's an older home, it was built off the road with a curving drive and a large front lawn. I used to tease Aunt Tilly that she'd have to leave me enough money to have some yard help, but I'd grown to love the physical labor. The interesting thing about the property was that it could be approached from the front or the back. It covered the entire block. Frank and I had gotten in the habit of going in through the back, since that's where the garage was located, but I only meant to stop for an hour at the most, so when I reached the block I headed for the front.

Just as I turned the corner I saw the burgundy Caddy sitting down the block two houses from mine. There was a big man in the front seat, and he was looking right at me. Panic was my first reaction, and then I got a grip on myself. I'd been driving the mini van. Did the driver of the Caddy know my conservative sedan? I could risk it by simply driving by. My only alternative was to turn around and beat a hasty retreat—behavior that might alert the watcher. One thing I didn't want to do was incite him to draw out his gun and try again to kill me on the street.

It took all of the grit I could muster to drive along as if I weren't nearly frozen with panic. It's funny how the street seemed to pass in slow motion. There was Betty and John's home, the live oak tree that I loved so much, the bump in the sidewalk where the roots of another tree had pushed up the pavement, and finally my own home. It all went by so slowly. Yet every time I looked at the burgundy car, I felt as if I were being pulled headfirst toward it at a hundred miles an hour.

The man behind the wheel didn't move. He was wearing wraparound sunglasses. And a bulky jacket, maybe leather. I looked with as much discretion as possible while forcing my foot to keep a steady thirty-five on the accelerator.

Somewhere in the distance I heard the long wail of a siren. A fire engine, maybe. It was sporadic, not like a dire emergency. I heard it yet it had nothing to do with what was happening to me. I was almost at the Caddy. Twenty yards, ten... My fingers clenched the wheel. There was the glint of sunlight on something at the man's ear. An earring! Was it possible? Was it a diamond? I couldn't get a clear look.

I was staring directly at him when his head turned and his expression shifted to disbelief. I could see nothing except his mouth and that he was young and Caucasian. I could also see that he recognized me. I hit the gas pedal with everything I had, clutching the wheel even tighter in an effort to keep control of the car. The tires squealed and the smell of burning rubber churned around me as I shot forward.

The man in the Caddy was right behind me. He swung his car up in the front lawn of Mrs. Ingram's house, rampaging over her azaleas and bridal wreath. In a few seconds he was back in the street and headed in the proper direction to chase me. Without any evidence, I knew he was the man who'd tried to kill me on James's porch.

The intersection of Devine and LaCamp is never busy, so I took the risk and shot across it. To my amazement, a patrol car was headed directly for me. I barely made it past the officers. They were traveling very fast, too, with the siren and lights going. They cornered in directly behind me. I was driving so fast that I ran up the curb and almost smacked into Mrs. Hamilton's prize chestnut tree before I could regain control. I gladly pulled over. The burgundy Caddy shot past and kept going.

I tried to get out of the car, but my legs were rubbery. I knew if I stood I'd simply fall onto the pavement. It was better to wait. I didn't care if they took me in. I would have kissed them for an arrest.

"Ms. Devlin!"

The voice was strangely familiar, but it seemed to come from a distance. There was the prickle of tiny ant bites all over my head and I knew that I was about to faint.

My car door was pulled open and I was assisted out of the car.

"Sit down and put your head between your knees."

The voice ordering me was firm and panic-free.

"Everything's going to be okay. Now just relax."

In a few moments, my head cleared and the burning sensation on my scalp faded. I looked up to find an anxious Sergeant Vesley looking down at me.

"You nearly got yourself killed," he said, and a frown darkened his eyes. "You went right through that intersection. And that Caddy was hot after you. What's going on?"

"That man was going to hurt me." I knew I should think everything through before I said more. I had a habit of saying just enough to make matters worse.

"Did he threaten you?"

I cleared my throat. "Not exactly."

"Then how did you know he intended to hurt you?"

Here it was. I couldn't tell the sergeant that the same car had been involved in trying to gun me down at Marla's house. I'd already lied by omission when I didn't tell the police that I was at the scene of that crime. What should I say now?

"Ms. Devlin, why do you think the person in that car was going to hurt you?"

"He started chasing me. I was going home, and when he saw me, he turned around in the street and started chasing me."

"You didn't know the man?"

I shook my head.

"Sergeant, I got a plate number on the car. Want me to run it?"

The second police officer was standing at Vesley's elbow. He was a younger man with a kind face.

"Sure," Vesley said. "Let's find out who owns that car. I want a warrant put out for him. Reckless driving, running a stop sign, possible DWI. That should be enough to pull him over and bring him in. Then we can ask him in person why he's harassing Ms. Devlin."

I nodded weakly. "Thanks."

The younger officer walked back to the radio in the patrol car while Vesley helped me to my feet.

"We were coming to talk with you, anyway," Vesley said. "If you feel up to it, I have some questions."

Now was definitely not a good time. I wasn't certain I could think clearly enough to keep all of my lies in place, but I knew Vesley wasn't going to take no for an answer. He might appear to be a kindly desk sergeant, but beneath that soft exterior was a man who had some sharp questions.

"Certainly. We could go back to my house and have some coffee. I could use a jolt of caffeine."

"You wouldn't happen to know where Marla Devlin is, would you?"

I looked up too suddenly. "What do you want with Marla?"

"Ms. Devlin, there are a lot of unanswered questions. I have two dead bodies. One of them is Marla Devlin's husband. I have a shooting at a local business, where a top employee is still listed as a missing person. I have a drive-by shooting at Ms. Devlin's residence, and now a harassment attempt on you. I can think of at least fifty reasons why I need to talk with Marla Devlin."

Before I was forced to respond, the young officer came back to us. He rubbed a hand over the bridge of his nose. "This is sort of interesting, Sergeant," he said.

"Go on, Conner, spit it out."

"That car was registered to Carlton Frazier."

I swallowed. Now I was really tied in to the whole mess, and there was no way I was going to explain any of it to Vesley's satisfaction.

He looked at me. "If this were a movie, I'd say the plot thickens. Since it isn't a movie, I'll just say that you've handed me one more headache, and I intend to get some answers. Conner, drive Ms. Devlin's car to her house. The lady will ride with me."

Without further ado, I was handed into the front seat of the patrol car and we headed back to Aunt Tilly's.

While I made the coffee, Sergeant Vesley and Conner sat at the bar. They waited patiently while I chatted on and on about the greeting card business. They simply let me talk until the coffee was made and I ran out of nervous chatter.

"Where is Marla Devlin?" Velsey asked as he spooned three sugars into his coffee and poured liberally from the pitcher of Half-and-Half.

"I'm not certain, Sergeant Vesley."

"That's a lie, Ms. Devlin. You were over there bright and early this morning. She put some suitcases in her car and disappeared just after you left. She didn't even take time to comb her hair."

Good for Marla, I thought. She at least took her own warnings seriously. "Sergeant Vesley, I'm concerned for my sister-in-law's welfare. I have no intention of telling anyone where she is."

"Ms. Devlin is a witness in a murder case. She was told not to leave town. We can arrest you as an accessory in her flight."

"Marla didn't tell me she was told not to leave town." I thought about it for a minute. My reluctance to keep Marla's destination a secret was because I wasn't certain who was after her—and me. But Sergeant Vesley was the most trust-worthy person I'd met, outside of Nathan. I watched the expressions shift over his face. He was waiting, as patiently as possible for him. "She's headed for West Palm Beach in a few hours."

"She was tailed to the airport. We checked the flights out. She isn't listed as a passenger and there was no ticket charged to any of her credit cards."

"Nice to know you're so efficient." I smiled and received no response. "I booked the ticket under the name Jasmine Rose and I paid cash for it."

He nodded. "It's probably best to get her out of town."

"You're glad she's gone?" I was certain they'd make her return, especially if she was a material witness.

He shrugged. "We can find her, now that we know where she went. I'll alert the West Palm P.D. to keep tabs on her."

I gave him the details of her "vacation," and waited for his response. He finished his coffee but failed to get up to leave. "Is there something else I can tell you?" I asked, indicating what I hoped was my eagerness for them to leave. "I have some errands I need to run."

"What do you know about Carlton Frazier?" Vesley asked.

"He was an executive at South Trust Savings and Loan."

"Did you have business with him?"

I let out an exasperated sigh. "We've been over this before. I—my friend—applied for a loan and was turned down."

"There was no loan application on file," Vesley said slowly. "We checked."

"Well, we didn't actually get around to applying. Mr. Frazier said there was no point."

"What did you want a loan for?"

I felt the noose tightening. "That's personal business, Sergeant."

"It's police business now."

My warm, sunny kitchen had suddenly become a chess board where my opponents sat across the table from me and waited for some break in my verbal strategy. "I had considered selling my stock in a company, and the potential buyer needed financing."

"Micro-Tech stock?"

"Yes," I answered stiffly but couldn't help myself.

"Is Mr. Yeager aware that you want to sell your stock in Micro-Tech?"

"He is not and I don't want him to know." At last my anger showed. I had no intention of selling my stock and I didn't want Benny worried by the police.

"Ms. Devlin, were you aware that the same gun was used to kill James Devlin, Carlton Frazier..." He paused. "And your husband?"

My first reaction was that I hadn't heard him properly. "Frank?"

"I found it a little hard to believe myself. Seems hard to swallow, doesn't it?"

He was watching me. It was almost as if his eyes were trying to read my thoughts. It didn't matter. I was so shocked by his revelation that I could only register my confusion—and surprise. "How can you tell?" I managed to ask.

"With Mr. Devlin—your husband—we noticed that the bullet was marred. It's a technical thing, but the cylinder on the murder weapon had been scratched. The forensic boys have determined that the weapon had been loaded with the wrong calibre bullets at one time or another. See, a .357 can take a .38 load. Since it isn't exactly the correct ammunition, there is some damage to the cylinder when the weapon is fired."

Vesley's explanation was difficult to follow, but I grasped the basics. "So you can prove the weapon was the same in all three shootings?"

"Modern science is wonderful, isn't it?"

"It would be if you could find the man who pulled the trigger." The glint of sunlight on something that closely resembled an earring came back to me. The man in the Caddy. Was it possible the multiple murderer had been sitting outside my home, waiting for a chance to finish me off?

"You okay?" Vesley asked.

I slipped onto a stool at the bar. "Yes, I'm okay. It's just that the information is disturbing."

"We've reopened your husband's case, Ms. Devlin. That's one of the reasons I'm here. It seems more than a little odd that you were poking around in that just days ago, and now there's a rash of new murders committed with the same gun. Is there something you'd like to tell us?"

How would Velsey like the story that I'd begun probing the circumstances of my husband's death because his ghost was visiting me and making my nights a hell? I didn't think the tough cop would buy that story a bit.

"No. I've told you everything I can."

"Have you told us everything you know?" he asked.

Vesley was a sharp man. He sensed that I was holding something back. "Sergeant, there's nothing else I can tell you now. If you don't have any specific questions, I do have some personal business that requires my attention."

Vesley rose, followed by his sidekick. "What I want to know is how Wilson Asphalt and Nella Colson fit into this. We've got an APB out on Ms. Colson. If you happen to hear from her, let us know."

"Certainly." I would have agreed to walk over hot coals barefoot to get them out of the house. There was something very obvious that I was overlooking, and I needed time to think. Vesley's little bombshell had rocked my foundations.

"Ms. Devlin, are you sure you're okay?" Vesley asked. He'd made it to the doorway before he stopped.

"I'm fine," I insisted. I forced myself to smile. "It's been a very strange morning, Sergeant. I'm not in the habit of helping my sister-in-law flee the state or of being chased by someone in a dead man's car."

"Those points are well taken," Vesley said. "I guess my job will be to find out why these things are happening to you." He tipped his cap and walked out the door, his fellow officer at his side.

As I watched them walk down the drive, I felt a stab of longing for Nathan. What I wouldn't give to be able to talk over these new events with him. I was about to close the door when I saw Vesley turn around and head back. I was tempted to slam the door and lock it, but I knew I couldn't. When he was about twenty yards away, he spoke. "By the way, I'm going to have some officers posted outside your house. Just for your own protection, you know. We don't want any more strange men harassing you."

Before I could protest, he turned around and walked to the patrol car. When I finally closed my door, I was already thinking of a plan to counteract Vesley's guard. He might want to protect me, but he was also interested in keeping me under his watchful eye. The man was smart. He hoped I would eventually lead him to the people he wanted to find.

Before I had a chance to think it through too carefully, I called a cab and asked them to meet me two blocks over. I gathered up my purse, the keys to Marla's car, and as much cash as I could find in the house. Before Vesley had a chance to sic his watchdogs on me, I intended to be gone.

Thank goodness for Aunt Tilly and her fondness for vegetation, I thought as I ran along the front lawn and crossed the street, cutting through the neighbors' yards until I was a safe two blocks away from my house and looking for my cab. When it finally arrived, I asked the driver to take me to the airport. Marla would certainly have left her car there, and, lucky me, I had the spare set of keys that James and Frank traditionally exchanged with vehicles.

As the taxi pulled away from my neighborhood, I couldn't contain a small victorious smile. Vesley was smart, but this time I'd outfoxed him.

Marla's sports car was a good bit flashier than my old sedan, but I could understand her appreciation for it as soon as I drove out of the airport parking lot. My car was reliable and comfortable. Marla's car was fun. My escape from Vesley had given me a little edge of daring that wore off all too quickly. I'd escaped my home—and the police. But what about the people who might be trying to kill me? And what if Nathan tried to call me at home? He'd be worried to death if I didn't answer the telephone sometime tonight. My euphoria disappeared in a cloud of worry.

As my first chore, I went to the main library and took a copy of the city directory over to a quiet table. I quickly looked up the address of the house that Marla had visited the day after James was murdered. It belonged to one Bob

Galwind. I cross-checked in the telephone directory. The information seemed correct. Maybe it was time to pay Mr. Galwind a little visit.

I decided to assume the guise of an insurance salesperson when I rang the bell. Expecting a man, I was a bit surprised when a middle-aged woman answered the door.

"Mrs. Galwind?"

"Yes. Who are you?"

"I'm Emma Remington with the Hanover Insurance Company." I spoke with clarity and assurance. "I'm here to see your husband about a policy he ordered."

"Bob? Insurance?" She laughed. "That'll be the day. That oaf hasn't worried about insurance since he signed on coaching sports. He thinks the Davis County Junior College system's going to take care of his family."

"Maybe he's turned over a new leaf. He was interested in our comprehensive health plan."

"Does that include a free trip to Vegas as an incentive to sign up?"

"Excuse me?"

"If you've promised my husband some gambling trip, you can forget it. He scammed two condo companies last year and managed to get free trips to Vegas and Atlantic City. If you're offering some kind of bonus like that to get him to sign up, let me save you a lot of time and expense. He won't take the policy. He'll take the trip, go out and spend every penny we have, and then some, and then he'll come back here and screw your company just like he did those others."

Before I could say anything else, she slammed the door as hard as she could. I had the distinct impression that she was standing on the other side, crying.

I walked back down the steps to Marla's car. So, Bob Galwind was a chronic gambler. And he had a wife who was on the edge. The clue worth pursuing was his employment. As soon as I got in the car I headed toward Davis County

Junior College. It might be interesting to find out what kind of person Bob Galwind might be.

"MR. GALWIND'S OUT on the field. He can't be disturbed," the student working in the athletic office informed me. "Come back at three-thirty. Football practice will be over then."

I thanked the coed as I left the office. She'd been more than helpful. Not only was Galwind a coach, he was also an appointee on the advisory board for the entire state junior college system. And Marla had been in charge of securing athletic equipment contracts for Sportsplex. It wasn't hard to figure where she might have learned a few tricks about negotiating state contracts. A lot of different angles had begun to pull together. But just how deep was Marla in? How had she become involved with Steve Gray in the first place?

The answer was as clear as a sunny Mississippi sky. Nella Colson! I'd be back at Davis County at three-thirty. I had a few of my own questions for Bob Galwind before I called Sergeant Vesley. But first I wanted to go back to Marla's house to look for some clue to the whereabouts of Nella Colson. Her disappearance was beginning to look more and more like foul play. The kind of foul play that ended in murder.

Chapter Fourteen

My second search of Marla's house netted nothing new. My only other ambition was to be on hand at three-thirty when Bob Galwind came off the playing field. I thought of calling Sergeant Vesley to help question the coach. But that would surely blow the whistle on Marla, and I wanted to give her a chance to try to explain before the authorities got involved with her.

No, I decided. It would be better to go after Galwind alone.

There was still almost twenty-four hours before Nathan would be back. And I had no way to contact him. I was on my own. I would check out Bob Galwind on the playing field. Sometimes you can learn a lot about people by watching them work.

Once I got to the Davis County Junior College playing field, I parked under a newly leafed oak. The air was filled with different scents. Wisteria and Magnolia were two of the most distinctive. The Junior College had a horticultural program that taught teenagers the rudiments of lawn and garden care and landscaping. It was one of the state systems that had maintained its rural ties. The college hadn't produced the best scholars in the state, but it did have quite a reputation on the gridiron and the garden. Two years before Frank was killed, we'd purchased a load of plants from the school. I hadn't been back to the campus since that time.

I'd failed to notice how beautiful the day was until I was forced to sit in the car and watch the young men in spring practice. The black and gold uniforms against the green grass and blue sky reminded me of long-ago days. It was a pleasant memory until I saw the man I determined to be Bob Galwind.

He was coaching a defensive line, putting the tackles at the dummies again and again. His right jaw was distorted by a wad of tobacco. He spit at least every minute, and he yelled constantly, when he wasn't spitting.

Galwind strutted the line, his florid face moving from a soft red to crimson as he reprimanded the players. I knew it was all part of the sport, but it was still a bit of bullying. Bob Galwind was a distasteful man, and I wondered what Marla could possibly have in common with him, unless it was illegal.

I got out of the car and sat on the hood. Now that I'd tracked Galwind down, what was I going to do about it? The seed of a plan started to germinate. By the time Galwind sent the defensive line to the showers, I was ready for him.

Just at the edge of the playing field he got rid of the tobacco. I waited until he was walking past the car.

"Coach Galwind?" I called out, sliding off the hood and walking to meet him. "I'm Emma Devlin, Marla's sister-in-law." I waited for a response, but he said nothing. It could have been my imagination, but I thought his eyes narrowed slightly.

"I'm sure you heard that Marla's husband was killed, and... well, I've decided to help her in the business for a while. She recommended that I come by here and talk with you, seeing as how you've been such a good customer in the past."

"Get out of here." He started to walk away.

"Excuse me, Mr. Galwind. I don't think I heard you correctly."

He stopped and slowly turned to face me. "Get off this school property. I told your sister-in-law the last time I saw her that I wouldn't do business with her again. It's too dangerous. Those cops are going to be looking for a motive for her husband's murder. That's the kind of examination I don't want or need."

"Marla obviously isn't worried. She sent me here. Something about equipment for the weight room."

"Damn!" Galwind's face crimsoned. "I can't! I can't risk it, and neither should she."

"Marla said there isn't a risk. It's the same cut that you got before." He'd edged all around it, but I hadn't gotten him to admit anything!

"You've got to be nuts. Get out of here!" He looked around as if he expected someone to pop out from behind the oak tree and arrest him.

"What would you find acceptable?" I was so close. I had to find out one way or the other.

"Hey, I don't know." He looked around again. "I've got to go. I have to meet with some students before they leave." He edged away.

"How does thirty-five percent sound?" Was that enough to keep him from walking away?

"Keep talking." His eyes looked up as his mouth moved. He was making the calculations in his head. "That would be a nice chunk of change," he agreed. His eyes shifted left and right again. "Can we talk about this somewhere else?" His face flushed hot red. "I can't believe Marla would send you over here! She must be losing her mind completely. You'd better go."

"But you'll meet me?" I asked.

He nodded. "Make it Barney's Bar and Grill. Five-thirty. You know the place?"

"I know it." What a dive. I could easily imagine that Bob Galwind was on a first-name basis with every roach in the joint. It almost made me shudder to think about it.

As I watched Galwind walk away, I could only hope that his wife wouldn't give him a description of the insurance saleswoman who'd come calling that very morning.

I got back in Marla's car. What was I going to do until time to meet Galwind? If only there was some way to get in touch with Nathan. I missed him more than I ever thought possible.

THE JUKEBOX in Barney's was blaring a Randy Travis oldie. I settled into the vinyl booth I'd picked as having the best vantage point and waited. Galwind would be an easy man to spot.

It was impossible to believe that a beautiful spring day was ending just outside the greasy-looking door of Barney's. Inside the bar, it was as if spring and sunshine were fantasies. I checked out the three other customers—a woman in stretch pants and a fuzzy red sweater, and two men in jeans and plaid shirts. They drank in silence, all three at the bar.

Galwind was ten minutes late, but he pushed through the door and saw me immediately. He took his seat across from me in the booth and signaled the waitress with his index finger. She brought him a beer.

"I don't like this," he said. "Where's Marla?"

"She had to go out of town."

"I'll bet," he said, sipping the beer with a loud noise. "She'd better have taken all of her records with her."

I remembered her trip to Sportsplex just after James's murder. She'd probably been clearing out her own files then. No wonder her business activities couldn't wait until after the funeral.

"Marla isn't a fool. She's taken care of everything."

"Easy for you to say. It's my neck on the line if she gets caught." He put a finger in the collar of his shirt and loosened it.

"Well, you know the old saying, Mr. Galwind. In for a penny, in for a pound. You're already involved in this, so why not make a little more money?"

His eyes bored into me. "What kind of equipment you got? It's got to be good stuff. I can't take any chances anymore. I'd rather cut the profit margin and get good stuff."

"I'll make sure of it." I'd done a little research at the library in the hour I had to kill before going to Barney's. I owed the library a big donation when all of this was over. "Cybex. Top of the line. We'll work it the same way we did before. You have complete control of the athletic funds?"

He shook his head. "Marla knows I don't have control, just influence. Anyway, we've taken in almost twenty-five grand for the weight equipment."

I'd got him! "When do you want it?"

"Give me two weeks. That'll put the equipment in there before school lets out. Give the kids a chance to use it some, and it'll be there for those who want to work out this summer." He nodded. "Now it's Cybex, right?"

"Only the best."

"Thirty-five percent, right?"

"That's our agreement." I felt suddenly sick. Now there was no doubt that Marla had stepped over the line. And now that I'd proven it, what had I accomplished? None of this tied in with Frank's death. At least not that I could see.

I stood. "Thanks, Mr. Galwind. I'll be in touch." I walked out before he could say anything else.

Climbing into Marla's car, I made a decision. I was going to Vicksburg. It didn't matter that Vesley had asked me not to leave town. I only knew that Nathan was the one person I wanted to see. Had to see. It was exciting and very scary that I'd developed such strong feelings for him.

It was an hour's drive, and I was coasting into the river city. Ravenwood loomed dark and uninhabited in the night sky. No matter how many times I saw it, I still couldn't suppress the pang of sadness I felt. A way of life had ended in the old plantation house. A family had been devastated by war and grief.

The apartment above the kitchen was like going home. I'd missed the coziness of the small place. I took a long shower, changed clothes and decided to hunt Nathan on the battlefield. It would be fun. Reenactment forces would be camped around the area. The men would be gathered around the campfires, talking and eating. If I wanted, I could pretend it was the past.

I left the lights burning in the apartment and a note for Nathan on the door—just in case he happened by. He'd have no reason to believe that I was in Vicksburg, but we had a strange communication between us. He might ride his horse through the estate.

The Military Park parking lot contained several trucks and campers, as well as a scattering of other vehicles. As I parked and started walking, I could see the campfires glowing along a ridge.

The men were very friendly as I walked from group to group, asking about a dashing cavalry colonel who rode a big gelding. I was surprised to find that some of the reenactors had brought wives and girlfriends, who'd assumed the roles of local women or nurses.

I learned that women in the confederacy were very active in all phases of the war. A handful even went to battle, but the prejudices against women on the battlefield were so strong that most women worked in a nursing capacity, as suppliers, and as spies. That latter category intrigued me, and I stopped for a while at a campfire and listened to stories of the past.

My quest for Nathan was leisurely. I took my time, experiencing the reenactment where he spent a lot of his time—when he wasn't running all over Jackson almost getting killed with me. I wandered through the park, careful to keep my bearings on the paved road that would eventually wind and circle all the way around. When I came upon the silent man astride a powerful horse, I thought for a moment it might be a memorial. It took only a few seconds of staring to recognize Nathan's jawline, the breadth of his shoulders and his carriage.

"Seen any Yanks?" I asked from the shadows of a large Magnolia.

"Not a one, ma'am," he answered. He shook his foot loose from the stirrup and held out his hand, offering me a ride on the big chestnut. With his help, I mounted behind him, and Frisco set off at a ground-covering walk.

"I thought you might return to Ravenwood," he said.

"I wanted to see you." My arms circled his waist and I held him tight. I had the crazy sensation that he would disappear at any moment. Why was our time together so bittersweet? I pushed that thought aside and concentrated on enjoying the night and the feel of Nathan in front of me.

Frisco took us unerringly along the path and we left the campfires behind. Soon we were alone in the starry night.

"Do you know where we're going?" I teased him.

"There's a roundabout path to Ravenwood."

"But Marla's car is at the park."

"You modern women, can't make it a night without a set of wheels," Nathan teased. "We'll explore the park and then I'll take you back to your car."

"Will you come back to Ravenwood with me? Can you?"

He shook his head and caressed my hand with his gloved one. "Not tonight."

"I know you've got a lot to do. You've missed so much already, helping me."

"I've done what I wanted to do, Emma. Since the moment I met you, I've done exactly what I wanted to do. Don't ever think otherwise."

I rested my head on his strong back as the horse carried us on. I wanted to tell him about what had happened during the day, but I didn't want to add that element of danger to our time together. Maybe when all of this was over we would be able to spend a weekend or a week simply getting to know every last detail about each other.

"You haven't mentioned what brought you to Vicksburg today," Nathan said. "Something happen?"

I sighed. It was pointless to try to pretend it hadn't happened. I started slowly, telling him about searching the house. I ended with the burgundy Cadillac and my feelings that the man behind the wheel meant to kill me.

"Emma, I should have been there with you."

"You're here now, Nathan." I pressed against his back, unbelievably comforted by his presence. "That's all that matters. You're here now. Sergeant Vesley will probably skin me tomorrow when I go back to Jackson, but I wanted to see you."

Nathan was silent for a long moment. "I can't stay with you tonight, Emma, but I'll be by to check on you."

"I'm perfectly safe at Ravenwood," I replied, swallowing my disappointment. As we rode through the night, I realized that Nathan had duties, responsibilities that even now he was ignoring. Just being with him for a brief time had made me feel so much better.

"Of all the places I could be, Ravenwood feels safest," I assured him. "I'd love to have your company for the night, but Ravenwood will do. Besides, I can always call my brother Shane to come and stay if I get silly. He'd do it." I gave him a hug. "But I'm not concerned about the rest of the night. Tomorrow, when I go back to Jackson, then I'll be worried."

Nathan didn't say anything for a while. "Remember when you told me about the books being scattered in James's study? Did James ever build his boat?" he finally asked. "I've always wanted to sail."

"I don't know." I tried to remember. "I know he hadn't when Frank was still alive, but since then, I really don't know. I haven't been in contact with the Devlin family like I should have."

"Marla would know, wouldn't she?"

"I would hope so."

"Then call her tomorrow and ask."

"Why?" I couldn't see where Nathan was heading. So what if James owned a boat. It wouldn't do him much good now.

"It has occurred to me that maybe we've found where Nella Colson is hiding. If she was in James's study looking for something, then maybe she found out about the boat. It would be the perfect place to hide, especially if no one really knew about it."

"Absolutely." I hugged him even closer. "How can you be so handsome and smart to boot?"

"It's the breeding, ma'am," he replied. "Southern gentlemen are always..."

"Don't even start that," I said, laughing and hugging him harder.

"Check out the facts about the boat in the morning, and then I'll be there at lunch," he said. "But you have to promise to wait for me before you go running out to any boat yards."

"Okay," I agreed. Who was I to argue, especially when I felt so much safer when he was with me.

Frisco broke though a curtain of willow limbs and we found ourselves on a kudzu-covered ridge. The vines had grown up the side of the hill, climbing trees and creating gigantic monster shapes in the night. I shifted closer to Nathan, glad for his warmth in the cool night air. My hands played across the planes of his chest and muscled stomach, dipping lower.

"Why don't we give Frisco's back a rest," Nathan suggested as he gripped my legs and pulled me closer against him.

"Sounds like the humane thing to do," I answered, sliding off on the left side of the horse. My hands trailed suggestively over Nathan's body.

The kudzu made a natural shelter from any prying eyes. In the chill night, I could feel my heart beating. Anticipation made my blood sing. Nathan slid off the horse and stood beside me. He let the reins fall on the ground, knowing that Frisco would remain grazing near us.

There was no need for talk. We embraced and kissed eagerly. Using the kudzu as a shelter and a blanket, we made love beneath a vine-covered tree.

Nathan pillowed my head on his arm. He'd thrown his shirt over me to ward off the cool night air, and I was content, snuggled against him.

"In the next few days, they'll start the cannons and the weapons. Vicksburg will never be the same again," he said.

"Will you come back here next year for the reenactment again?" I hated to ask any questions about the future. If Nathan wanted me to know his plans, he would tell me. If I had to pry information from him, then it was no good. Still, I had to know something.

"It's hard to tell, Emma. If I knew myself, I'd tell you." He kissed the top of my head. "Especially you."

At the sound of someone moving through the woods near us, Frisco lifted his head. Nathan retrieved our clothes without any wasted motion. He pulled on cavalry pants and boots while I struggled into my jeans and sweater.

The sound of someone coming through the vines grew louder. I hadn't noticed that Nathan carried a gun on the right side of his saddle, but he pulled it out. In the moonlight it looked antique.

"Will it fire?" I asked in a whisper.

"Very accurately," he replied, holding up his hand for silence as he listened to place the direction of our intruder.

"Identify yourself," he called into the night.

There was a nervous shifting. "Excuse me, sir. It's Private Wes Gabbins. I was, uh, looking for some privacy."

A young boy stepped out of the woods. He was dressed in the uniform of a Confederate private. He saluted Nathan smartly, perfectly ignoring me as I sat on the ground and tied my shoelaces.

"You've wandered pretty far from your posting, Private" Nathan said darkly.

"Those guys," the private started to explain. "Every time I try to get a little privacy, they play some kind of trick on me." He threw me a sheepish look. "Excuse me, ma'am. The men are havin' a good time is all."

Nathan's posture relaxed. "Well, this secluded position is already... covered." He grinned and his teeth flashed in the night.

"Excuse me again." The private saluted Nathan, then tipped his hat at me, backing into the vines as he did so. "I'll just find some other private place that isn't already taken."

There was the rustling sound of the young private making his way through the thick underbrush, and then it was silent again.

"I'd better get back to my patrol," Nathan said softly.

"And I should get back to Ravenwood." I hated the idea of leaving him.

He mounted Frisco and then assisted me up behind him. It seemed only fifteen minutes before Frisco was clip-clopping across the paved parking lot. The urge to cling to Nathan was so strong that I deliberately cut our goodbyes short. I didn't want him to see how much I wanted him, needed him. He had already made it clear that he viewed our time together as temporary. It was up to me to keep my end of the relationship in balance. I would destroy what we had if I let on how much I loved him.

He was standing with Frisco beside him as I drove out of the parking lot and turned toward Ravenwood. It was only about eleven, but Vicksburg had shuttered itself and drifted into sleep. I drove around the town, trying to calm my emotions. I knew I wouldn't be able to sleep, and I didn't want to go back to Ravenwood in an agitated state.

When I first noticed the car behind me, I was driving parallel to the river. I'd been so absorbed in my thoughts, I hadn't noticed when the car had fallen in behind me. But it had kept a careful distance for the past ten or fifteen minutes. I couldn't tell if it was following me, or if it was simply going the same way I was.

To test the theory, I took a right. The car followed. I turned back left. My eyes watched the rearview mirror. The car followed suit. I couldn't help but think of the man who'd been sitting in the burgundy Cadillac waiting for me at my house. There had been the glint of jewelry in his ear. It could have been Diamond, the man who'd killed my husband.

Sweat made my hands slick on the steering wheel, and I gripped it tighter. One thing about Marla's car, it could maneuver.

The road I'd turned onto was dark and unfamiliar. I had the sense that I was once again paralleling the river, but I couldn't be certain. In my efforts to lose the tail, I'd also gotten myself lost.

I decided to take the next left turn and attempt to get back to Riverroad. At least then I could circle back toward town. It seemed I was driving farther and farther away from Vicksburg—and away from people. That made my heart pound even harder.

I came upon the turn so sharply that I almost missed it. The little sportscar swung hard and held the road, and I was shooting back toward Riverroad, or so I hoped. When I chanced a look in the rearview mirror, the road behind me was empty.

Completely empty.

I let a shaky laugh escape, more nerves than humor, and tried to ease my grip on the steering wheel. It felt as if my fingers were embedded in it.

So, no one had been following me. I'd imagined the entire thing because I saw headlights behind me. As if no one had the right to drive on the same road I did. I thought of Nathan, and the amusement he would show at my display of raw courage. At least we'd laugh about it at lunch tomorrow.

I came upon the intersection to Riverroad and turned back toward Vicksburg and Ravenwood. I was no less agitated than when I'd started my drive, but I'd come to the conclusion that I could unwind with a glass of wine and a hot bath in the safety of my Ravenwood apartment.

The flare of lights in my rearview mirror alerted me that another car had turned behind me. I smiled to myself. I'd already played that little mind game once. This time, I'd ignore the car. This time, I wouldn't behave like a simple-minded ninny.

Chapter Fifteen

The lights in the apartment signaled to me like a beacon.
Ravenwood would never be my home, but it was part of my
heart now. It was where I'd met Nathan.

I drew a bath and soaked for half an hour, reveling in the
hot water and a chilled glass of wine. My thoughts were
filled with Nathan. How could I be so lucky to have known
two such wonderful men as Frank Devlin and now Nathan? I had learned such a valuable lesson at Ravenwood—
to live for the present, not the past or future. Whatever
happened, Nathan had given me a tremendous gift.

After my bath I found I was incredibly tired. I'd thought
I'd never be able to get to sleep after the day I'd had, but I
drifted off instantly.

The coral netting cocooned me as I let consciousness slip
away. I slid almost immediately into dreams. I was walking
down a shady path. I sat down on a tree root to wait for
someone to meet me. I was looking up an avenue of trees
and shrubs when I felt a hand on my foot, jerking at me.
There was the sound of breaking glass and I suddenly became afraid and started to struggle to stand.

The draped bed swirled into view as I fought off the
shroud of sleep and opened my eyes. My heart almost
stopped beating. Frank stood at the foot of the bed. His
hand was on my foot.

"Beware, Emma," he whispered. "Beware."

He stepped back from the bed, disappearing into the coral drapes, disappearing completely.

The room was empty except for me.

I could hear the rush of breath in and out of my lungs, the rustle of the bed curtains in a gentle breeze. Outside the open window, leaves whispered.

"Frank? Please come back." I sat up in bed and pushed the netting aside. "Frank?"

There were so many things to say, so much I wanted to share with him.

"Frank?"

He had gone.

I sat on the edge of the bed, unable to sleep.

Frank's warning still sent legions of chill bumps marching along my skin. "Beware," I whispered out loud to no one. "Beware."

Of what? Did Frank know that I was in some danger? His message could mean almost anything. He hadn't visited me since I'd started the hunt for his killer. Was this visit something to do with my hunt, or was it something else? I remembered his hand on my foot, and there had been something else that had awakened me. A noise.

I pulled my feet back up in the bed and snuggled under the covers. The smartest thing would be to try to get back to sleep.

I'd closed my eyes and was searching for sleep when I heard it again. Glass shattering.

It wasn't coming from the kitchen below me, so that meant it had to be from the main house. Someone was trying to get into the old house. I listened quietly for several minutes. A male voice called something indistinguishable into the night, then there was a laugh and the sound of something smashing.

He was inside Ravenwood. He was breaking the priceless antiques and heirlooms that had once belonged to Mary and the Quinn family. I had thought that it was Frank who'd awakened me, but it was the sound of the breaking glass. I remembered it from the dream.

I got out of bed without bothering to look for shoes or clothes. I was driven by a cold fury. The idea that someone had broken into the old house simply to destroy inflamed me. The telephone was in the kitchen, and I sneaked downstairs to use it to call the police. The vandal had to be stopped before irreplaceable heirlooms were destroyed.

It was an older rotary phone, and I dialed 9-1-1, listening to the clicks of the rotars. Then nothing. I hit the switch hook several times. Nothing. The telephone was dead. My good sense told me it wasn't just a coincidence. Whoever was in the main house wreaking havoc also knew that someone was in the guest apartment. He knew and he thought he'd silenced me.

The possibility that the intruder knew me—had come specifically because of me—was like a rock hitting a windshield. I felt the first impact, and then the little tracers of fear spread wider and wider until I thought I would shatter.

Grabbing a handful of candles and a flashlight, I went back upstairs. In total darkness, I dressed. I had to be prepared to survive. Looking out the bedroom window I saw that Marla's car had two flat tires. I knew, then, that whoever was in the house was no juvenile burglar or petty hoodlum. I'd already been shot at and chased down. If he'd come to Ravenwood breaking and destroying without any attempt to hide himself, he expected to have his way.

As if he read my mind, the intruder's voice echoed in the night. "Hey there, pretty lady. Ready for some fun?"

The voice taunted me. I had never felt such fear of another human being. This man was cruel, a bully with a weaker child at his mercy. He intended to torture me.

"Come out and play with us, pretty mama."

The voice seemed to come from the gentleman's parlor in the main house. From the vantage point, the intruder had a

clear view of my apartment door. I had no choice but to go
through the main house on the second floor and attempt an
escape from there. The second story breezeway that connected the buildings was mostly windows. On hands and
knees, I started the long crawl.

I had to make it to the estate grounds, or at least inside
Ravenwood. There were a million places to hide there. And
I'd toured the premises during daylight. The main house had
no electricity, but I'd be at no worse an advantage than my
tormentor.

"Emma! Come here!"

The voice sent dread through me. He was so supremely
confident that I was securely in his clutches, he thought I'd
obey him without a fight. He'd cut off the phone and crippled my car. I was merely something he was going to take his
time and enjoy toying with. The thing that terrified me most
was his use of my name.

"What's the matter, Emma? Maybe I should tell you that
we have mutual acquaintances. See, I knew your husband."

The full realization of who I was dealing with struck
home.

"Your husband groveled like a dog, Emma. He wal-
lowed on the dirty floor and begged me not to kill him."

Impotent rage caused tears to fill my eyes. What he said
wasn't true. I knew the truth. But I wanted to make him shut
up. I wanted to make him pay for what he'd done to Frank.
He was only trying to goad me into the open. So he
could...what? I swallowed hard. It would be foolish if I
didn't assume that he was going to try to kill me.

Hired assassin.

Someone who killed for pleasure and profit.

The man who'd killed my husband with no more thought
than as if he'd stepped on a bug.

How could someone like me stand a chance against him?

Because I wanted to live! The surge of energy that came with that realization gave me a sense of power and strength that I'd never felt before. No one had a right to cheat me of my life the way Frank had been cheated. Or James. Or even Carlton Frazier. Frank had been executed on the floor of a liquor store. And James and Carlton Frazier had been caught by surprise. But me, I was warned. I felt certain the man inside Ravenwood intended to kill me if he could. And he was so sure of himself and his abilities that he didn't even consider it worth his while to be wary of me.

I forced myself to keep moving. Terrified that I'd make a noise and give myself away, I opened the door to the sunroom and slipped inside. I was in Ravenwood, at least. Now, to find a weapon.

There was a bronze statue on an upstairs table that would leave a gruesome dent in someone's head. Guns? There had been several antiques locked in cabinets, but I didn't think they'd have any shells, and I wouldn't be able to load one. Why hadn't I listened to Robert at the liquor store when he'd tried to talk me and Frank into learning to use a weapon?

Why? Because no one in his right mind would ever expect to find a greeting card verse writer from Jackson, Mississippi, cowering outside an antebellum plantation house afraid for her life.

I suddenly remembered something that Nathan had told me—that in hunting for Frank's murderer I'd taken a stand and refused to be a silent victim. If that were true, then I'd drawn the man inside Ravenwood to me. I should have been better prepared to deal with him. But I wasn't willing to pay with my life because I wasn't prepared.

"Don't make me mad, pretty lady. Come on out. There's no way for you to escape."

I stood perfectly still, trying to force myself to think.

"Okay, I'll try not to lose my temper. We'll make a game of it. We can play until dawn. I just thought I'd tell you that I left my cousin down at that front gate. He's a bad one, he is. He has a real fondness for the ladies. Only sometimes he hurts 'em. Know what I mean?'' His voice, tired from the harangue, broke.

Chills swept over my body. This man was sick. Really sick. I didn't know whether to believe he had an associate or not. It didn't matter, because I'd never attempt to get to the front gate. If anything, I'd cut through the woods and down to the river. I'd rather risk the Mississippi than a meeting with one of these guys any day.

I thought again of the guns in the downstairs cabinet. Maybe I could load one. Without a doubt I could use it if I could figure out how. I made a silent vow. If I lived through this night, I was going to sign up for lessons in gun use immediately.

The sound of breaking glass made me cringe.

''Uh-oh, pretty lady. That was an expensive one I'll bet. One of those little statues. I think they're collected by people with expensive taste.'' He laughed. ''Look here, I found another one.'' There was another crash.

There was now a raw edge of fury in the man's voice. Fury and a need to make someone pay. I had to act fast.

The second floor was centered by a stairwell that swept down in a graceful curve. I eased into the hallway that circled the stairs and provided access to all of the upper floor rooms. This was the most dangerous part. If the intruder came up the stairs, he'd find me. I moved as quickly as possible until I made my way around to Mary Quinn's old bedroom.

''I'm getting tired of this silly game. Come on out like a good girl. If I have to hunt you, I'm going to be very angry. You won't like me when I'm angry.''

I looked around Mary Quinn's room, hoping for some inspiration. There was the lightest flutter of a breeze near the windows and the mosquito netting on the bed blew against my arm. I couldn't believe the window had been left open.

In fact, when I'd checked the house once before, I'd made sure all of the windows were locked. Maybe this was the entrance the intruder had used. That thought made my skin crawl.

I slipped behind the draperies to find the open window. But when I checked, they were all locked. The view outside the window was startingly bright. I hadn't realized how much moonlight there was. I'd have to make my break fast and trust my luck in the gardens where the plants would give me some shelter.

I felt something brush my arm again, and turned to see the mosquito netting settling back into place. There had been no draft. The window was shut tight. I reached out for the flimsy material and my hand settled on the cord that pulled it up and down. It was the perfect tool. If I could only tie it to the staircase, then I could lure the intruder up the stairs, jerk the cord and trip him. While he was stunned by his fall, I could knock him out and tie him up! It was a brilliant plan. I'd have surprise and the stairs on my side.

It took all of my patience to disengage the cord, but I managed. The room was flooded with moonlight—plenty to work the cord free.

Before I could think of a reason not to do it, I slipped out of the bedroom and to the stairs. They were beautifully curved, magnificent. And there was only one location where my plan might work—the very head of the stairs. I'd have to tie the cord to a massive table just to the left of the staircase and then run the cord through the spindles to the right. If I held the end, then I could jerk up on it and trip the intruder when he got to the top of the stair. He'd land face-first on the top steps, but I didn't think the fall would disable him for very long at all. I'd have to be ready to hit him.

I secured the cord and tried it several times. When I yanked really hard, the cord pulled taut across the staircase about eight inches above the step. It would be perfect—if the intruder fell for the bait and came after me. I selected the statue of a robed female from the hall table. She was heavy enough.

"Listen, woman, I've had enough. Get in here! Now! I'm getting tired of breaking this expensive junk."

Another crash followed.

I gripped the cord in my left hand and took three steps back from the staircase. I cut loose with all the power I had. "Okay, you big moron. I'm here. Right upstairs. If you can find me."

"What the hell?" the man said.

He was smart enough to show a little concern. I hadn't behaved in the expected fashion. I hadn't come crying and groveling for my life. I'd come after him. I clenched my hand around the cord and let the feeling of satisfaction grow. I needed all of the confidence I could muster.

There was the sound of rapid footsteps, heavy footsteps. He was a big man. He came toward the stairs. The curve of the stairway hid him from my sight, but I could hear him coming.

I wanted to cut and run, to throw my hands over my head and cower in some dark corner, hoping he wouldn't find me. But I couldn't do that. I tightened every muscle in my body and stood my ground. This had to end now. If I didn't stop him, he'd kill me.

The top of his head came around the curve, then his dark eyes, his face and broad shoulders. He paused long enough to grin at me. In the dim light that filtered from the upper floor, I could barely make out the white of his teeth.

"I've been waiting a long time, Emma Devlin," he said as he continued up the stairs. "I always knew it would come to this." He laughed as he took two more steps. "I knew, eventually, you'd begin to think that your husband's death was a little too pat, a little too convenient. I told 'em you'd have to go, too. I told 'em you'd figure it out.''

"Told who?" My voice shook. I couldn't help it. He was only seven steps below me. The heavy statue was against the wall to my left, within easy reach. "Who wants me dead so badly? And who killed Frank?"

The man laughed. "Is this like one of those movies where I'm supposed to confess everything just before I do you in?" He laughed again.

"I'm not going to be as easy to kill as you might think, Diamond." It was pure bravado. I felt as if he could crush me like a beetle.

"You Devlins are a fiesty bunch, you know." He took another two steps. "So, you know my name. You aren't stupid, either."

"Tell me who," I demanded.

"Why should I?"

He enjoyed playing with me. He was simply a cruel and evil man. I felt a total revulsion I'd never felt for another human being. My fingers gripped the cord so tightly that I thought my hand might be permanently paralyzed.

"Why shouldn't you?" I parried. "If you're going to kill me, what would it hurt to tell me who? Unless, of course, you aren't certain you can kill me."

His hand lifted, and I saw the gun. Perhaps I'd pressed him too hard. He could shoot me at this distance just as well as point-blank.

"Nice gun, huh?" he asked. "I've had it for a couple of years now. A real collector's item." He lifted it up and then aimed it directly at my head. "Shame to mess up that pretty face." He lowered the barrel to point at my heart.

I fought the urge to fall back, but I couldn't help myself. My feet moved backward two steps of their own accord. My body was screaming for me to run, to make an effort to live.

But I had to hold the cord. If I was ever going to survive, I had to make my stand here.

"Coward!" I lashed him with the word. "Slimy, murdering coward."

"I love it when you snarl," he said, laughing. "People usually react in one of two ways when they're faced with certain death. They either beg or they snarl. I much prefer the snarlers, don't you?"

He took three steps closer. Two to go!

"You won't tell me who's behind this because you're afraid I'll escape. That's what a coward you are. You have no confidence in your ability to kill me."

"Maybe I don't want to kill you. At least not yet."

He lunged then, unexpectedly. He'd taken one step before I knew what he was doing. I jerked the cord with all of my might—and nothing happened! It had jammed around the spindle.

"I'm going to enjoy killing you," he said, and there was no humor in his voice or eyes. "I like my targets to fight a bit. Otherwise this work gets so tedious. I'd give you a chance to run, but that might be stupid on my part."

He took the last step onto the landing. I reached for the statue, but my fingers, made clumsy by fear, couldn't get a grip. His hand lashed out, coming down on the bend of my arm. It felt as if the bones had broken.

"That's a naughty girl," he said.

I turned to run, and his hand caught my shirt. He dragged me back against him, ignoring my flailing arms and legs. His fingers laced around my throat, brutally shutting off my air supply.

"I didn't want to shoot you, anyway. It's too messy for such a lovely woman." He increased the pressure and I felt pain in my throat and head. My lungs burned and I couldn't control my arms or legs. He was choking me, and I lost all power to fight. There was a red blur behind my eyes and a roar in my ears. I fought to live, but I wasn't strong enough. I still held the cord, but I felt my grasp begin to loosen.

A blast of frigid air struck me, and the fingers on my throat suddenly weakened.

"No!" Diamond said, as if he were speaking to himself.

I was dropped like a sack of potatoes, and I fell onto my knees. A rush of wind blasted down the hallway, wind laced with the delicate perfume of flowers.

"No!" This time he screamed. He stumbled away from me, back toward the top of the stairs. Gasping in a crumpled heap on the floor, I looked up at him. He was staring behind me as if some fiend from hell had come after him.

I caught a strange movement in a mirror across the hall. It was as if a wave of fluid swept under the surface of the glass. Diamond's hand reached out, as if to ward off a blow. His mouth opened and his eyes widened. He took two backward steps.

I yanked the cord for all I was worth. It pulled taut, about eight inches above the step. Just enough to catch his calf as he stepped backward. His own momentum carried him all the way over in a complete somersault and he tumbled down the stairs. The gun discharged once and then crashed into the wall.

I couldn't move. The cord slipped from my fingers and dropped to the floor. I couldn't get enough air. It was as if there was no oxygen and I started heaving, pulling in great lungsful.

I looked at the mirror again, but it was empty.

I knew I had to go downstairs to see if Diamond was alive. After that fall, I doubted he'd survived. It must have broken every bone in his body, and I didn't want to confront the sight.

A chill brushed over my skin, and the air was filled with a sweet perfume. It was a violet scent, as light and airy as spring.

Turning quickly, I found only an empty hall. But several feet behind me there was a yellow rose on the carpet.

Chapter Sixteen

My fingers closed around the rose. A sharp thorn on the stem pricked my thumb, and a single drop of blood trickled down my hand. Mary Quinn had saved my life. It wasn't possible, but it had happened. No one would believe me if I tried to tell them. No one except the man at the foot of the stairs, and I felt certain he was dead. I forced myself up. My throat burned and ached, and my legs betrayed me with rubbery bones. I'd found the man who killed my husband, but I still didn't know who was behind it. I was only half finished with my quest.

I started down the steps, stopping only long enough to pick up the weapon that had been thrown from Diamond's hand. The handle was hand-carved, designed to fit a larger hand, a man's hand. I remembered what Robert Mason had said about the weapon used to kill Frank. This might be the one. Frank and James, and Carlton Frazier. A murderer's weapon of choice. It made me sick.

Diamond was at the bottom of the stairs in a crumpled heap. His right arm was twisted under him, and he was lying on his stomach, as if he were dead. I was almost certain he had to be. Kneeling beside him I checked his pulse. To my surprise, it was steady and strong.

I noticed his long hair pulled back in a ponytail. My hand brushed from his neck and touched something hard near his ear. The base of the stairs was in deep shadow. I went to the dining room and got a candle and a match and returned to the intruder. I knew I should have felt more concern for his physical condition, but I wanted to see what I'd felt. I had to see.

I struck the match and lit the wick. In the flickering light of the candle the diamond earring winked back at me. A man of many talents—and torments. In the light of the candle I recognized him as the same man who'd chased me in the burgundy Cadillac.

I prayed that he wouldn't die. If he would only live long enough to tell me who'd had Frank killed. That was all I asked—that he live long enough to tell me and the police a few details.

I stood and blew out the candle. I still clutched the pistol. Diamond would never get his hands on it again.

From outside the front door the sound of running footsteps came to me. I'd forgotten that Diamond had said he had an associate. He must have heard the gunshot and come to his cohort's aid.

There was a small alcove behind the staircase. I slipped into the space, clutching the gun and praying that I'd have what it took to use it if I had to.

"Diamond!" The man outside the house called. "You okay?"

He waited for an answer that would never come.

"Diamond! Get the woman and let's get out of here! We don't have time for games this time."

My trigger finger pulled at the little metal lever. These were the men who'd killed my husband. All I had to do was step out of my hiding place and shoot them. It would be justice to kill them. Real justice.

I took a deep breath and pressed deeper back into the alcove.

The front door opened, and there was the sound of a sharply indrawn breath. "Son of a—"

I couldn't stop the smile at the thought of what he'd found.

"Diamond?" There was the sound of a body being dragged away from the steps. "I'll go get the car. I'll, uh, be back."

I knew the gate was locked. There was no way to get a vehicle into the estate. It was clear to me that Diamond's accomplice would take off and leave him, which was exactly what I wanted. Diamond could probably be convinced to blow the whistle on all of his dirty little playmates, including the one who was getting ready to abandon him.

The second man's steps retreated in the foyer and the front door slammed after him. For a few seconds after that I could hear his feet crunching on the white shells outside the front steps. Then silence again.

I cautiously entered the gentleman's parlor, opened a window and checked to make sure there was no one around the apartment. The moonlight was undisturbed. Reluctantly I hid the gun in Marla's car. As much as I wanted to take it for protection, I knew that I couldn't conceal it very well, and I'd never be able to flag down a car. No one would ever stop to help me if I carried a weapon.

The estate was surrounded by a wrought-iron fence about six feet tall. Since I didn't want to risk running into Diamond's buddy at the gate, I cut across the front yard. I'd have more cover if I stayed clear of the driveway, too. With the help of a small oak, I made it over the fence. I urged my tired body into a steady jog.

Ravenwood is set off from Vicksburg, but it isn't what would be considered isolated. There was a paved road running up to the property, and I ran along this, listening carefully for the sound of a car in the still night. The darkness, the road, the emptiness seemed to stretch into eternity.

I was feeling the strain of the jog, and I knew that soon I'd have to slow even more. An unexpected thought gave me another jolt of energy. What if Diamond knew something about Nella's disappearance? What if they were holding her hostage? My jog became a run. I couldn't allow myself to tire. Nella's life might depend on it.

At first I thought I was imagining it, so I slowed just enough to listen. I heard the distinct sound of someone—or something—running after me.

I thought I had nothing else to give, but my body surprised me. I spurted forward, sweat running down my face and chest. I'd gone what seemed like a million miles. Up ahead was a store with a telephone. It wasn't far. I could make it.

The pounding behind me grew louder. Heavier.

Tufts of torpedo grass snagged my feet, and the terrain was rutted and dangerous. I darted off the road toward the dark line of trees that offered shelter.

"Emma! Wait!"

I stopped, unable to believe my ears.

"Emma!"

Nathan's voice was choppy. He was riding Frisco hard toward me. I couldn't believe it. I wanted to laugh, except the sound came out like a cry. "Nathan!"

He brought the gelding to an abrupt halt at my side. His face was as sweat-covered as my own. The gray wool uniform of the Confederacy must have been stifling.

"I went to Ravenwood on a break. I saw the man at the bottom of the stairs. And then I couldn't find you."

"We have to get help." I was panting, but my hope was renewed. "That's the man who killed Frank and James. We have to get him to a hospital before he dies. We have..." I had to stop.

"It's only a little farther to a phone," Nathan reassured me as he reached down to pull me up behind him on the horse. With pressure from his legs, he sent Frisco into a ground-covering gallop.

It didn't take us even five minutes to get to the store and to place the call to the police and an emergency crew. As I hung up the phone I felt a rush of relief.

There were so many things to tell Nathan. There was the rose and Mary Quinn. He'd believe me. If no one else ever did, Nathan would know that I hadn't imagined the whole thing.

"Nathan..."

He didn't give me a chance to talk. He pulled me against him and held me tight. His heart was pounding, and I knew it was as much from fear for me as exertion.

"Listen, Emma. I have to get back." Nathan's brow was furrowed with worry. "I hate like hell that I can't stay, but I just took a few minutes to stop by and check on you. I left a lot of things hanging."

Nathan cast a glance up and down the road as if he expected to see something terrible.

"I'll be back. As soon as possible. Will you be okay?"

I'd never seen Nathan so near panic. Whatever he'd left must have been very important, he was obviously torn. I wanted him beside me. I needed his strength to get through the ordeal of Diamond and the police. But I loved him more than I needed him.

"The worst is over, Nathan. I'm a bit shaken, but I'm not hurt."

His fingers traced my neck and I couldn't control the flinch.

"He hurt you, the bastard." Nathan growled the words.

"He tried, but I had a little assistance from Mary Quinn." In the light of the phone booth I managed a smile. "I'm fine, Nathan. Go on."

"I can't leave you alone." His face was anguished. "No matter what the cost, I can't leave you."

"But I'm not alone," I whispered, touching his cheek. I didn't understand the turmoil that had beset him, but I couldn't stand to see it. "I have Mary, and Frank stopped by for a visit, too." I made my voice lighthearted. "The worst is over. In a few minutes the police will be here, and they'll go back to Ravenwood with me. Take care of your business," I urged him. "I'll be fine. I promise."

"It kills me to leave you, Emma," he said, and his hands moved over my shoulders and back, pulling me into his embrace. "I want to stay with you and make sure that no one ever threatens you again."

I braced my hands on his chest and gently pushed back. "That man never will again. You can count on that. I think we're on the way to solving this entire riddle. Soon we should know who was behind Frank's murder. All of this will be resolved, and we can begin to lead normal lives."

"Oh, Emma," he whispered as he kissed me lightly on the lips. "You're a very strong woman. You'll never know how much I love you."

"I only know how much I love you."

"True love is a powerful weapon," he said, kissing my forehead. "I'll be back as soon as I can."

He mounted Frisco, wheeled and was gone, swallowed by the night with only the echo of Frisco's hooves left behind. I was left with the sound of the sirens drawing closer.

SITTING ACROSS from Sergeant Vesley, I had the distinct impression that I was in deep, deep hot water. The Vicksburg police had called the Jackson Police Department as soon as they heard my name. Vesley had been more than angry when he found that I'd shaken my police tail and slipped away from Jackson. He'd been so angry that he'd put out an APB for me. Once alerted to my whereabouts in Vicksburg, and the circumstances of my current situation, he'd taken it upon himself to get up in the middle of the night and pay a visit. He was beyond irate. It was more in the way he wouldn't look at me than in anything he said.

Dawn was just breaking through the windows of the apartment at Ravenwood. I'd made coffee and had two cups. Sergeant Vesley was on his third. Every few minutes his glance went back to the gun sitting in the center of the kitchen table.

It was the only evidence—along with the shattered figurines—that anyone had been in Ravenwood other than myself. By the time I returned with the Vicksburg police, the man I thought was Diamond was gone. So was his companion. They'd vanished without a trace.

"How do you know it was the same man who murdered your husband?" Vesley asked for the tenth time.

"He said so. He said that he always knew I'd have to be killed, too." I'd decided that nothing Vesley said was going to rattle me, but I was getting awfully tired of his questions. And his doubts.

Vesley picked up the weapon.

"If there were any fingerprints on it, you've managed to rub them out." I knew I was snapping, but I was exhausted.

"The Vicksburg crime lab's taken all the prints we'll ever need and turned the weapon over to Jackson." He looked at me. "Did you know this was the same type of gun used to kill your husband, your brother-in-law and Carlton Frazier?"

I didn't know, but it didn't surprise me. "I just told you that man killed my husband. You've told me the same weapon was used in all three murders. Therefore it's logical." I felt as though I was arguing with a three-year-old.

"It's a very handsome gun," he said, as if talking to himself. "Very handsome, indeed. Why don't I give you a ride back to Jackson, Ms. Devlin?" He turned his attention back to me. "Seems to me if you'd'a stayed in Jackson, you wouldn't have gotten into all this trouble."

"It seems to me the police should be more interested in finding a critically wounded man who is a multiple murderer than worried about where I spend my mornings."

Vesley smiled. "At this point, I'm not so worried about where you are as what's going to happen to you. If what you say is true, you've been the target of a near assassination. That man—Diamond or whatever you want to call him—may try to kill you again."

"I don't think he's in any condition."

"And I don't think you're any judge of that." Vesley stood. "Gather your things. I'll drive you back to Jackson."

"I'm not going anywhere without Marla's car, and as you plainly see, the car's in no condition to be driven."

"One of my men will have the tires repaired and bring it home to you. And you'll get the bill," he added. He folded his arms. "Better pack your things. I need to be at ballistics when we get the first report. If everything matches, you may have found a big piece of the puzzle."

"Will you be able to find Diamond?" I couldn't believe that a man so severely injured had managed to escape. But he had.

"Eventually. But until we do, I'm going to put you in protective custody."

Before I could argue, Vesley signaled one of the patrolmen who was outside the apartment. "Help Ms. Devlin gather her things. Then we'll be on our way. It's going to be a very long day."

It was almost eleven o'clock before Sergeant Vesley consented to let me out of his clutches. I was dropped at home, and Marla's car was returned, as promised, with both tires repaired and a bill attached. I didn't even try to shake my police tail as I made my way to the Magnolia Café to meet Nathan. I'd been forced to leave him a note, since Sergeant Vesley wouldn't hear of leaving me behind in Vicksburg. I felt like the prize egg in a hunt.

As I sat in the Magnolia, I could see two police cars, unmarked of course, watching. Vesley did think someone would attempt to kill me. I'd given it some thought. If Diamond was alive, then he knew I could positively identify him. He was no longer an anonymous killer with no trail. Now the police had fingerprints—and bait.

Me.

Nathan arrived just at noon, and even though we felt as if every bite we took was being scrutinized, we ate a healthy lunch. I filled him in on everything that had happened. When I got to the part about the rose and how Mary Quinn had appeared to save my life, Nathan smiled.

"You don't believe me," I said. In the light of day it did seem a bit improbable. My husband appearing was one thing, but a perfect stranger? It was a bit hard to swallow.

"It's not that I don't believe," he said. "It's just that you've wanted to see Mary for so long about your husband. What a time for her to pick to show up."

"Believe me, I won't quarrel with the timing of her visit. She saved my life."

"She was like that." He chuckled. "Or at least that's what I've read about her. It was due to the legend of Mary Quinn that I ended up in Vicksburg, and Mississippi College," he said.

"You knew about Mary *before* you came to Vicksburg? I didn't realize her legend was more than regional."

"Oh, I'd say that it even crossed the Mason-Dixon line. Charles Weatherton wasn't the only handsome young swain to vie for Miss Quinn's hand. She was something of a celebrity before her engagement."

"She was a child!" I was fascinated, and relieved that we'd found something to talk about about other than the horrors of my immediate life. The distinct scent of the perfume I'd smelled came back to me.

"By today's standards, she was a child. By those of the 1860s, she was a marriageable young heiress. Remember, she was Canna Quinn's only child, and he was a very wealthy man."

"You make it sound as if she were virtually auctioned."
I wanted to know everything I could about the young
woman, dead for so long, who had saved me from death.

"Oh, believe me, Mary had a mind of her own. She went
to formal affairs from one end of the South to the other.
And she even traveled into Washington, Philadelphia and
Boston in search of the perfect ball gown and an acceptable
husband. But it was homegrown Charles who took her
fancy, and then there was no doubt about whom she would
marry."

"So Mary Quinn was well known outside the South?"

"There was a rumor that a very prominent Republican
courted her."

"Oh, scandal!" I said, laughing.

Nathan's hands covered mine. "The sound of your
laughter makes me happy. I haven't heard enough of it
lately."

"You're more than likely going to hear the sound of my
snores. I didn't get a lot of sleep, and I know you didn't, either."

"We could go home for a nap."

The suggestive twinkle in his eyes made me blush. I turned
my hands palm up inside his and laced my fingers through
his bigger ones. "There's nothing I'd like better than to go
home with you right now, lock the door, and not come out
for days."

"Then that's what we should do."

I shook my head. "I have to go by Micro-Tech first. It
won't be long before Benny hears about what happened.
He'll know that I'm looking into Frank's death. I'd rather
tell him myself, someplace where we can have some privacy. I don't want him to do anything rash."

"Like what?"

"I don't know. He might go out looking for Diamond
himself. Benny might get...irrational. He worshiped
Frank." I found the understanding I sought in Nathan's

eyes. "I know it's hard to believe that two men could have such a close relationship. They were like brothers. Really, they were even closer than Frank and James."

"I do understand," Nathan answered. "As a student of history, I've seen many cases where a bond that was stronger than anything else grew between two people. Most of the time, it's between a man and a woman, but I've seen it happen between friends."

"I'm afraid for Benny. What happened to James... Maybe that was my fault for starting all of this."

Nathan's hands tightened on mine. "We've been through this, Emma. And you remember what Diamond said. It was a matter of time before he came after you. These past two years, they've watched you and your family and friends. You were never safe. And neither was your family nor the people you love."

As brutal as his words were, I needed to hear them. My resolve to end this tragedy strengthened. "Let me go and talk with Benny. I'll meet you at the house, okay?"

"I'll be waiting," he promised.

I left him on the sidewalk. He said he'd get a cab to the house. He wanted to stop by and talk with Sergeant Vesley on his way, to make sure that the protection around me was adequate, and to see if any new clues had turned up.

The fingerprint check on Diamond had come up negative. He didn't have a record, according to the information Vesley could find. Nathan said that it only went to prove that he'd never been caught. Not yet.

I drove straight to Micro-Tech and found that I was a little surprised to see Beth sitting behind the receptionist's desk. She looked unhappy, and I smiled encouragement at her. She was a sweet kid.

"Where's Benny?" I asked.

"He had an appointment with Marion Curry," she said. "He's going to be in that calendar of hers. The one about single men. He was dressed in a really expensive suit. He even bought a Rolex. And had his hair styled. And put in his contact lenses." There was a note of worry in her voice.

"That'll be good for Benny. He needs to develop some self-confidence where women are concerned. Sometimes he can't see a good thing when it's right in front of his eyes."

"Benny needs self-confidence?" she asked, amazed. "He always seems so..."

"Shy?" I supplied with a laugh. "Frank and I worked for years to find him the perfect girl. We finally had to give up."

"He'll be back any time now," Beth said, looking down at her hands.

I realized then that I'd probably stepped all over her feelings. A pang of sympathy went through me. "Maybe Marion can teach Benny the value of what a wonderful receptionist he has," I said. My reward was a beaming smile.

"You can wait in his office, or in Mr. Devlin's office," she said.

"I'll do that. But I can't wait long. If he doesn't return soon, I'll leave him a message."

"If I can get you anything, let me know," she called after me.

Frank's office was exactly the same. I had the strange idea that I could enter there in twenty years, and it would all still be exactly the way it was now.

I sat behind his desk and opened the drawers, again. Nothing had changed. I thought about calling Marla, but I didn't. Not from the office. Benny might walk in and make a delicate situation even worse.

I picked up a book from the stack on Frank's desk. *Lady Adventure* was the title. It was the story of a man who'd built his own ship and sailed to the Cayman Islands. I flipped the cover, wondering when Frank had decided to read a book on sailing, and why. Then I saw the inscription. "To my brother, James. May his dreams of adventure come true."

This book belonged on the shelf in James's study, along with his other sailing books. It was no wonder I didn't remember it. Frank must have bought it for a present for James and never been able to deliver it.

I flipped through the pages and a piece of paper dropped into my lap. Out of curiosity, I picked it up. On it were the words "*Lady Adventure,* Berth 21."

My hand was shaking when I reached for the telephone directory. There was only one body of water big enough for a sailboat, even a small boat like the one on the book jacket. I looked up the yacht clubs and docks on the Ross Barnett Reservoir and I started calling. It was at the third one that I found the boat. The *Lady Adventure* was docked there, and she belonged to James Devlin.

Chapter Seventeen

Growing up in a town has certain advantages. I knew the area extremely well, I knew people, and I knew I had to lose the police who were guarding me. The *Lady Adventure* was bound to hold some of the answers I'd been hunting, and I wanted to find them. The only problem was that I wasn't certain if the police had tapped my phone line. It was possible. That would make it impossible for me to get Nathan, or even tell him where I was going.

I had no idea what I'd find at the *Lady Adventure,* but I wanted to look at it myself before anyone else did.

Frank would never be involved in anything illegal. Not deliberately. Or knowingly would be a better word. That was a given. Somehow, through James or Marla, he might have become involved in a bad situation, though. Something that hadn't looked illegal on the surface. If Micro-Tech was involved, I wanted a chance to find out how, before it all came crashing down on Benny's head.

If Micro-Tech—through Frank and James—was involved in anything, I knew where it had all started. Marla. She had always been one of those people who lost sight of right and wrong when it came to something she wanted. I had her nailed dead to rights on the athletic contracts. That would eventually have to be taken to the police. What else had she gotten involved in?

And how had James been able to afford a boat? I didn't think I could answer that until I saw what she looked like. The Southside Yacht Club was the most prestigious, so the *Lady Adventure* couldn't be too shabby. Maybe she was a rental. My mind cast about for explanations that wouldn't put James in the category of a crook. It was difficult to believe that about a man I'd always liked and admired, but I knew when it had come to his wife, James could be terribly blinded.

My fingers itched to dial Nathan, but instead I made a phone call to an old high school friend. Again I was thankful I'd grown up in Jackson. Ann Lincoln, a clerk for Coastal Airlines, was the one person I knew who would do anything I asked. A sweet, married, mother of three, she had always been the kind of girl who trusted too easily and would do anything to protect her family or friends. She readily agreed to my plan to trade cars for the day, and I drove to the airport where she worked. I parked Marla's car and walked in as if I were expecting to meet someone just flying into town. Ann met me in the ladies room. With a minimum of questions, we exchanged keys, and she created a minor disturbance outside the rest room while I slipped out to get her car.

The drive to the Southside Yacht Club was an indistinct blur since so much of my attention was spent making sure the police weren't tailing me.

It took me a few minutes to find the *Lady Adventure*, because I wasn't expecting a boat of her size. She must have been thirty feet. Definitely not something James could have afforded, unless she was something he'd taken on lease for a year or so.

Several of the berths around her were empty, so I assumed that the owners had taken advantage of such a beautiful day and gone out on the water. The *Lady Adventure* was a magnificent sight with her tall center mast and her

freshly painted trim of red and black. She was everything
James had ever dreamed of, and more.

Marla had to have known about her, but she'd never said
a word, I thought grimly as I boarded. As soon as I finished with my examination, I intended to call the police.
There was no way I could protect Marla, the Devlins, or
Micro-Tech from this. Besides, it was time for everything to
come out. No matter what the cost.

The companionway to the cabin was narrow and steep. It
had been a mistake coming here alone. Now that I was here,
though, I wanted one quick look around. Wouldn't it be
something if I found Steve Gray's files and contracts hidden on the *Lady Adventure?* If James was going to go down
as some kind of crook, I wanted everyone else to sink, as
well.

Even with the boat docked and land only a few feet away,
claustrophobia closed in around me as soon as I started
walking down the passageway. Up on top, I didn't mind the
idea of being confined on a boat so much. Below deck, it
was a torment.

I decided to go to the end of the passageway and work my
way back. That way I'd be moving constantly toward light
and air and sun—and land. There was a forward hatch at
the end, which was locked. Hiding places were scarce. I
headed toward the sleeping quarters.

I was entering the bedroom when I heard the hatch above
me slam shut. I'd latched it firmly in the open position. It
couldn't have swung shut on its own.

The exact stupidity involved in coming to this boat alone
dawned on me. Especially after the night I'd spent at Ravenwood. My muscles went into spasm and I froze. I had
absolutely no control over my body.

"Emma?"

I didn't recognize the voice, or at least, I couldn't place it.
Even though I knew it was impossible, I'd expected to hear
Diamond's taunting tones.

"You shook the cops, Ms. Devlin, but you couldn't shake me. I've got something for you. Something Diamond wants you to have."

I realized then that I knew the man. I knew him from Ravenwood. The man descending the stairs was Diamond's associate.

I slipped into the bedroom and closed the door. What was I going to do? The room was too tiny even to try to hide. A dark blouse thrown in the corner of the otherwise immaculate room caught my eye. I picked it up, discovering that it was crusted in dried blood. A hole had been torn in the shoulder. I recognized the blouse. It was Nella's. So, she'd been on the *Lady Adventure*. Had it been voluntarily or against her will?

"Don't hide from me, Ms. Devlin. I'm going to take you to see an old buddy. You've been looking for her, and I'll bet she'll be glad to see you."

I made my decision. Wrenching open the door I stepped into the narrow passageway. "So here I am," I said.

The man at the end of the hall was about five foot eleven, slight of build with a scraggly beard and mustache. He bore no resemblence to the well-muscled Diamond. He exactly fit the description of the second gunman that Robert Mason had given the police.

"You were so eager to find me, I hope you're just as eager to spend the rest of your life in prison. My friend and the cops will be here in a matter of minutes."

"I don't think so." He smiled. His gun was tucked into the waistband of his jeans and he pulled it out. "Now let's get going, and don't try anything smart. If you hadn't had some help last night, we'd have got you in Vicksburg. And by the way, Diamond's a little sore about his trip down the stairs." He laughed. "Sore, get it?" He laughed again. "He wanted to be here himself, but he wasn't up to it."

"I'd hoped his neck was broken," I said coldly.

"Nah, just some ribs, a leg and his arm. He'll be fine in a few weeks."

I cursed my luck.

"You should have killed him while he was down, because he's really mad at you now." He laughed again and motioned me up the ladder.

"Since your friend goes by Diamond, what are you called? Topaz?" I asked.

He laughed. "You're pretty funny. Too bad. You can call me Jake."

I climbed the stairs, hoping that someone would be on the dock and I could get their attention. Surely this lowlife wouldn't be able to kidnap me in broad daylight from one of Jackson's most exclusive yacht clubs.

But when I broke into the sunshine, I saw no one.

"It was Diamond's idea to leave that book there for you. He said you'd figure it out and go running like a rat for the cheese." He pressed the barrel of the gun into my spine. "Now don't try anything dumb," he said. "There's a black car over by the clubhouse. Just walk toward it and get in, normal-like. We're going for a ride."

"Where's Nella?"

"Oh, she's just fine. A little weary of our hospitality. She'll be glad of some female companionship."

"If you've hurt her—" I didn't get a chance to finish.

"Seems to me you'd better spend a little time worrying about yourself instead of Nella Colson."

"You aren't going to get away with this." It was straight out of some Edward G. Robinson movie, but it was the only threat I could think of. I was in a bad spot and I knew it. *Why hadn't I told Nathan where I was going? Hell, why hadn't I let the cops follow me?*

"We were going to blow you up in the boat, out in the reservoir. That would have done the trick, but the boss decided it would stir up too much of an investigation."

I got in the passenger side of the car and Jake walked around. The idea of calling that man by his first name made my skin crawl. "Roach" would have been more appropriate.

"Mr. Gray prefers things neat and tidy, does he?" I knew it had to be Steve Gray behind all of this. The connections were too well placed. Nella Colson was the key. If they were holding her hostage, it had to be because Wilson Asphalt was deeply involved.

Jake laughed. "You're a smart one, aren't you? Diamond said you asked a lot of questions. Good thing he didn't answer, either. That's what he told me, to keep my mouth shut."

"How did you manage to get him out of Ravenwood? And how did you find me?"

"Easy." Jake looked away from the road long enough to grin at me. "We've been following you for a while. Ever since you went to the police department and started poking around in the past."

"How did you know?" My eyes must have widened. "Not Vesley!" I'd trusted the cop, at least as much as anyone other than Nathan.

"We got our ways. Your friend at the liquor store started asking around, too. If he isn't careful, we'll have to take care of him."

"If you hurt me or anyone else, questions will be asked. You can count on that. You might stop me, but I have friends who won't rest until they've nailed you."

"That new boyfriend of yours? Well, I wouldn't count on him helping out. He had a little surprise waiting for him when he went back to your house. See, we were expecting him. Even last night in Vicksburg. That's why I was waiting at the gate."

"What have you done to Nathan?" My terror was complete. I'd been frightened for myself, but it was nothing like the fear I felt for Nathan. I couldn't bear it if anything happened to him. I couldn't.

"Didn't your mama ever tell you that meddlers pay a high price?"

Jake's laughter seemed to go on and on. He refused to answer any more of my questions, and I was left alone with my growing worry for Nathan as we entered Jackson's city limits.

NELLA LOOKED as if she'd been run through the wringer. Her curly hair was matted, and the dark circles under her eyes were evidence that she'd had little sleep.

"Emma," she whispered when Jake thrust me into the bedroom with her. "I'm so sorry."

There was a noticeable lump under her shirt where her bandage was. Had she even had medical attention? I suppose if they intended to kill her they wouldn't be concerned that she might lose the use of her arm.

"Are you okay?"

She nodded. "For the moment. I guess you've figured it all out."

"Some." I took a seat on the side of the bed while she paced the room. "What happened to you?" I wasn't quite yet willing to volunteer information. I wasn't certain if she was part of the original plan or as innocent as I was.

"I shouldn't have run from the hospital," she said slowly. She stopped pacing long enough to look at me. "They started asking a lot of questions. Carlton Frazier was dead, and I was afraid they'd try to pin his murder on me. I didn't know what Steve Gray might have tried to blame on me. My only thought was to escape."

"So you called your good friend Marla." I knew this part.

"That's right. She brought some clothes to the hospital for me. Marla had gotten me the job with Steve Gray. She said he was a business associate and that he respected her opinion. Whatever they had going, he did hire me on

Marla's say-so. That's why I was in a bad position there. I knew Marla and Steve had some outside business interests, but I didn't know what they were.''

"He was teaching her the fine art of defrauding the state school systems," I said dryly.

"I suspected it might be something illegal. Marla had a lot of money at times." Nella sighed. "I just didn't ask because I didn't want to hear the answers. And the day I met you and Nathan, that wasn't an accident. I knew you were coming. I knew your connection to Marla. She'd made a few references to you. I felt that you were honest."

"Why didn't you ask Marla to help you get the goods on Steve Gray?"

Nella looked startled. "I did. She went berserk. She said Gray would destroy her if she tried anything. That's when she told me about the boat. She said she'd planned on surprising James with it this summer, for their anniversary. She had enough money tucked away out of the States. She wanted to sail away with him. She was going to have the boat hauled to Florida and set out from there. The Caribbean or somewhere like that. She said she owed James that much, at least."

"James didn't know about the *Lady Adventure?*"

"I don't think so. Marla bought her."

That was an interesting twist, and one that relieved me a little.

"So you were hiding out at Marla's and what happened?"

Nella started pacing again. "I was worried sick about what had happened to Frazier. I knew then that we were in way over our heads. Marla had gotten up early, and I thought I was the only one in the house. Then I heard arguing."

Nella stopped talking. Pain and fear washed over her face. "It was terrible. The argument was coming from the study, and I recognized James's voice."

"And the other was Steve Gray, right?"

"That's the odd part. It wasn't Steve's voice. I didn't know who it was. He was saying terrible things about Marla, about how she was a tramp and how she'd stolen money from the schools and how Sportsplex was going to be ruined.

"James was arguing just as loudly, calling the man sick and insane. He said he was shocked to hear such accusations from someone the family had known and trusted for so long. That's when the man demanded the records that Marla had stashed away."

"What records?"

"That's what James asked. Then the man said he wanted the records or there was going to be serious trouble. James said he didn't know where they were or what he was talking about."

Nella's pacing became even more frantic. "That's when I realized that the stranger was going to kill James. There was just something in his voice that was cold, without any feeling or compassion. James was a dead man."

Nella's words struck fear in my heart. I'd had that same feeling before, and it involved one man. Diamond. But when had he ever been a trusted friend of the Devlin family? His only connection, as far as I knew, was paid executioner.

"What happened then?" I prodded Nella. "Was it the man called Diamond?"

"I don't know," she whispered. Tears started down her cheeks. "It all happened so fast. There was a scuffle, and then a gunshot. I tried to run back to my room, but the man heard me. When I was trying to get into the bedroom he came and struck me with the butt of his gun. That's the last thing I remember. I woke up here."

"Do you know why they've kept you here?"

She nodded. "If all else failed, they planned on using me to draw you out. They knew you'd come to rescue me, if you thought I was in danger." She was crying in earnest now. It wasn't hard to follow her thoughts. Now she was expendable. Diamond and his associates gave the distinct impression that as soon as someone's usefulness was up, so was his life.

"Don't worry, Nella. Nathan will do something."

Nella started sobbing. "They're going to kill him, Emma, and they're going to make you help. That's what that horrible Jake told me when he left to get you."

"We'll see about that." I sounded a lot bolder than I felt. I had to keep up my confidence in Nathan, if not in myself. He'd figure it out. If they contacted him in any way, he'd know what to do.

"They're going to kill us, too," she whispered, her voice breaking. "Soon. They're going to make it look like I tried to kill you and that we shot each other. They have some of the records from Wilson Asphalt. They showed them to me and they're orders I signed. They'll put those in your hand as if you caught me in something illegal, and I killed you."

As farfetched as it sounded, I knew it could very easily be true. They had to do something with us, and turning us loose didn't seem to be a real alternative.

"Where are we, anyway?" I didn't know the neighborhood we were in. The house itself was isolated, and it was in the general direction of Vicksburg. I hadn't paid as much attention as I should have when Jake was driving, and now I rued my inattentiveness. There wasn't a shred of doubt that Nella understood the situation correctly. If we didn't escape, we were going to be killed.

The house was a modern ranch style with the windows in our bedroom shuttered from the outside. I tried the heavy wooden door. It was locked tight.

"I've tried everything. When they let me go to the bathroom, that creep stands at the door."

"How many are in the house?"

"There's Jake and the one they call Diamond, but he's banged up pretty badly. He fell or something." She looked at me. "Why are you smiling?"

I waved a hand, knowing that she would never believe Diamond had been trounced by a ghost. "I'll tell you everything later. How many others?"

"I can't be certain. There's at least one more, but he doesn't stay here all the time."

"Is it Gray?"

"No." Nella took a seat in a straight-backed chair. "I haven't heard Gray's voice at all. He's the kind of guy who would be in here telling me how I was going to die and exactly why. I've been expecting him since they've had me."

"What about Marla?"

"She's out of town, which is fine with these guys." Nella looked worried. "I know she isn't your favorite relative, but I get the distinct impression they think she's on the death list. They talk like they're going to kill her."

Marla was a loose cannon. If she knew as much as I thought she knew she was in terrible danger. "So there's one wild card, the unseen man."

Nella nodded. "Now that we've figured all of this out, how is that going to help us escape?"

I nodded to the chair on which she was sitting. Nella looked puzzled, so I began to outline my plan. "Right now, the only one we have to worry about is Jake. Diamond's crippled and I didn't hear or see anyone else when I came in. They won't expect an escape attempt so soon."

"What do you think we should do?"

"I think you've double-crossed me, right? So I attack you. Your wound reopens and you start bleeding profusely. Jake comes in and tries to restore order, I bop him on the head with that chair, and we're out of here. Can you run?"

"My feet have wings. Just give me half a chance."

"Okay, Nella. Ready for a cat fight?"

At her nod, we went after each other, screaming and hair pulling with as much vigor as possible. We did our best not to damage each other, but if our plan was to work, we had to look convincing.

"My shoulder!" Nella screamed. I slammed myself into the wall and she screamed again.

"She's killing me!" Nella cried out.

"You're gonna pay for double-crossing me," I cried out. "I'm going to rip your hair out."

"Help me!" Nella's cry was competely convincing. She sounded as if I was tearing her limb from limb. "Help me!"

"Hey! You two in there!" Jake pounded at the door. "Break it up. Diamond says if we have to come in there he's going to give you something to scream about."

"Louder," I whispered to Nella. With rage in my voice, I called out, "I'm going to kill you, you lying tramp!"

"Get her off me," Nella begged. "Please, help me! My shoulder's bleeding." She started to cry and scream.

I picked up the foot of the bed and thumped it into the floor several times. "I'm going to break your head open like a melon." I couldn't remember what television show had featured that incident, but I was glad I'd seen it.

"Hey! Break it up!" There was the sound of a key in the door, and I fell on Nella, grabbing her hair. I lifted her head dramatically.

"Hey!" Jake grabbed my own hair and dragged me backward, flinging me into the wall with a seriously painful thump. I thought for a minute I was going to black out, but I forced myself to stay conscious. My head was spinning. The chair was only a few feet in front of me. Jake was bending over the thrashing and moaning Nella. She was making it as hard as possible for him to look at her.

"Hold still," he ordered her. When she continued to thrash around, he slapped her hard across the face. "Now be still."

That finally got me to my feet. I picked up the chair and swung it, all in one fluid motion. It came down on his head and back with all the force I had in me. Jake collapsed across Nella's chest in a limp heap.

Although he wasn't a big man, it took all of my strength to roll him off her. She was still panting when she got up. "I ought to kick him where it hurts, just for good measure," she said, rubbing her jaw.

"I won't tell," I answered. "But let's just get out of here."

"Not so fast, ladies."

It was unbelievable, but Diamond was leaning against the door frame. In his hand was a neat-looking little gun. It was pointed directly at my heart.

Chapter Eighteen

"I should kill you both right now," Diamond said. He was struggling to stand, but his aim didn't waver. "But I owe you." He waggled the gun at me. "And I'm going to have my fun. I'm sure that my old buddy, Jake, there, will want his pound of flesh, too."

I was still holding the chair in my hands. A moan came from the despicable creature on the floor. If I didn't do something soon, we'd never have another chance. We were going to die, anyway. That's what I had to remember.

My hands slid down the back slats of the chair until I had a grip near the flat bottom. I slung it sideways at Diamond. Since one arm and a leg were in casts, his balance was precarious. When he tried to dodge the chair, he lurched backward. He couldn't prevent himself from toppling over.

Before he could regain any balance, I rushed out the door, picked up the chair and brought it down with all my might against his face. He screamed once and brought up his hands to fend off my next blow. With my right foot I kicked his gun from his hand. The weapon slid down the hallway.

"How does it feel to be a victim?" I asked. I was panting and I felt a surge of shame at my own emotions. I wanted to hurt him. I wanted to bring the chair down on his bleeding face again. I wanted to stomp and exterminate this mean and cruel creature who had killed my husband in cold blood. "How does it feel?" I demanded.

"Don't! Damn you! Stop!" His voice was muffled by the blood from his nose.

"Emma?" Nella was standing in the doorway, her eyes wide open with awe.

I lowered the chair. "Let's drag him into the bedroom and lock them in." I took his broken leg and Nella took the other and we hauled him into the room in which we'd been held prisoners. Jake was starting to moan and come around again. I didn't say a word as Nella picked up a lamp and brought it down on his head.

"That should hold him for a while," she said.

The key was in the door and we locked it. "Let's get out of here," Nella said. "There should be a car out there."

"Let me call Nathan first." I was worried sick about what might happen to him because of me. Steve Gray still figured into this, and I knew he was a ruthless man. Jake had also implied that someone in the Jackson Police Department was involved, possibly Sergeant Vesley.

I dialed my house, not caring if the police had tapped my line. In fact, I was going to tell Nathan to call the police. It was time the entire can of worms was dumped out for public inspection. "Run out and see if you can find a street sign or some address," I told Nella.

She disappeared as my shaky fingers dialed home.

The voice that answered was familiar, but it wasn't Nathan's.

"Benny?" I couldn't believe he was at my house.

"Emma! Thank God." He spoke away from the phone. "Nathan, it's Emma. She's alive!" Then he came back. "Where are you? Nathan called the office when you didn't show up at home. Beth said you'd been there and left. Oh, Emma, we've been worried sick."

Benny actually sounded as if he might cry.

"I don't know where I am, but I'm getting ready to get out of here. Please put Nathan on the phone."

Nella came back in. "It's 125 Oberton Road. Know it?"

I shook my head. "Benny?" He was still on the line. "You know the city better than Nathan. We're at 125 Oberton Road."

"I know that area," he said. "My aunt Margaret has a house out that way. It's pretty isolated out there. Used to be a lot of farm property, but it's growing up."

"Not around this house, it isn't. There isn't a neighbor around for miles," I said. Nella nodded in confirmation.

"Stay there, Emma. Let me and Nathan come after you. That would be the best thing. We'll call the police."

"How long will it take?"

"Fifteen minutes, twenty at most. If you don't know where you are, some of those roads lead around in circles."

"Fifteen minutes?" I was asking Nella as much as myself. She took one look toward the room where Diamond and Jake were locked up.

"Not a minute longer. Then I'm getting in one of those cars and I'm getting out of here," she promised. "I can't take it here. This place makes me think I'm going to die."

"Okay," I said into the receiver. "But make it fifteen minutes. Break the speed limit and bring every cop you can find with you. These guys are murderers."

"I know, honey," Benny said. "Now here's Nathan."

"Emma!"

His voice was tight with worry, and for the first time I thought I was going to cry. After every horrible thing I'd been through, it was the sound of Nathan's voice that brought me back to reality.

"I love you," I whispered, afraid to speak aloud because he'd hear how scared I was.

"Meet me at Ravenwood, Emma," he said.

"Ravenwood?" I didn't understand what he was saying

"If anything goes wrong, meet me at Ravenwood."

"Nathan?" I didn't fully understand.

"Excuse me, you two, but we need to go," Benny said impatiently at Nathan's shoulder.

"I love you, Emma," Nathan said.

"See you in a few minutes." I replaced the receiver.

"Something wrong?" Nella asked.

"I don't know. It's just Nathan. He sounded so...odd."

"I think our prisoners are beginning to wake up," Nella said. There was a pounding on the bedroom door in the back.

I walked down the hall and picked up the gun I'd kicked from Diamond's hand. The pounding grew louder.

"Open this door!" Jake demanded. "Diamond's bleeding in here. He looks like he might die."

"That's too bad," I answered coolly. "If he does, that'll just save the state from having to bring him to trial."

A series of expletives erupted behind the door.

"Emma." Nella paced nervously along the hallway. "What if they get out? I mean, they might. I've been here for days! I don't know if I can take it if I have to stay here any longer."

She was clutching her arms and pacing. "Nella, where would you go?" I asked gently. "Benny and Nathan will bring the police. We have to talk with them now. We have to bring all of this out in the open."

"I know that, but does it have to be here?" She looked down the hall, her eyes wild. "Let me go to the police station and wait. Maybe I can hurry them up to get here."

"The police? You promise?" I was only slightly afraid she'd cut and run again. It would only make it worse on her.

"I have something to do first," she admitted. "Then the police."

"What do you have to do?"

"I heard the guys talking, and I think I know where Steve Gray's secret files are kept. I think I can get them."

That would be the final evidence we needed, in black and white. "Okay. Where are they?"

"They're hidden somewhere, but it's on the way to the police station." Nella's face and voice had immediately brightened at the prospect of escape. "I'll call the police and then bring the files to them. That's a promise."

"We should be right behind you."

Nella looked down the hall. The bedroom door was vibrating under Jake's pounding. "Are you sure you want to stay here alone with those guys? They're evil."

"They are, indeed." I checked my watch. "But reinforcements should be here in another eleven minutes. You go on. I'll be fine. And I have the gun." We moved into the kitchen, and I put the gun down on the counter within easy reach. If I stayed, then should Diamond or Jake make a break, I'd be able to stop them. If I left, Nathan and Benny would be entering the house without any idea of what had transpired. Jake might be able to trick them. I had to stay, no matter how much I wanted to go.

Nella picked up a set of car keys beside the gun. "There's only one car." She hesitated.

"Go! Get those records before somebody else finds them."

Nella didn't stay for a second invitation. She was gone.

With ten minutes to wait, I stayed in the kitchen. Nathan would be with me soon. All I had to do was think about what it would be like when his arms encircled me. I could relax against his chest, lean on him for just a moment. And in a matter of hours, we would be alone together. All of this would be behind me. Frank's death would be avenged. I knew that he would rest easy then. The past would be settled once and for all. Maybe then I could look forward to the future.

Nathan's suggestion that we go to Ravenwood was an excellent idea. We could retreat there and hide out for a few days. My two-week visit was still valid. At least for a few more days. And after that? Well, I wouldn't think that far ahead. Nathan had his own agenda. He'd made that perfectly clear. But once he'd finished what he had to do, maybe we could see if there was something permanent for us. If there was any hope, I'd wait for him.

The sound of a car brought me out of my own thoughts. Jake was still pounding on the door.

"You'd better shut up," I called to him. "The cops are pulling into the driveway."

That did the trick—instant silence.

I didn't wait. I flew out the door and down the drive. Nathan was sitting in the passenger side with Benny driving. I tore open the door and half dragged Nathan out.

"You're here," I said, hugging him. "You're safe and alive." I'd been more concerned than even I'd realized. "Oh, Nathan." I buried myself in his arms. Nathan was stiff, unnatural, and I pushed back from him, embarrassed by my open display in front of Benny. In my emotional state, I had forgotten that Benny was completely unaware of my feelings for Nathan. Benny's loyalties were with Frank. It might be difficult for him to understand that I'd grown to love someone else.

"Emma..." Nathan grabbed for me but I was already moving away.

I went around the car to Benny. "I'm glad to see you." I hugged him and kissed his cheek. I still held the gun in my hand and I gave it to him. "Take this, Benny. I hate it!"

"Get back in the house, Emma," Benny said slowly. "Now."

"What?" There was something terribly wrong. I looked at Nathan and saw his face ashen, his blue eyes worried.

Benny was pointing a gun at me and Nathan, and he tucked the one I'd given him into his belt. For the first time I noticed the gun he held. It was beautiful, with a carved handle, exactly like the one Sergeant Vesley had taken into custody in Vicksburg. I knew then that I was a dead woman. "What are you doing, Benny?"

"Get back in the house."

Nathan's arm at my elbow pushed me toward the door. "I had to come with him," Nathan said. "He knew where you were."

"Benny?" The terrible truth was beginning to emerge. "Not Benny." I looked to Nathan for the denial I wanted to hear.

"I'm afraid it was Benny," he said gently.

I stopped and turned back to the man I'd known for years. My husband's most trusted friend. "You betrayed Frank," I said, unable to control the quiver in my voice. "You betrayed your best friend and the man who loved you like a brother. That's why Frank couldn't rest. It wasn't just that he was murdered. He was betrayed!"

Benny pushed the gun in my stomach with enough force to make it hurt. "Get in the house. This is the last time I'm going to ask."

"My God, Benny. What have you done?" I planted my feet and refused to budge. It was Nathan who took my arm and moved me toward the house, always careful to keep his body between me and the gun.

"Save all your questions, Emma," Benny said. He was undisturbed. "If you hadn't come poking into this, you wouldn't be in this mess. It isn't my fault you weren't content to let sleeping dogs lie. Diamond wanted to kill you two years ago, but I wouldn't let him. I had to get rid of Frank, but I had a soft spot for you."

"Why?" I could only stare at him, wondering what kind of twisted mind would allow a man to kill his best friend.

"I hated Frank." Benny's gaze didn't waver. "All of those years, pretending that I thought he was so wonderful. I hated him. He thought he was so much better than me. He patronized me, and the whole time he was using me to make himself rich. But I was getting richer. I was the brains behind the bidding scam. Me, not Frank."

"You were partners, Benny. You shared in everything."

"Not everything." Benny's lip curled. "Frank was so charming, so personable. The clients all asked for him. They preferred him. The women, too." He took on a sly look. "He had you and they still came on to him. Even Marla."

"Frank never encouraged them. You know that. Most especially not Marla." I talked as we entered the kitchen.

"They never looked at me, except as some kind of computer geek, some nerd who slipped into the room and made the computers run. All of that is changing now. Marion Curry, the photographer. That's just a start. When I'm rich, they'll come after me."

Nathan shifted forward slightly, and Benny thrust the gun in my face. "Move again, Mr. Cates, and you'll see Emma's brains splattered all over the kitchen wall."

"I thought you had a soft spot for her," Nathan said sarcastically.

I thought about Micro-Tech. "He had a soft spot for my shares of the stock. If I died, my heirs might sell them to someone other than him!" I stumbled back against the wall. "What did you do about that?"

"That did present a little problem, until I convinced Marla to forge your name to a new will, which she witnessed. She was easy to convince once she knew we had evidence on her." One corner of his mouth twisted down. "I was going to give you a choice, Emma, until I saw you with him." He waved the gun at Nathan. "Then I knew it was hopeless. You liked the pearls because you thought Frank had bought them for you. And when you were over him, you took up with someone else. There was never a chance for me. Never."

"Benny, there are people who can help you." I kept my voice calm.

"Where's Nella?" Benny asked suddenly. He swung the gun around the room.

"She's gone." I felt a moment of sheer triumph. "She went to get the cops."

Panic swept over Benny's face. "That's too bad, isn't it? No time for pleasantries. Drugs would have been nicer. But a bullet will have to do, Emma. If the cops are on their way, I don't have time for anything else."

"This is madness," Nathan said softly. "They'll catch you, Benny, and they won't hesitate to kill you. Give yourself up. You're a sick man. They'll help you."

I had to help Nathan. "Frank caught you and Steve Gray, didn't he?" I asked Benny. "You set up Gray's system. You invented some way to keep those crooked contracts from showing."

"I didn't invent it, Emma, I just implemented it. But I did discover that Steve and I made a good team. And Frank had such high moral standards. He said he was compelled to report Steve for stealing from the state. Compelled!" Benny spat out the word.

"So you got Marla to start cheating on athletic contracts with schools."

Nathan shot me a look. It was true, there was nothing I could do to change it. Marla wasn't as deep in this as I'd thought, but she was still plenty dirty.

"She was easy. Marla saw a way to make money and she didn't ask a lot of questions, until she was in way over her head. She thought she could make it up to her husband with that boat. She actually thought she could escape out of the country." Benny took a deep breath. "She couldn't leave when I needed her, though. She had to help me hide those records from you meddlers. Then when I went to get them, James was waiting. She'd told him that we'd corrupted her, and he was going to 'talk sense into me.'" Benny eyed his watch. "He sounded just like Frank. So I shot him."

"And Frazier was just unlucky enough to be in the wrong place at the wrong time?" Nathan asked.

"Oh, he wanted in at the beginning. But when it got hot, he wanted to bail out. Steve Gray owed him a lot of money. If Wilson Asphalt went down, then that S&L would be on precarious ground. Frazier was going to turn us in, I believe. He was after the same records you wanted."

"How much does a good hit man cost?" I asked bitterly.

"Enough." Benny shrugged. "The trouble with Diamond was that he didn't want to get off the gravy train. He and his cousin have been like leeches. They even demanded this house, my Aunt Margaret's house." He looked around the room. "Where are those bad boys?"

"In the bedroom," I answered.

"Should I kill them first, or you two?"

"You can't kill Emma," Nathan said softly. "Benny, think what you're doing. She's been your friend."

"Shut up or I'll kill her first," Benny said without a shred of emotion in his voice. "I'm only doing what I have to do to save myself. But I think you'll have to die first. Then Diamond and Jake." He looked at me. "Killing you won't be a pleasure, Emma, but those two—" he rolled his eyes "—will be a delight. You have to agree, the world will be a better place without them."

"He's over the edge isn't he?" I asked Nathan in a whisper.

"Yes, I'm afraid so. He's been hanging by a thread since Frank's death. Now he's gone."

"Stop that whispering. You think I'm nuts, but I'm not." He aimed the gun at me. "Goodbye, Emma."

At the same time that I heard the blast, Nathan dove in front of me, pushing me back and down to the floor so that I fell behind the counter. There was the sound of a scuffle as Nathan torpedoed himself into Benny and both men tumbled to the floor. The bullet must have gone through Nathan's torso. He'd jumped straight into the line of fire.

"Nathan!" I scrambled to my feet. He and Benny were struggling. Benny still held one gun. The other had been knocked out of sight. The weapon he held was pointed at Nathan's head.

"Stop it!" I screamed. I tried to dart forward, but they rolled and suddenly Benny was on top. I could see the blood seeping from Nathan's abdomen.

"Benny! Stop it!" I moved in again, picking up a rolling pin. It was marble and heavy. Just as I started to swing, the two men rolled and Nathan was on top.

"Run, Emma," he commanded. "Get out! Get help!"

"No!" I was crying. I could taste and feel the tears, even though I didn't know when they'd started. "I won't leave you, Nathan."

He looked at me for one second, and before my eyes the vision of Nathan Cates, Lieutenant Colonel in the Confederate army appeared. The blue jeans and paid shirt he was wearing disappeared. In their stead was the hat and gray uniform of the Seventh Cavalry. The red splotch of blood seeped through the gray wool of the uniform just below Nathan's heart.

"Nathan!" The sound was torn from my throat. He was dying in front of my eyes.

He held Benny down against the floor. "Go, before I weaken."

"No."

He struggled to hold Benny down, but his breath was coming in shallow gasps. "Mary Quinn sent me to help you."

"Nathan!" I hefted the rolling pin. I saw my moment and brought it down hard on Benny's head. He was stilled instantly. To my horror, Nathan slumped off him and onto the floor. His entire chest was covered in blood.

"Nathan." I removed his hat and held his head in my lap. "Don't leave me. Please." My tears dripped on his face and I wiped them away.

"I could never have stayed, Emma. That's why I couldn't marry you. I should never have touched you, but I couldn't help myself. I love you so much. I hope you can forgive me, but I couldn't deny myself your love."

"I'll call an ambulance. A doctor." I struggled to rise, but his fingers clutched my wrist and held me.

He shook his head as if he were terribly weary. "Don't leave me. There's nothing you can do."

"Don't go." I was begging. "Or let me come with you."

"You can't go where I'm going. You have a lot of living yet to do, Emma. Remember, I told you that once. I always knew that when the mystery of Frank's death was solved, I had to leave."

"Not like this, Nathan. Not like this." I pressed my hand against the wound, hoping to staunch the flow of his blood.

"It's an old wound, Emma. You can't stop it." He smiled, and for a moment the sun and the summer sky were in his eyes. "I got it at Vicksburg, in the gardens of Raven-wood. I was defending the Quinn family."

It was so hard for him to speak, and yet I had to keep talking or he'd leave me. "And you really knew Mary Quinn?"

"She was a beautiful girl. Not as lovely as you, but with a lot of the same spirit, and the same capacity to love."

"I love you, Nathan. With all of my heart."

"You have a lot of love to give, Emma. Don't hide from it. That's what Mary wanted me to tell you. Don't run away from love. Frank doesn't want you to, and neither do I. You're a kind woman with a generous heart. You need to love."

"Can you come back to me? Even for a little while?" I could see that he was weakening. "Please, Nathan. Just for a while. Please." I couldn't help myself.

"I love you, Emma. Remember . . ."

He closed his eyes and his body grew heavy in my lap. I held him for a long moment, unable to accept what had happened. A shaft of afternoon sun struck one of the buttons on his coat, and I realized I could see my leg beneath him. I thought I was imagining it when he started to fade.

It took several moments before he completely disappeared.

Chapter Nineteen

It was raining at Ravenwood, a clean spring shower that would revive the flowers and make the grass grow at least an inch. I stood in the window of the upstairs apartment looking out over the grounds. Behind me, my bags were packed and ready to go. I had only to take them down to my car, load them, and drive away.

The rain beat a steady rhythm against the glass, and for a moment I allowed myself to imagine the plantation alive with one of Mary Quinn's famous parties. The delicious smell of baked ham wafted on the spring air. The sound of fiddles cut the night in a lively number, and dancers laughed and clapped. The gardens were ablaze with lighted torches, and one couple, hopelessly in love, kissed beneath the sheltering branches of an old oak. I could see it all so clearly. That was a gift from Nathan, the ability to open myself to the past.

I turned away from the window, ending my daydream. Maybe one day I'd turn my imagination to writing a novel. I had a million choices to make about my future.

I'd come back to Ravenwood in the hope that Nathan might return, even just for a moment. Our telephone conversation had haunted me. He'd told me to meet him at Ravenwood if anything went wrong. Wrong by whose definition?

By the time Sergeant Vesley had arrived at the secluded house that did indeed belong to Diamond Crane, I was holding Benny Yeager at gunpoint.

Nathan Cates was gone.

The floor where he'd died was bare. There was not even a drop of his blood.

Vesley took it at face value that I'd overwhelmed Benny single-handedly. He'd completely ignored Benny's ravings about a dead man who'd disappeared. Diamond and his sidekick, Jake, were still locked in the back bedroom. True to her word, Nella Colson had called the police and given them directions to me before she took off for the reservoir. After a lengthy search, she'd found the incriminating records linking the illegal activities of Wilson Asphalt and Micro-Tech hidden behind a wall in the *Lady Adventure*. Nella had delivered those records to the police that very afternoon.

Marla had been extradited, and Sergeant Vesley had assured me that things would go easier for her if she testified for the state against Benny Yeager and Steve Gray, who were due to spend a long, long time behind bars. Marla had readily agreed, and even won a measure of my sympathy. She'd gotten in way over her head, but she'd never thought anyone would be hurt. Especially not James and Frank.

It seemed that all of the loose ends were tied. It was over.

And Nathan was gone.

He'd vanished before my very eyes, leaving not a trace that he'd ever existed. In fact, he had not. In the modern world of 1993, Lieutenant Colonel Nathan Cates had never lived. He was a transient spirit, a visitor from a distant time who'd given a few historical lectures at a small Mississippi college, and who'd saved my life.

He'd also taught me that the past and the future can sometimes take on a life of their own, but it is only the present in which we actually live. Nathan had given me so much, of pleasure and of pain. I would not have traded a minute of our time. And I had no regrets or remorse. I had loved him with all of my heart, and now I would miss him forever. Just as I missed Frank.

I turned from the rain-splattered windowpane and lifted my bags. There was nothing left to do now except go. The insurance adjustor had been by. The damages at Ravenwood were not astronomical, and the Quinn estate included a provision for damages and vandalism. In fact, the insurance adjustor told me that my night of horror with Diamond, a multiple murderer, would be added to the folklore of Ravenwood. It gave me pleasure to think that I had become a small part of the fine old plantation's legend. After all, I was keeping the best of company.

In coming to Ravenwood, I'd hoped to see Nathan again. I knew it would be only for a moment, but it would be enough to see him whole and smiling. And I'd also hoped that Frank might visit me. My sleep had been strangely deep and untroubled by any dreams. Now, in the emptiness of the old house, I accepted the fact that Frank Devlin would no longer trouble my sleep. He was at peace.

I threw the bags into the trunk of my car and impulsively darted to the main house for one last look. I'd never come back to Ravenwood. I knew it in my heart.

I slipped in through the kitchen and made my way to the dining room. Nathan had almost frightened me to death here one night. I'd been anticipating a visit from Mary Quinn, and I'd found Nathan instead. If I'd suspected he was a ghost, would I have held back my heart? No. I could not have.

"Goodbye," I whispered to the old plantation house and to Mary Quinn, if she was listening.

"Emma."

Nathan appeared at the foot of the stairs. His gray uniform was immaculately pressed. There was no trace of any injury. He held his cavalry hat in his hand, and his boots were polished to a black gleam.

"Nathan." I threw myself at him, headlong into his open arms. Beneath my hands and lips he was solid, warm and real. "Oh, Nathan." I ran my hands over the planes of his face, memorizing each detail with my fingertips. I would remember him always.

"I love you, Emma Devlin," he said, kissing me with a poignant gentleness that told me how brief our time was.

"I'll never forget you," I whispered, holding him as tightly as I could.

"No, you'll never forget. Not me, or Frank, but you have love and life to give, Emma. That's what Mary Quinn wanted me to tell you. Don't hide from the love you can give." He tilted my chin up so that our eyes met. "And I can see in your eyes that you will not."

"Remember me, Nathan." I made no effort to cling.

"How could I forget?" He smiled. "Live long and happily, Emma."

He gently stepped back and the walked out the front door and toward the grounds near the river.

I stood at the door and watched him, knowing that Lieutenant Colonel Nathan Cates had died of a gunshot wound to the abdomen while defending the plantation of Ravenwood. It was his unit that had saved the plantation and a handful of Vicksburg citizens from an assault by a Union advance force.

As I watched, he disappeared into the rain-drenched gardens. In the patter of the rain I heard the distant sound of artillery, the roar of cannons, and the scream of a terrified horse. The sulfuric smell of gunpowder drifted in with the rain.

I closed and locked the door of Ravenwood, and then I drove away.

Epilogue

The neat stack of pages beside the printer grew steadily as the machine buzzed line after line. Emma Devlin stood, leaning forward slightly, as she read along with the printer. When "The End" came up on the last page, she took her glasses off the end of her nose and sighed. It was done. Nearly two years had gone into the research and writing of her first novel, and it was due on the editor's desk in less than three days.

The old Victorian house on Devine had suffered a bit of neglect, she noticed as she went to the window and rubbed a finger on the pane. Well, it was April. Plenty of time for a good spring cleaning. And it would be fun to throw herself into the house and some gardening. She'd been a prisoner of her computer and a cast of characters who'd become almost flesh and blood.

She smiled at the thought and walked back to her desk. Beside the keyboard were two pictures, one of a handsome dark-haired man with an open collar and wind-tousled hair. The other was a ferrotype, a worn image of a Confederate Cavalry officer. The insignia on his uniform showed him to be a lieutenant colonel.

"Okay, guys, I'm done," she said. For a moment she almost allowed herself to wish that they were present to celebrate with her. But that was living in the past, something she'd vowed not to do. It was the least she could do—for them.

All that remained now was to copy her manuscript, slide it into a mailer, and kiss it goodbye. Maybe on the way back from the post office she'd stop by Robert Mason's liquor store and get a bottle of champagne to celebrate the completion of the book. It had been years since she'd indulged in some really good champagne, and it would be fun to see Robert. He'd been a great support to her during the past two years when she was going through Benny Yeager's trial for the murder of her husband, her brother-in-law James, and Carlton Frazier.

Benny's conviction hadn't given her the sense of justice she'd once thought it would. She was only glad that he was behind bars, unable to hurt anyone else.

Micro-Tech had been sold, and she'd realized a handsome profit, enough to allow her the time she'd always wanted to write.

Emma picked up the manuscript and began shredding the sides from the computer paper.

The knock at her front door was completely unexpected. Everyone in her family knew not to disturb her during the morning. That was her most productive writing time, and her relatives had been more than generous in leaving her alone. Even her mother, who always had a list of things that she wanted Emma to do—chiefly among them, date some nice man that she'd met.

Walking down the stairs to the front door, Emma allowed her imagination to bloom. Maybe it was the mailman with a certified letter. Or it could be a courier with a sweepstakes check. She was almost smiling when she opened the door.

A tall, dark-haired man stood with one hand on a little boy's shoulder. The child was about seven, and his eyes were swollen with tears.

"I'm John McNaught," the man said, "and this is my son, Kevin." He indicated a house across the street. "We just moved into the neighborhood, and I'm afraid Kevin's puppy slipped through a hole in the fence and ran under your house.''

The little boy hiccuped back a sob and turned his face into his father's leg.

''Kevin's very attached to the pup,'' the man explained.

Emma clearly saw the sadness in the man's eyes, and the little boy was terribly upset.

''Why don't we get a flashlight and look under the house?'' she suggested. ''I'm sure if the pup's there, we can get him.''

''His name is Buster,'' the little boy said. At the mention of rescuing the dog, he'd turned back to look at Emma. ''I tried to call him, but he wouldn't come.''

''Since it's a new neighborhood, he might be a little confused and afraid,'' Emma said gently. ''Moving's hard on dogs—and boys, isn't it?''

The boy nodded and took a tentative step away from his father. ''Can we look now?''

''Let me get the light.'' Emma found a flashlight in the downstairs desk and led the way around to the side of the house. As soon as she found the opening under the porch and bent down, she could hear the puppy crying.

''Daddy, he's hurt,'' the boy said, his voice breaking. ''We have to get him out.''

John McNaught moved closer to the opening, but it became apparent that his wide shoulders would never slip through.

''Why don't I try?'' Emma asked. ''I'm sure I can fit.''

''We'll get some food and lure him out,'' John said. ''This is too much trouble.''

''He's crying, Daddy,'' the boy said, his voice about to break.

''Kevin's mother died six months ago. Until we got the dog, he wouldn't talk,'' John said, his big hand stroking his son's hair.

"I'll be right back." Emma took the flashlight and slipped under the house. She found the dog in a matter of minutes. It took a little longer to win the animal's trust, but she soon had it cuddled in her arms and was crawling back toward the opening. When she handed it out, Kevin McNaught cried out in happiness.

She came through the opening to a chorus of thank-yous. John assisted her to her feet, and then brushed a cobweb from her hair. The April sun shifted through a leafy pecan branch and struck him full on the face. His eyes were the color of a summer sky, and he was staring at her.

"Kevin and I would like to take you to dinner tonight, if you have time," he said. "We're new in Jackson. I've taken a job teaching history at Millsaps College."

Emma Devlin faltered. "That won't be necessary. It's enough reward to see that smile on Kevin's face." She knew her voice sounded odd, but she felt as if her balance had suddenly disappeared.

"It may not be necessary, but I think it would be a pleasure," John McNaught insisted gently. "I've been told all my life that an act of kindness is the mark of a generous heart. You have a good heart, Ms. Devlin."

Emma felt the blood rush to her head. For a moment she thought she might faint. She was dimly aware of John McNaught's hand at her elbow, steadying her.

"Are you okay?" he asked, his blue eyes shadowed with worry.

She smiled at him. "I'm perfectly fine, John. Better than I've been in years. In fact, I'd love to have dinner with you and your son. I finished a manuscript today and I was thinking when you rang the bell that I wanted to celebrate. I can do that and welcome my new neighbors at the same time."

"We'll pick you up at eight?" John asked.

"Make it seven-thirty. We'll have a glass of champagne at my house before we go. And some root beer for Kevin."

Their eyes met over the top of Kevin's head. Neither spoke nor moved until the boy restlessly tugged at his father's hand. "Let's go, Dad. You said you'd find the hole in the fence and fix it."

"Moving to this neighborhood may have been the smartest thing I've done in a long, long time," John McNaught said as he hefted puppy and son into his arms and looked again at Emma.

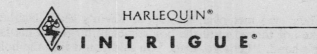

1993 Keepsake

CHRISTMAS

Stories

Capture the spirit and romance of Christmas with KEEPSAKE CHRISTMAS STORIES, a collection of three stories by favorite historical authors. The perfect Christmas gift!

Don't miss these heartwarming stories, available in November wherever Harlequin books are sold:

ONCE UPON A CHRISTMAS by Curtiss Ann Matlock
A FAIRYTALE SEASON by Marianne Willman
TIDINGS OF JOY by Victoria Pade

ADD A TOUCH OF ROMANCE TO YOUR HOLIDAY SEASON WITH KEEPSAKE CHRISTMAS STORIES!

HX93

HARLEQUIN CELEBRATES
THE SEASON OF SHARING
AND FAMILY WITH

Friends, Families, Lovers

Harlequin introduces the latest member in its family of
seasonal collections. Following in the footsteps of the popular
My Valentine, Just Married and *Harlequin Historical Christmas
Stories*, we are proud to present FRIENDS, FAMILIES,
LOVERS. A collection of three new contemporary romance
stories about America at its best, about welcoming others into
the circle of love.... Stories to warm your heart ...

By three leading romance authors:

KATHLEEN EAGLE
SANDRA KITT
RUTH JEAN DALE

Available in October, wherever
Harlequin books are sold.

THANKS

Relive the romance...
Harlequin®is proud to bring you

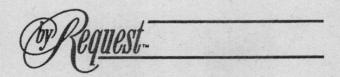

A new collection of three complete novels every
month. By the most requested authors, featuring
the most requested themes.

Available in October:

DREAMSCAPE

They're falling under a spell!
But is it love—or magic?

Three complete novels in one special collection:

GHOST OF A CHANCE by Jayne Ann Krentz
BEWITCHING HOUR by Anne Stuart
REMEMBER ME by Bobby Hutchinson

Available wherever Harlequin books are sold.

Calloway Corners

In September, Harlequin is proud to bring readers four
involving, romantic stories about the Calloway sisters,
set in Calloway Corners, Louisiana. Written by four of
Harlequin's most popular and award-winning authors,
you'll be enchanted by these sisters and the men
they love!

MARIAH by Sandra Canfield
JO by Tracy Hughes
TESS by Katherine Burton
EDEN by Penny Richards

As an added bonus, you can enter a sweepstakes contest
to win a trip to Calloway Corners, and meet all four
authors. Watch for details in all Calloway Corners books
in September.

CAL93